www.puggrumble.com

This book is a work of fiction. The characters, incidents, and dialogue are drawn from the author's imagination and are not to be construed as real. Any resemblance to actual events or persons, living or dead, is purely coincidental.

ISBN: 978-0-9890058-9-0
First Edition, November 2020

Cover designed by Cutlip, www.cutlip.com

Ouch

by Pug Grumble

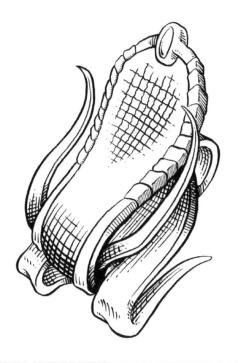

A Comical & Quirky Tale
About a Masochist, a Sadist,
& a Klutz

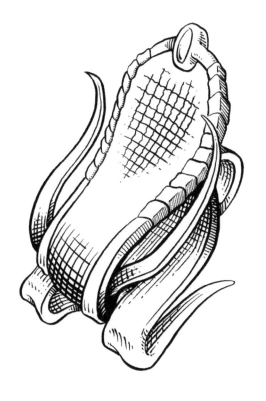

Part 1
Felicia

CHAPTER 1
ALARM CLOCK

The cigarette danced through the air, its glowing smile blazing the way for its tail of dribbling smoke. A step to the right, a turn to the left, a pirouette back around, and then straight south, crushing itself out with a final hiss in the small of his back.

Sylvester howled in pain; a howl that in its second second curved to a smile as the pain passed and the pleasure began, the gift of some odd and intrinsic foible.

Felicia leaned over him, her nails digging into his shoulder, three other lit cigarettes still dangling from her mouth, mumbling her voice. "You're running out of space back here. We may need to start doubling up. Retrace some scars. Or maybe we try cigars? The scar of a cigar… I like the sound of that!"

Sylvester was pillow-faced on the bed, his stippled and beaten body and its hundreds of scars grinning back in her direction. Half of them she'd caused and the others she knew the names and stories behind.

"You're so pretty…" she said with a loving smile as she traced over his scars, a fingertip kiss goodbye before spitting the fluppering stubs into the ashtray and flopping herself on the bed, a prop of pillows cushioning her landing.

Sylvester sat up and rubbed his eyes, kneading away the last of the sleep that tickled its edges, chasing away the dreams. He had the world's most painful alarm clock and he was happy about that.

Felicia squinted crookedly at his back, a hint of hope in her voice as she poked at it, "I think it's gonna get infected."

"Good," he said as his fingertips traced along his cratered back.

"Want me to clean it?"

"No thanks," he said with a flirting smirk, "I can see you using steel wool."

"You're all out. Remember you let me de-whisker your chest hair last week?"

"Oh yes! That's still not fully healed, so it seems a *thank-you-very-much* is in order."

"I do good work, what can I say?"

Sylvester smiled, flirting happiness dancing through his mind, "OK, we'll save the wool fun for the weekend. I'll be rebellious today and go with the 'antibiotic and bandage treatment'. Make me feel like I'm in a convent being taken care of by nuns."

"I could be a nun!" she added helpfully.

He paused and widened one eye before leaning over to give her a nibbling kiss. "I'd love to see that."

His right hand reached into a bowl by the bedside and emerged with a handful of Legos, casually tossing them across the floor as if preparing to read tea leaves, before hopping off the bed and making his way to the bathroom, being sure to step on each one as he went.

He brushed his teeth and gave himself a quick look in the mirror, a droopy and ragged face staring back, his beard stipple coming in a bit greyer than he was ready for. He saw the beginnings of a pimple on one cheek and gave it a good poke before trying to pop it, then twisted around to examine his newest burns in the mirror. He was surprised to see blood trickling away from one. He was getting old; he never used to bleed.

His hands dug deep in the medicine cabinet, shifting around boxes of medical supplies, surgical tapes and ointmented creams, and even a small suture kit in a well-worn box, before he found the empty space he was expecting to be filled.

"Are we out of those adhesive gauze pads?" he shouted back into the bedroom.

"Yeah, we used the rest of 'em last week on that game with the fire poker," came her response.

Sylvester thought back and smirked. It was a fun game. Well worth a few adhesive bandages. But he'd need to refill his supply before work or risk bleeding through to his uniform. Carl didn't like that. '*Unprofessional,*' he'd say.

He pulled on an overly tight t-shirt that looked to be the dominant one in the relationship, before synching his belt three notches too tight and wedging a few sleeves of staples into his pockets. He tossed a pebble in each sock and horned on his small sneakers, before finally shoving a biker-spiked wallet into his pants (spike side in), hopeful that there'd be a bus seat to grind into. Worst case, he could twist an ankle or something.

Felicia was still in bed, a marker in hand as she flipped through farming fixture catalogs circling fanciful bargains and registry items. Sylvester smiled, a chuckle escaping his lips at their overlapping taste in dangerous mail order, before leaning in for a kiss, which she happily delivered with enough ferocity to crack his lip.

"Need anything?" he asked, "I'm gonna do a big bandage grab."

Felicia looked off and pondered, scratching at her neck absently in thought, before getting excited as an idea arrived, "Ooh! See if they have any more acupuncture kits! Sturdy ones, though. We broke the last three we got."

Sylvester nodded and waved, "I'll look."

And then he was off, a meandering pace down the hall and the stairs, his thumb prodding every exposed nail, his arm grazing every unsanded edge, his head bumping every doorjamb, his elbow funny-boning every banister.

He knew all the spots and made sure they never got worn too smooth, the nails never hammered in too deep, the tease never fully removed.

After all, what fun would that be?

CHAPTER 2
SUPERMARKET SUPPLY RUN

The streets were empty at that time of night, a few luckless locals digging through trash cans and testing door locks the way people used to check phone booths for forgotten quarters. Sylvester waved to them as he passed, a quick *'Hello'* or *'How do you do?'* to the ones he was friendly with. They waved back, giving him cheery whiskey smiles.

He aligned himself with the parking meters and put his hand out, letting it slap hard against each one as he went, brief surges of smiley pain dancing along his arm while his off-hand played pocket games with nail clippers.

A few blocks later he arrived at the bus stop, happily crashing onto the bench and grinding his walleted-hip into the wood before adjusting himself, an addict in search of an untapped vein.

He ground his teeth. He bit his tongue. He nibbled his lips. He dug his long nails into his palms and played his little games of cringing and smiling, back and forth, back and forth. Pain and happiness.

At ten past eleven the Green Line bus pulled to a stop in front of him, briefly waking the homeless man sleeping under the bench, who in turn rolled over and adjusted his newspaper blankets. Sylvester hopped on, happy to see an empty bus and his choice of available seats.

"H'llo Marty," he said to the driver, a waspishly segmented older gent who swayed in his seat and always seemed on the verge of sleep or death.

Sylvester walked his way down the aisle, his eyes searching for the most unflattering seat he could find. There were plenty that were roughed from disrepair, some fusty from flatulent folks, while others he swore were gang-affiliated and watching him, ready to pull a switchblade from their cushions the moment a fight broke out. In his mind he always pined for the seat with the stray comic spring poking through the fabric like a crackerjack prize.

There was no prize tonight though, so he sat on the flattest and most worn-down seat he could find, once again grinding himself into his wallet while his fingers wrapped around the seat bottom, searching out screw points and sharp edges, delicately avoiding the stores of hardened gum.

His mind wandered back to Felicia, who he knew was likely sitting at home planning something insidious, although not necessarily directed at him. Just as his mind always wandered to his own pain, hers always wandered to the pain of others.

She made her living doing bad acupuncture and angry massages, with a side of sticky waxing. He never understood how there was a market for it, but there was, and she did well on her untaxed tips. Far better than he did, with his endless list of fry jobs and broom pushings. His appearance gave away his addictions. Hers were neatly veiled.

The empty bus jerked to a stop as Marty seemed to awaken and accidentally slam the brakes, bigotingly announcing that they were *"somewhere bright and smelling of coffee and Asians,"* which Sylvester knew to mean his stop. He patted the man on the back, a mild form of cautionary CPR, before he quickstepped off the bus into the refreshing night air.

The Wong Chen Supermarket was lit up like a holiday, the only 24-hour supermarket in town and the one with the cheapest prices on everything from fresh fish to potted plants to kitchen furniture. It was also, notably, especially affordable for people using vast quantities of medical supplies, importing some questionable brands and pharmaceutical curiosities not found in your local chain supermarket.

Sylvester grabbed a cart and pushed inside, nodding at the happy gentleman who certainly didn't speak a word of English, manning the lone register in the hours where nobody noticed.

He wandered through the fresh vegetable rows, window shopping and eyeballing the strange ingredients he couldn't identify and had no idea how to prepare. Strange crossbreeds of broccoli and mushrooms, still alive and moving days after being removed from the earth.

He paused briefly at the durian fruit and the pineapples, their strange and pointy protrusions warning predators to stay away, but he made a point to squeeze and juggle them as if testing their ripeness, before putting them back, satisfied and unpurchased, and moving on with pockmarked palms.

He grabbed a bundle of carrots for snacking ($1!) and then moved on to his target aisle at the back end of the store, just past the rice cookers and the plastic kitchenware, but before the frozen food section filled with seaborne animals he was certain would come flopping back to life after defrosting.

His eyes hopscotched down the pharmacy aisle, past the endcap of towering canned fish, surveying the large variety of bandages, band-aids, antiseptics, and assorted oddities with labels printed in a language unknown even in Asia.

He grabbed a couple of tubs of ointment ($3!), a few yards of gauze from the unsanitary rolling dispenser, some unnamed brand of cotton swabs that had a hook on the end, and a few boxes of some strange mint-smelling cream that he seemed to recall did well on burns and in soups.

He spent a few minutes examining the small unmarked drawers of the apothecarian witchcraft wall, filled with roots and fungi and what he was certain were bat wings and newt eyes, unsure how to use them and doubtful they worked even when you knew.

Then he lined up his cart before the bandage section, a supermarket sharpshooter on the hunt for volume. He slid his hand behind the second level of boxes as he gave the cart a small push, meandering along behind as he scooped two of every type of bandage off the shelf and into his cart like a waterfall. After fifteen feet he stopped, his cart now brimming to capacity and the shelves devoid of all but a few stragglers.

He smiled to himself like a landscaper who'd just finished mowing a large lawn, proud and satisfied with the grill marks.

A loud crash pulled his attention back down the aisle as his eyes caught a sight both comical and confusing – a smallish girl in her thirties with dark hair and cracked glasses sat sprawled amongst the remnants of the canned fish tower, looking for all the world as if the tower had suddenly decided to attack her and had struck the first blow. This seemed particularly aggressive of the tower seeing as the girl was already in rough shape.

Her arm was bandaged to the fingertips and in a sling, her legs crisscrossed with medical tape that held in place a variety of gauze pads and peeling band-aids. Even her face seemed to have taken the brunt of some unknown battle, a small bit of white gauze wrapping her ear and a Totoro band-aid tracing the curve of her jawline.

Sylvester's immediate thoughts were a toss-up between leprosy and a horrific car accident that involved a window launch (although he did briefly tantalize his mind with the idea of her being himself in female form).

She had the vibe of a Frankenstein's monster made in the era of sticky white tape instead of stitches, although crafted with an exceptionally bad sense of fashion, a crushed bearskin cap on her head and a winter coat three seasons too warm around her shoulders, double-stuffed with down, an ostrich in training gear.

After a moment of watching the canned tuna roll down the aisle and the dust settle into its place, his wits returned, and he jogged down the aisle in a helpful mood.

"Are you OK, miss? Anything…reinjured or reopened?" he asked, unsure of etiquette.

"Oh no, no, I'm fine, thank you. Just clumsy old Natalie," she responded, her eyes nervously twitching about, as if she were infested with the spirit of Chicken Little.

Sylvester knelt down, collecting cans to make it easier for her to stand (and if he happened to crush his fingers between them, so be it).

"Were you trying to pull from the middle?" he asked. "I always do that, as if it's the magic can with a smelly golden Wonka ticket in it."

The girl giggled a little snort, amused. "No, I was actually trying my best to leave a few feet of space between me and the cans, but as always, I seem to have my own gravity well that pulls things towards me."

"This happens a lot does it?" he asked.

The girl tried her best to hold up her bandage covered arm as she gave him a cockeyed expression of disbelief. "Where do you think all of this came from?" she asked.

"Towers of tuna?" Sylvester snarked with a smirk.

"And juice towers and stacks of cheese wheels and barrels of twisty pretzels and even little Christmas displays full of twinkly lights and paint-by-number houses. If it's on an endcap, it's likely to fall on me." She paused, calculating briefly in her mind, before adding, "Except paper towels and toilet paper. Those never seem as aggressive."

There was no scent of animosity in her voice, only a small sprinkling of reserved expectation, as if she was damned regardless of her own personal hopes and dreams. As Sylvester looked on, as if to underscore the moment, a dozen more cans slid off the display and dribbled across her foot like ants on a hill.

"Steel toe," she said, as he looked with open eyes at her mildly unchanging expression as one bounced firmly and angrily off her shoe.

As he instinctively reached down to pick up the new escapees his eyes wandered across her legs, scar-covered between bandages, a few dozen stitches visible to a moment's inspection.

As he stood up he noticed her eyes briefly dance across his own arm of Jackson Pollack-like scarwork, a look of curiosity and acceptance fleeting across her face.

"You have some nice tattoos," she commented, pointing towards his other, non-scarred arm. "I don't often see people with tattoos of arms on their arms."

Sylvester lifted his tattoo arm and twisted it toward himself as if he'd only just stepped into this body and now needed to identify what she was talking about. Midway down his forearm was a tattoo of, strangely enough, a forearm.

"Oh…I'm not sure I even noticed that one before," he said.

"Didn't notice?" she giggled, "Was it tequila or Mad Dog?"

Sylvester nervously slipped his hand back into his pocket, fumbling with his nail clippers and trying to distract himself.

"Oh no, I mean…well…ummm…I get a lot of tattoos. I don't really care what they're of. I get them removed every few months, something else put in their place. My buddy that does the ink…he…well…he sometimes leaves jokes for me to find."

"A human Etch-A-Sketch, huh? So why bother getting a tattoo if you remove it? Why not stay a clean slate?" she asked.

Sylvester's tongue untied and rewet itself as he pondered the ceiling, "I enjoy it? It's relaxing. Don't care much what it's of, as long as it takes up space and time. And I sorta enjoy getting 'em removed, too. We all have hobbies, right?"

"Most of mine revolve around couch sitting and traffic dodging," she said.

"If you chased your tail and peed on fire hydrants you'd be a ringer for my old dog."

She glanced at him for a moment, trying to decide if he genuinely didn't realize that he'd just insinuated that she was a dog. Then she let it go.

"Well, thanks for helping me pick myself up and for clearing a path for me. Best of luck with your inking hobby."

And then she started walking down the aisle, a small limp to one side, her opposite foot dragging a little. She had the look of someone in a movie, heroically walking away before something blew up. He couldn't tell if these were new injuries from her fall or if she was still indulging the past, but it somehow gave him a smirk of appreciation and respect.

He watched her shuffle halfway down the aisle before he awkwardly realized he'd have to walk past her to get to his cart. He thought briefly about looping around down the next aisle and swinging back for it, or even wandering off to fetch milk and look busy.

But then she paused and glanced up and down at the empty spot he'd left in the bandage area, her head swiveling back and forth trying to take in the sudden break in merchandise where she'd been intent on shopping. And then her eye caught his cart, parked strangely towards the end, unclear if it was a customer's planned purchase or a pile of returns not yet restocked.

Sylvester quickly jogged to his cart, passing her as he went, before wheeling it back around with a squeak. She watched him curiously as his eyes wandered guiltily while he tried to explain, "I'm sorry, did you need some of this? I didn't mean to take it all. Well, I mean, I did, but if you needed it, I don't need it…today. Ummm, I mean…"

He squibbled as he searched for words.

"I shop in bulk," he added, as if this explained it all.

His eyes swiveled around towards the ceiling and avoided her gaze as he tried to imagine why the average person would have a cart filled to brimming with enough supplies to stock an ambulance. He stole a glance and saw she was smiling faintly at him, the corner of her mouth upturned in amusement.

"I needed some butterflies in the green package. Recyclables. Spare any?" she asked.

Sylvester dug into his cart, rifling through the green boxes looking at pictures on the outside and ignoring the cryptic alien lettering. He pulled a couple out and handed them over.

"Anything else?" he asked. "I have some, uhhh…"

He felt like a briefcase salesman, digging through his wares, desperate for a sale, trying to be helpful without seeming greedy. He pulled out another package absently, looked at it briefly, then kept going.

"…some moleskin? Umm…it sticks really well for a while and won't come off in the bath. Those are good…or some nice white tape…"

"No, this is all I needed for tonight, thanks," she said.

He gave her an unintentionally sad but accepting look, as if she'd just cost him his monthly sales quota and his final, fleeting, chance to get that ski trip vacation he was after.

She caught it and added, "I buy my moleskin in bulk and have a big stack at home already. It is good stuff."

"Oh."

"Sticks well in the shower," she agreed with a flirting smirk.

"Yeah, good stuff," he said.

"It was nice to meet you. Bye-bye."

And then she turned the corner and was gone, her two boxes of butterfly bandages in hand alongside his piqued interest and curiosity.

Sylvester stood frozen, his fingertips tensely gripping themselves into his hands on impulse, his heart beating faster than it normally would. He had a good girlfriend. There was no explanation for the pitter-pattering away in his chest. But for some reason it was there.

The silence was quickly broken by another loud crash from around the corner, followed by a curtly exasperated mutter of "Ugh," and then immediately pursued by a tinkle of broken ceramics.

Sylvester stepped around the corner to see the girl slogging through a fallen stack of broken sake cups, giving the appearance that a display from the far side of the aisle had leapt in her direction on a suicide mission.

She gave him a wave as if to indicate she was fine, and then cautiously stepped into the checkout line while a small elderly woman appeared with a dustpan and began sweeping up the chipped bits of cup.

Sylvester's heart gave another brief thump. He wasn't normally tongue tied after meeting a pretty girl, but this girl intrigued him on a different level. He'd always felt his perfect mate was someone like Felicia, someone who dished out the pain he craved so readily, and yet here was a girl who didn't seek it out. Instead she hid from it. Avoided it. And it chased after her with reckless abandon.

She made him curious. And jealous.

He reached down and picked up a piece of the sharp, jagged sake ceramic that had slid across the floor and squeezed it tightly before turning to finish his shopping, curious about acupuncture kits and wondering if they'd be shelved near the lockpicks.

CHAPTER 3

THE JOB

Felicia was sitting comfortably at the kitchen table by the time Sylvester returned, an array of traditionally non-sharp objects in the midst of being sharpened. Some, like the old and dulled-down salad forks, an argument could be made for. Others, like the screwdriver, the business cards, and the ballpoint pens, seemed less in need of sharpening.

"Oh, thank god, I was afraid our...ballpoint pens...were getting too dull..." Sylvester began.

"Seriously?" she interrupted, "You're giving me shit about sharpening things? Wait, no, I'm almost certain it wasn't *me* who was caught, twice, attempting to sharpen the *doorknob*."

Sylvester feigned innocence, "It was getting dull..."

Felicia tilted him a quixotic, lopsided smirk. "I trapped you a lunch. Sandwich at the bottom."

"Oh?"

"Your favorite, with bacon, on sourdough."

"The occasion?"

"An urge to lob over some lunchtime fun? But no peeking!" she said, squinting him a comical evil eye.

He flicked the bag with his finger as he passed it, setting off the hard snapping sound of a mousetrap nestled within.

"You peeked..."

"Shoddy construction."

She smiled broadly, her teeth sunbathing, both of them knowing that she'd reset it while he was in the shower, better and more stable, capable of surviving more than a finger flick and a bus commute. He realized he may need to start inspecting between the bread slices for traps.

He often wondered how far she went with her clients and whether she'd do well to have malpractice insurance or a rainy-day lawyer fund for the almost certain day when she went too far and hurt the wrong person.

But for now, he thought little of it, concentrating more on the ticking clock and his impending work shift that began at 1am at the local Fry Daddy House (Home of the Calamari Cuttlefish Clam Bake!). Third shift paid better than second, which paid about the same as first when you balanced the tips out. Not necessarily tips in the conventional sense of money left for good service and a quick meal, but the tips drugged and drunken people left when they were overly excited about the prospect of getting fish sticks and french fries at three in the morning.

Sylvester set his alarm and hopped in the shower, flipping the heat to 'scalding', ice cold to start before turning to blistering heat a minute later. His skin was used to it, a calloused crust from years of being beaten upon. He imagined this was how turtles evolved shells long ago.

He looked down at the tattoo of the forearm on his forearm and chuckled to himself. It was certainly different; he'd give Socket that.

There were a variety of other tattoos spread around that he gave a glance to, hoping to ensure he wasn't caught again in such a strange conversation about his own skin.

He was generally in tune with the specifics; where each scar came from and the number of stitches it took to fix. He was a pop culture trivia expert on his own body, the lone exception being the ink he'd gotten changed so often that his skin matched the cracked, leathery look of the beaten old boots he sometimes wore in the snow.

He traced his hand up his left arm as he went, passing by the silly self-referential forearm, noting a couple of birds flapping around, a small dragon breathing fire at them playfully, a few trees twisting around like snakes, the mustachioed logo from the local pizza place, and the few core staples he never had removed - Calvin & Hobbes playfully operating a transmogrifying box and a small drawing of Obelix, the menhir delivery man, carrying a tall stack of Roman helmets that toppled toward the underside of his wrist. Those were his first tattoos and he viewed them as proper scars.

His right arm was balanced with a web of crisscrossing scars and bruises in various states of healing. The one on his elbow that looked like a waffle iron was from a skateboard accident when he was twelve.

The one in the shape of Captain Hook's missing hand was a burn from a hot lighter. The dozen indentations near his wrist were from a radiator he leaned against for a good minute after it began to singe and smell funny. His inner forearm was scarred with a shape that he swore Prince stole when he changed his name. There was even a large discolored area near his bicep from a lumberjacking incident that reminded him of Gorbachev when the temperature dropped.

The damage went on and on, weaving in and out, mimicking a topographical map of the Grand Canyon with its gullies and crooked donkey trails. There was little truly left untouched at this point, and what there was he wanted occupied by the right things, his last bits of canvas, the final scraps of paper in a world without trees. Those places he saved to be scarred in memorable ways he hadn't yet discovered, not simply another knife prod or lighter burn or bit of staple-gun mischief. Everything else could be doubled up or reused if need be. Let him pincushion the backside he could never see and throw scars on top of old tattoos. Those were already lost causes and blighted lands.

There were also a few spots he kept roped off and tried not to damage, the most obvious being above the neck and below the belt (although on occasion he was known to allow Felicia to dabble and play). After all, he still needed to interact with the rest of society, job hunting in particular being a challenge when he arrived with a bandaged bloody ear that drew condescending squints from interviewers.

His shower alarm went off, pulling him back from his rambling dream state, signaling he was about to run out of both time and hot water.

He dried himself quickly and then shaved, happy that the razor was worn down and the stubble stuck in the blades. The fact that he had permanent razor burn was of little concern to him, often birthing the fun distraction of tiny pimples to pick at.

He broke the seal on the new box of adhesive gauze pads and fastened a fresh one to his still bleeding cigarette burn and pulled a fresh beater on over it, throwing his work shirt in a bag that he tossed over his shoulder.

Felicia was now busy playing with wires and pliers at the table, rigging something to a coffee pot that did not belong to their apartment. He reached down and grabbed a 9-volt and put it to his tongue, giggling at the buzz.

"I need that at full strength," she ordered, snatching it back from him.

He smiled and leaned in to kiss her goodbye, at which point she electrocuted him with an exposed wire, followed by another electrocution, and then a third before he finally insisted he needed to be out the door or he'd miss his bus.

*****

The ride was uneventful, Marty once again his late-night escort, continuing to drowsily nap most of the way, occasionally stopping only long enough to open and shut the door and spout something racist, before continuing on his meditative driving tour. He may have missed a few stops.

"Hello Carl," muttered Sylvester as he walked behind the counter at work, waving weakly to his supervisor who stood proudly at the register, waiting patiently, a huge happy grin prepared for the next early morning muncher who craved fried fast food.

Sylvester had little respect and no understanding for Carl, who seemed to live for the place. Show up early, take extra shifts, and be sad when he's sent home early and unneeded. It wasn't like he was in it for the money, already being the highest paid peon in the place, inching up the seniority ladder for 15 years so that he outpaced even the day managers. He quite enjoyed his big fish status in the bathtub-sized pond he lived in. Sylvester often wondered what his home life was like, finally deciding he didn't want to know, imagining it a sad cacophony of loneliness and masturbation that culminated in eBay auctions and post office deliveries. If there was one goal Sylvester still had in his life, it was to not end up like Carl. Marty seemed to have a better life sleep-driving a bus.

A young couple sidled into the place, hanging on one another and giggling profusely while peppering each other with sloppy kisses and groping hands, excitedly discussing the odds of such a fine establishment as this not only being open late, but also being located directly between the bar and the motel that rented by the hour.

Sylvester got used to these people, the staples of his working life. It was the rare oddity that came in wanting nothing more than a midnight meal and a place to rest their legs. Instead, it was generally the late-night hookups, the faces forgotten by morning, the homeless who'd found a fiver and needed to spend it before they lost it, the cops and the cabbies who needed a pick-me-up on a double shift.

"It was just a job," he told himself time and again; a way to pay for his vices and keep the debtman at bay. Maybe one day something better would come along, but for now, this was enough of an outlet, a gathering of available inflictions not to be found in deskbound brain work. Blue collars were always more burlap than silk.

Sylvester pulled on his work shirt and took his place at the grill, his opening ritual to starting the games. He checked the sharpness of his knives, the sizzle of his fry oil, and the sear of his grill plate, his index finger getting slightly cut, fried, and sautéed in the process.

He always inevitably returned to the oil as if it were a Siren calling to him from the open ocean. The oil teased and tantalized him, bubbling like a molten welcome card, an amber bath that promised heat and happiness. Maybe one day he'd take the perilous plunge, but for now he sacrificed plastic lids and pasta bowls he'd watch shrivel like Shrinky Dinks.

"Here comes Biggie Berwick," muttered Carl, who spoke so often with exuberance that you knew this was the low point of his day.

Bastian Bottlewock Berwick had a way with making an entrance.

The bell rang on the door and in walked a huge peacock feather, followed soon after by a slight man with an invisible entourage. He was ostentatiously dressed in primary colors with large, dark sunglasses blocking his eyes and giving the air of having a bevy of women under his employ, but what he actually did and who with, none could be too sure.

He often kept conversations with those who weren't there and maintained friendships with people who may not exist, but they seemed to enjoy him all the same for the attention he gave them. And for the owl-eyed fry guys he ordered a lot of calamari that helped keep the late-night shift alive.

He announced himself at the register in his own language, "I am hip-hop chilling Biggie Berwick, master see-foo, kwan to-fu, samurai blackbelt defender of chin yen, and the robemaster of Wembly Hall."

His words danced with rhythm off his silver tongue. It was full of both melancholy and excitement, and tasted like something fresh and new, even if it meant nothing.

Carl looked at him confused, unsure what the proper response was to the code he'd just heard, fearful that the wrong response may loose something far worse. He defaulted to programming.

"Welcome to the Fry Daddy House, would you like to try a Fry Daddy Platter?" asked Carl with formulaic sincerity.

"Me and my crew be lookin' for FOUR Daddy platters. Make three ta go, put the fourth on a plate. Extra slaw and pickles."

Carl leaned into the microphone and repeated the order. Sylvester scowled at him from three feet away.

Biggie Berwick paid with a crisp couple of twenties, the lone contents of a shiny money clip emblazoned with fake diamonds in the shape of a ladybug.

Sylvester threw down the order in the fry basket and watched it bubble away, his hand slowly tractoring itself towards the oil, letting the spitting spray tickle his palm.

Biggie Berwick settled himself and his entourage into a corner booth, giving his phantom friends their choice of seats. Watching him work his strange voodoo was simply that – strange. At times Sylvester felt this must be what it was like to live in an asylum, surrounded by crazy people and their imaginary friends.

Yet Berwick was allowed out into the real world, wandering on his own without supervision. It gave Sylvester flashbacks to being a child with a five-dollar bill, loosed in the mall with a passionate penchant for comics and candy.

The fry timer dinged, and he pulled up the basket to drain, his finger teasing down the side of the metal mesh until he felt the oil's sting. He scooped voluptuous amounts of coleslaw into overflowing plastic tubs and speared more pickles than Ishmael had whales, wrapping them up with the fried platters and sliding them out on a tray.

"Order ready, please," he said with a snark of conformity to Carl, who stood two feet away on the other side of the grill counter, staring him down in readiness, excitement brimming on his face like Christmas morning sunlight. Carl lived for conformity and rules. Sylvester even palmed the bell twice because he knew he could get away with it.

Carl slid the tray off and quickly loaded it with forks and knives and napkins and straws that he'd already parsed out and had at the ready, and then made a point of reorganizing the tray in the most pleasing way possible before walking over to Berwick's table and delivering it, seeming more like Bruce Wayne's butler than the register attendant at a midnight fry house.

"You need to settle the fries better next time," Carl said as he returned, "Those were too uneven."

"They're french fries. They don't care."

"The customer cares! The more pleasing it looks the better for business. If it looks like a mess, we'll be treated like we're a mess."

"We ARE a mess," Sylvester said with a smirk, waving his hands around the place as if indicating the obvious, hoping a ceiling tile would fall loose in sympathetic emphasis.

"If we aim to be a higher-class establishment people will learn from our example," Carl said with a huff.

Sylvester got the impression Carl had been reading self-help books.

The night dragged on for hours as it always did, mindlessly, customers trickling in every half hour in small, last-call bunches. Sylvester made the best of his down time by juggling forks and bending spoons and distracting himself with frivolous fun, but the work games were always limited when you had unexciting people to play with.

CHAPTER 4
BREAKFAST

"More coffee, please, Mrs. Mosquito!" shouted Felicia over the bustling din of the breakfast crowd.

Sylvester and Felicia were seated at their normal table at the Schneider Diner, a corner booth with a shallow side that forced Sylvester to wedge himself in. Their breakfast rendezvous had become games of legend. They felt public settings brought out the best in them.

Sylvester was always beaten down and tired, just off his long shift at Fry Daddy's, while Felicia was freshly showered and bound for work, brimming with aggressive ideas after hours of creative downtime with which to plan and prepare.

By the time the coffee arrived Felicia had already inflicted eleven different types of unexpected suffering on Sylvester, who was noisily sucking on a sore index finger still smarting from the electrified jukebox he hadn't been expecting.

"That was a good one," he said.

"Did you like that?" she asked, the happy smirk of wonderful gift-giving playing across her lips. "I've been laying the groundwork for weeks!"

"It was great! I wasn't expecting it at all. Socket would be so proud."

She was looking lovingly at the jukebox now, her mind ignoring his existence.

"I'm going to leave it…let someone else enjoy it…"

"Felicia, come on. You can't do that," he scolded.

"Why not? Things malfunction. People get shocked. It's not that big of a deal." Her voice had a tinge of childish anger as she pouted and batted her eyes a few times.

"And what if it's a little kid? Or some old guy with a pacemaker? I like this stuff. Most people don't."

She glared at him for a moment, seemingly weighing in her mind his anger versus her fun, before finally reaching under the table and starting to fiddle with the wires.

"Fine…but I'm not taking it apart. I'm still leaving it for us to play with."

"As long as it's only us."

A creeping silence spread over the table as they both glanced around absently, the conversation stalled without the torment to tether it. Sylvester started playing with an extra fork on the table that wouldn't be missed or needed.

"So…" Felicia began, hoping for a spontaneous conversation epiphany, "…how was work? Any frying incidents?"

"Nothing memorable."

"Still haven't pulled the trigger on the full hand submersion yet, huh?"

"No, not yet. Tough trigger to pull, what with the lifelong scarring and all."

"I'm always here to help. Ya know, if you need a push or a nudge…someone to hold your hand in the oil while you cry…"

He glared up at her with a grin. "Thanks. If I get cold feet, I'll call you."

"My birthday IS coming up you know. Nothing says love like…"

"…blistering skin?" he cut in.

She glowered at him, "I was going to say 'couples activities'."

"I'll keep it in mind."

Sylvester bent the fork tines back and to the outside as he started bending the stem around top, his fingers turning white under the pressure, small tine marks branding themselves into his skin as he twisted the fork under the table, leaning his arm strength into it. With gloves and pliers it was easy enough. With bare hands it was an imposing challenge.

"You look like you're laying an egg," said Felicia, mocking and mean. "Humpty Dumpty, The Dimwitted Fry Cook."

Sylvester glared at her, "You know I don't like you calling me that…"

"Oh, come on Dumpty, grow thicker skin!"

"This coming from the girl with nipple hair?"

Felicia's eyes lit up as she swatted at him angrily, "That's off-limits!"

"So's name calling. We talked about this; you get your off-limits, I get mine."

"Fine," she grumbled with a look of reserved disgust, a pout of immaturity racing across her face. "But yours is for wimps…"

Sylvester gave her another egg-laying look and then placed a fork bent into the shape of a cockroach on the table. The inner tines bent out and upward like antennae while the outer tines bent down like legs, the fork's tail wrapping around itself like a shell.

"Oh, another one?" she asked, her mood lightening as she gave it a playful poke. "You must have a whole intrusion by now! Surprised this place is still in business with their lack of stolen forkware."

"I don't take many from here. I like this place," he said as he slipped the metal critter into his pocket.

Felicia was already distracted, mixing salt into the sugar dispenser. Sylvester looked on, seeing his polar opposite mate in a polar opposite way. He liked to wreak havoc on himself. She liked to dish it out. It was a strange love, a strong hint of convenience and addiction tying them together.

But there were core differences that went beyond the barbarity. He was selfish with his obsessions, the fun being in the moment and his own skin. She was content laying the trap she knew would be sprung, even if she didn't savor the enjoyment of watching it happen.

If she had her way, she'd probably spend her days sharpening ketchup packets and kicking the walkers out from little old grannies. He didn't even want to know what she did when he wasn't around to instill a sense of morality. Hours left alone with a vicious hobby and an easily manipulated conscience? Maybe he should start reading the police log, just in case.

Sylvester gave a start. He wasn't expecting it when he felt something sharp and round poking into his knee. Felicia looked up from her sugar shaker, smirking to herself, both of her hands still visible on the tabletop.

He wiggled, trying to glance under his shallow side of the table, before spotting what looked like a boot spur rubbing into his knee.

"Were you wearing that all morning?" he asked.

"Nope. Put it on when I was supposed to be disconnecting the jukebox."

Sylvester gave her a crooked look and immediately reached for the jukebox, earning himself a shock twice as powerful as the first one.

"Enough! Turn it off. If you kill someone they're not gonna let you giggle it off with a charismatic smile."

She pouted and fell into a baby voice, "Awww, someone doesn't have a sense of humor this morning…"

"And someone else doesn't have a sense of humanity," he shot back. "Where'd you find spurs anyways?"

"Mail order."

"Well played, equestrian catalogs, well played…" he said with a nod of respect.

The waitress waddled over with a hot pot of coffee and topped off both of their mugs, setting the pot down on the table as she reached for her order pad. Sylvester's hand had already snaked out, his fingertips pressing against the scalding hot glass of the pot, his mind laughing at its failed attempts to melt off his prints. Felicia nudged it further toward him.

"Hey, kids, how was the food today? Scrumptious?" wheezed the waitress through her muffler mouth.

"It was great as always, thanks Mos," said Sylvester.

The waitress slapped the bill down on the table, "Here's your check. Don't forget, tip's not included."

Sylvester heard a twang in her voice directed at Felicia.

"Thanks Mrs. Mosquito!" Felicia said cheerily.

The waitress gave her a crooked look and walked off to another table.

"I like Mrs. Mosquito. She's the best waitress here," said Felicia as she pulled out exact change.

"Then why don't you ever tip her? She hints pretty heavily these days. I think you just like her name, which incidentally, isn't Mosquito. It's Mosquit."

"Close enough. I've never met anyone named Mosquito!" she said ignoring him. "And c'mon, you know me. I get a buzz from stiffing her."

"It's one thing to poke someone with a stick; it's another to be a cheapskate, especially to people who serve you food. Do you know what kind of looks I get when I come here by myself? It's anger and pity."

"Pity?" asked Felicia as she counted out the pennies.

"For having to put up with you."

"Oh, you know you love me."

"Only when the tips are good."

"Ha. Ha. You're a funny little man." She glared at him with a smirk in her eye. "I may have to make you pay for that later."

He smirked back. "Looking forward to it."

"OK, I gotta get to work now. Lots of pain and anguish to inflict on the unsuspecting," said Felicia, clapping her hands together and rubbing them.

"And I need a long nap," said Sylvester with a yawn.

"Vampire."

"Mr. Hyde."

They smiled at each other and leaned in for a quick kiss before Felicia slid off the seat and sashayed out the door, leaving him to extricate himself from the seat he was wedged into.

He paused, making sure she was gone, before throwing down a $5 tip and touching the jukebox, just to be sure.

CHAPTER 5
TATTOOS & LIGHT SOCKETS

Sylvester stared up at the ceiling, noting the cracks and water spots and the sagging signs of squirrel nests living in the walls. The house was old and rented to the kinds of people who wouldn't muster the energy or the interest to move; the ones who didn't mind scurrying neighbors and funny smells.

Light Socket had lived there for years now, fitting that bill and building his own nest. The squirrels probably saw him as nothing more than a large neighbor who shared their interest in winter storage.

His rooms were piled high with stacks and collections of various types and sorts, all seemingly on the verge of toppling should you wander too close or allow a gusty breeze to cross their teetering tops. Sylvester glanced to his right and picked up a newspaper from the closest stack and chuckled at the mid-90s publishing date. Yeah, Socket had been here a while.

For a few years Sylvester had called it home, his last vestige of bachelor normalcy before Felicia confiscated him away to her closeted apartment life of nightly pokes and prods. He smiled at his surroundings, evidence of the alternate universe his life might have taken without her.

"OK, Vest, you ready?" came a booming and squeaky and bearded voice as it wandered into the room, echoing around the canyoned walls of piled TV Guides and comics books and empty wooden booze boxes.

"Ready and waiting. As always. You keep to your schedule like a Wonderland rabbit with a timepiece."

Light Socket gave a hearty, mocking laugh, "Yeah, yeah, I get it. You're oh so witty."

Sylvester didn't have many close friends, but Socket was one of them, the odd remnant of high school who'd somehow slipped through to the rest of life.

They'd met in one of those science classrooms with the sinks and the gas spigots, the Bunsen burners and the strange things in jars. Back then Sylvester carried pliers to tease his early urges, a masochistic puberty, while Socket carried fuses and wiring for similar reasons. One day they decided to marry them together and have an electrical socket preside over the nuptials. The friendship really took off from there.

"So, what're you after today?" asked Socket as he leaned down, giving off the air of a barber offering haircut advice.

"I want you to fix this," said Sylvester as he lifted his tattooed arm, showing off the forearm within a forearm.

Socket laughed hard and howled. "Oh man, how long did it take before you saw it? I was bitin' my tongue something fierce when I was doin' it! That's what you get for zoning out..."

"Didn't notice it 'til last night. Someone at the supermarket pointed it out to me. Felt like an idiot."

"As you should!"

"Well, yeah. But now I want you to fix it."

Light Socket lifted the arm and looked at the tattoo with an analytical air. "It's still too fresh to be removed. Best I can do is add to it or cover it up, your call. It is a forearm though, so I could probably attach a body to it..."

"Anything would be an improvement. But nothing stupid. I don't want some dude spanking it or something."

Socket smirked knowingly at him. "I've been drawing a lot of the fairy tale folk recently; I could give that a go?"

Sylvester nodded, "As long as..."

"I promise! No self-indulgence."

Socket wheeled up a stool and pulled over an ottoman, piled high with magazines and paper pads and topped with a tray of inks and tattoo needles. The tray itself had a medieval feel to it, but one that was quickly undermined by an amazingly odd array of glittering gumball stickers stuck to it. Hello Kitty and car emblems mixed with hearts and butterflies, roses and daffodils, some adorned with saying like "Love is eternal" and "Mom" that spoke to cheesy teenagers and oedipal bikers. Socket clearly had other clients for his home-brewed tattoo services.

He turned his attention to Sylvester's arm and pulled up his sleeve, wiping it down with an alcohol-soaked rag while Sylvester smiled and looked off toward the squirrel nests, closing his eyes and wandering off in his mind to enjoy it, preparing to let the chills wash over him.

Sylvester couldn't fully explain why he liked getting tattoos. It reminded him of getting haircuts as a kid when he'd get goosebumps and excitement vibes as the hair buzzer hit his neck.

He felt Socket start some base scribbling on his arm and immediately tried to guess what it was. So far it only felt like squiggles; maybe when the needle hit it'd help.

"So, how's The Leash doing?" Socket asked as he leaned in, tightening a design on Sylvester's arm. "She run anyone off the road recently? Kick any kids in the shins? Swap acid in for holy water?"

"She's good. Same old, same old. Causin' stress and distress up and down the coast, working hard..."

"At that weird pain parlor of hers?"

"Yeah, she does OK with it."

"There're some strange people out there. Fetishists and convulsives."

Sylvester reached over to the closest pile and grabbed whatever was on top, "This coming from the guy with thirty copies of the 1987 Bugs Bunny Halloween coloring book?"

Socket paused, looking at him with wide eyes, as if his inner child had been offended, "Those're collectibles, man. Retirement fund."

"Yeah, keep telling yourself that," said Sylvester as he tossed it back on the pile.

"You never get worried about her, do ya?"

"Worried? Nah. She's great."

"Girl like that, I'd be afraid she'd kill me in my sleep or something. Fatal Attraction syndrome. Cut off something near and dear to me."

"'Licia's into pain, not damage. She likes to poke and prod, not chop and maim. The trap more'n the damage, ya know?"

"Something wrong with that girl, man, I'm tellin' ya."

"Nah, she's a good fit for me. Loyal, loving...just a bit mean-spirited is all."

"I wouldn't leave my ex's cat with that girl."

Sylvester rolled his eyes back to the ceiling squirrels and let them close, "She's not as bad as you think."

A moment later the whir of the kit started up and Sylvester heard some dabbing and rubbing on paper towels before the needle dipped into his skin and broke the silence of his mind.

Sylvester had never done hard drugs but suspected the feeling of getting inked to be similar, albeit drawn out slow and tortoise-like. His whole body was on edge, his nerves standing up, as if he'd somehow captured the moment before climax and stretched it to hours.

He didn't hear Socket's humming as he worked, and barely registered the three intervals when a pizza was ordered, delivered, and eaten, lost in his revelry.

After two hours something wet slapped into Sylvester's face, waking him from his ink daze.

"Blacks're done, but my hand's killing me from noodling all that crazy McFarlane detail you love. Come back in a week and we can fill the color in."

Sylvester looked down at his arm and saw a friendly tree goblin staring up at him, leaping and throwing seeds, twisting and turning around the established scenery.

"Nice," he said.

"You're a fun challenge to work on," said Socket. "Nobody else lets you ink the same spot again and again like a chalkboard. Will be curious to see that arm when you hit fifty; see if the skin just slides right off the bone."

"Like good ribs, right?"

"Exactly!"

"Got any alcohol to rub?"

"You know you're supposed to wait a little bit, right? Let it settle and heal?"

"Alcohol?" Sylvester repeated with a smirk.

Socket shook his head as he tossed him a plastic jug and a dry towel, the door squeaking as he walked out, "Just make sure you don't ooh and ahh too loudly. Don't want anyone thinking I'm running a brothel over here."

CHAPTER 6

THE GARGOYLED BOOKSTORE

Sylvester stood in the nail and screw aisle of the local hardware store killing time, testing out the various offerings found in little cardboard slide-out bins while lamenting that they weren't made as sharp and pointy as they used to be.

For whatever reason, nail technology was continuing to advance regardless of the lack of a need or desire for it. Blunted tips, new metals, various head sizes, twists and corkscrews of design, color, and even longevity were now mixed among the variants to choose from, a sure sign that the American culture of throw-away-personalization had infiltrated even the most absurd. There was even an entire row of multi-colored "ladies nails" that reminded Sylvester of golfing pro shops.

Felicia had a membership here, one of only a dozen they offered to frequent customers, herself being a popular purchaser of special ordered items most customers couldn't find a use for and often injured themselves with while trying to. In today's case, she was picking up a pneumatic drill attachment for boring holes in glass without causing cracks.

She'd been busy yammering away complaints at the checkout clerk for a solid twenty minutes now, her special-ordered sandpaper having still not arrived, while her latest pair of 'lifetime warranty' pliers had already worn down.

So for now Sylvester wandered up and down the aisles, playing with products and looking for injurious ideas, testing the strength of different ropes, wrapping bits of barbed wire around his wrists like bracelets, and teasing himself with a nail gun while wondering if he'd get more than one use out of it before he deemed it "too destructive".

He often had that problem, temptations that went past the pain and teased the line of outright danger.

Sylvester had only seriously injured himself twice, once when he was twelve and experimenting with a belt sander, and again when he was in his early twenties and trying to carve ice sculptures with a chainsaw. In both cases he ended up in the hospital with an earful from doctors and family about his irresponsible nature, their endless prodding eventually compelling him to give up his new toy.

He may enjoy and appreciate scratching his perpetual itches, but he wasn't an idiot; he didn't want to kill himself doing something stupid. He'd read the award books and knew there would be a chapter devoted to him if he screwed up impressively enough, so he tried to keep it simple and subtle, a vast many small sips of soreness rather than huge gulping draughts of damage.

His hardware wandering had taken him full circle to the exit, and across the way he spied a bookstore, quaint and small and nestled in a notch, far from the absurd warehousian chain monstrosities.

He always appreciated the small stores, his mother being a book lover who'd lose herself for hours in places like that, its muffin-like nooks and crannies stuffed with obscure books you'd be hard pressed to find at the force-feed stores.

He waved to Felicia, grabbing her attention as he walked his fingers through the air and motioned to the bookstore. She waved him off with her eyes and went back to screaming at the poor clerk, his face shivering on the verge of tears and ritualistic suicide. Sylvester knew her enough to suspect she had nothing on order and perfectly working pliers, but simply enjoyed torturing the poor man. She didn't limit her sadistic ways to the physical plane, knowing full well that an emotional toll often had a longer impact. This clerk would certainly remember her on the next visit.

Sylvester skipped across the street, stubbing his toes on the asphalt as he went, happy he'd made the decision to go with sandals instead of sneakers. Sneakers might've had the advantage of letting small pebbles settle in and grind away for hours, but open toes gave access to far more freedom of experimentation. He'd once impulse-kicked a pile of mulch and managed to get splinters in places he hadn't known existed. Ever since, he enjoyed competitive mulching as a pastime.

The door creaked and whined as he opened it, stepping him into a bookshop that looked like it'd been built in the 1800s. There were polished wooden shelves and banisters, shiny floors of worn oak, an intricate ceiling with exposed timbers, propping up softly turning fans that circulated the cool musty air, and nestled into the wooden beams all around, staring down like guardians, were dozens of carved and gargoyled heads.

The books lined the walls as he'd hoped, hardbacks and leatherspines waving at him from all around. If a bestsellers section existed, it was not to be seen.

He wandered and danced between stacks of American classics, old first editions behind panes of glass, ancient and worn leather chairs and small tables laden with tasseled books, teasing the reader to sit down and dive in and plan an expedition to a new world.

There was no coffee shop wedged in the corner, no vibrant children's room colored with stuffed animals, no music or movies or magazine racks devoted to pop culture. Only books, and more books, and beautifully ornate shelving to hold them.

There was a single cash register in the middle, old fashioned and mechanical, perched atop a podium desk that looked solid enough to have sunk the Titanic. Below its lip edge hung a small wooden sign with the phrase "Dog-ears are blasphemous" burned into its face.

And behind the desk, settled atop a tall stool like the oracle on her tripod, sat the klutzy girl from the supermarket.

Her head was still bandaged, her arms still wrapped, a long black and gold skirt dipping down to the floor concealing her legs, her mind deeply engrossed in a book she held delicately in her hands, the spine not even fully cracked.

Sylvester stared for a moment, not often a believer of the fates, and watched curiously as she carefully turned the page with a gloved finger.

Again, his hands nervously searched his pockets for something painful, wrapping around the forkroach he'd made at breakfast the previous morning, its long tendrilled antenna-tines poking into his fingers.

She looked almost the same as before, but somehow entirely different. More at home perhaps, in a bookstore, shelved with all the books and gilded spines of an older era.

The door behind him whined again as someone popped their head in, and she glanced up briefly and spotted him, her head cocking slightly to the side in puggled recognition. He immediately stepped aside, hoping to avoid the medusal gaze he was certain would freeze him to the spot.

He was standing now in a travel section, which he found comical, since it too was filled primarily with older books, only a few drab colors teasing their spines. He picked one up at random and started flipping through, noting black and white engravings that looked like something out of a Jules Verne novel. The writing itself was timely, scribed with old style flourishes like "a jaunt down to the seaside" and "shaking the dust off his spats" that seemed out of place in the 21st century, and some that were downright comical when seen in print, such as "beware of the galloping knob rot prevalent in the seedier districts".

He had the distinct feeling that the book was almost certainly printed before airplanes were in wide use and likely had a price tag far above what he made in a month, so he carefully slid it back in its place and softly walked on, as if fearing his hard footfalls would damage something he'd be expected to pay for.

He stepped around the corner and found himself trapped in a small wooden zoo of old-world fantasies, as Greek and Roman myths were carved into the crenels and leered down at him suspiciously. The room was tiny and felt delicate, a small velvet-cushioned bench in the middle that seemed like a museum piece daring someone to try sitting on it. He half expected an underpaid security guard to appear to ensure he didn't set off an alarm.

The shelves here were not full, but intentionally spaced, giving air to the books like one would to an elderly family member.

Sylvester scanned the titles with an inner voice that didn't even try to pronounce what he read. Euripides, Sophocles, Phrynichus, Aeschylus, and so on around, a room devoted to classic mythology as it was written down long ago in its original tongue.

He picked up one book titled *Philoctetes* and opened it, surprised to see symbols that looked more like math equations than a language.

"That one's in Greek, from the turn of the 18th century," came a voice from behind him, soft and casual and helpful.

Sylvester almost dropped the book, disguising the fact by putting his body in the way as he tried to regain his grip, turning his head and smiling like a magician's trick of misdirection.

"Just looking is all. I don't read Greek much these days…only when I'm on vacation."

The girl chuckled and smiled back at him, reaching out for the book and plucking it from his hand. She opened it to a seemingly random page and began to read, in Greek, her eyes flicking up to his as she went, stealing his understanding from them.

After a few lines she closed the book and gingerly handed it back to him, as if handling a newborn elderly person.

"But I only know how to read it, not what any of it means," she said as they both smiled and laughed, the awkwardness of the room lifting a little. Sylvester carefully put the book back on the shelf where he found it, still fearful of a lawsuit.

"So twice in the same week…" began Sylvester. "That doesn't happen often, meeting the same stranger. Unexpected and odd twists of fate."

"Is it?" she asked. "Or are we both simply memorable enough to remember?"

Sylvester thought briefly of Biggie Berwick and how unlikely he was to be forgotten.

"Maybe a little of both," he said as he looked around the small room, seeking both an escape route and a conversation topic. "This is a great shop…do you…uhhh…work here?"

It sounded stupid as soon as he said it, and she stared at him for a moment, the clockwork of her brain wondering whether his gears were in need of a cleaning.

"Yeah…?" she began, not quite quick enough to mock him properly. "It's my grandparents' store. My grandmother read books and my grandfather was a carpenter. When they came over they built the store and ran it for almost 40 years. Now they play cribbage in Boca and come back when they crave good lobster and the smell of old books."

"It's an amazing place. I saw it from across the street and had to come in and look around." He paused, feeling the need to explain his presence more. "I didn't know you worked here."

"You didn't? For a minute I wondered whether you were following me."

"If I was I would've come in first thing this morning," he smiled. "It's too hot out to stalk someone slowly."

She smiled back.

"I thought you said you hid at home on the couch and dodged traffic?" he asked as his eyes unconsciously wandered over her, his mind chuckling to itself as he realized he was more interested in her scars than her body.

"Well," she began, "we have a comfy couch in the History section I can hide in, and when you have a bookstore that doesn't carry paperbacks you don't have much traffic to worry about dodging."

"Do you carry anything written in the last century?" Sylvester asked, looking around the small room still, as if expecting to suddenly spy a cardboard display.

"Oh yes, plenty, but we try to only stock hardcovers that feel they belong here. A few Gaiman books, a bunch of Tolkiens, some Bradburys and Le Guins, a few nicely bound books of art...and I'd be lying if I didn't admit that there may be a couple of King first editions hidden away in an alcove, just to keep the regulars happy."

Sylvester smiled with the corner of his mouth, wishing he was well-read and could say something witty. The only Neil Gaiman he'd read was in comics and the only Tolkien he hadn't fallen asleep to was *The Hobbit*, and even with that he could be remembering a cartoon version.

He wasn't even sure why he was so concerned and trying so hard. He wasn't the straying sort and was already in a fine relationship with a great girl who hurt him more than any man deserved to be hurt. His hands searched his pockets for something sharp and distracting again.

She immediately broke the silence by losing her balance and falling, deftly aiming herself toward the velvet bench that, in turn, deflected her to the floor.

"Oh my gosh, are you alright?" he asked, his hand reaching out to help her up.

"Yeah, as we discussed, this happens often. At least here I'm used to it and fill the gaps with soft targets."

She stood and straightened her skirt, flattening the creases she'd created. Sylvester noticed she wasn't wearing heels or shoes of any sort – she'd lost her balance on bare feet.

"When my grandparents visit I have to move these to the back room and insist they're only used when we're busy," she added. "They don't believe in comfort while reading. Far prefer that Victorian ethic of sitting in a straight-back and being miserable."

Sylvester looked around curiously, "Busy…here?"

"I tell them we had an author signing with a long line of guests. They're old. They buy it"

Sylvester smirked at her, envisioning a batty old couple in Boca telling their friends over cribbage that Shakespeare and Lewis Carroll had swung by to sign some first editions.

The door whined again as loud plastic bags broke the moment, seeming to infiltrate the old-timbered interior with their 21st century newness.

"Vest? You in here still?" came Felicia's voice.

He turned to Natalie, his smirk now half-flipped, "I gotta run. But it was nice to help you up again. You have a great shop here. If I learn Greek, this will be the first place I visit!"

She smiled back, sadly, realizing his hand was taken, already missing him. "Thanks for the help up. I can now go back to hiding in my couch."

He smiled at her for a moment, seeing his own reflected confusion on her face, and then he stepped around the bookshelf, his voice carrying as he directed it to Felicia. "Yeah, I'm here. Let me carry some of those…you got another drill? Did we need it? Business expense, really? You're gonna get audited something fierce one of these years…"

And then the door whimpered closed and the bookshop was silent again.

CHAPTER 7
BIRTHDAY GIFTS

Felicia flipped through the assorted packages of sandpaper, fingertips rubbing across the surface of each as she fished for the proper feel. Not too firm, not too fine.

She settled on a heavy grit emery cloth, pliable and durable, with enough coarseness to be useful, while also being surprisingly waterproof. It had the look of being able to survive some punishment, which was a prerequisite in their household.

She tossed it on the table beside the spool of denim thread and a new package of needles she'd bought at the fabric store (and kept hidden from Sylvester, lest he use them as toothpicks). Felicia's inventive streak was branching off into tailoring now, age sending her signals and pushing her down the path of white picket fences and PTA meetings. She mentally kicked age in the shin.

She pulled out of storage the long-forgotten sewing machine, scrubbing it down and scraping it free from the dried and caked on failure of Sylvester's many experiments. It was the kind of appliance neither of them had much experience with and bought for all the wrong reasons.

When it was finally clean and threaded and sparkling new, Felicia braced herself with a vodka shot and slid open Sylvester's closet door. On the hangers hung his few nicer bits of clothing, the ones that had yet to be destroyed; a shirt, a tie, some slacks, and a jacket, together totaling one nice set of clothes, albeit completely unmatched.

Below these rested 'the heap', a mildew breeding entity that she swore breathed sulfur and ate Fraggles. Jagged bits of clothing emerged from all sides, many torn and shredded, various implements having been poked through them far too often to maintain their resiliency.

She hesitated for a moment, her eyes flitting about, hoping that her goal would reach out a hand, begging for rescue, but her charismatic charm held no sway on this creature, so with a deep breath of hope, Felicia dove in, searching and flinging, tossing aside clumps and piles and foul-smelling things she couldn't identify. She found t-shirts that appeared pink, bloodstained and bleached so many times that they fell apart in her hands. She pulled out a fleshy leather jacket that looked like it may have been plucked directly from a fresh cow with the ears still attached. She found grass-stained shoes that were shredded and filleted, trophies a victorious lawnmower may have once tried to stuff and mount on its mantle.

Finally, toward the bottom, she found her goal, an old pair of jeans still in workable shape, a gift from the previous year that'd been in the unfortunate position of being worn the day Sylvester discovered the magical bond between super glue and human skin, leading them to no longer possess the structural integrity needed to be worn in public.

They were perfect.

After a quick run through the laundry Felicia made her way to the sewing machine, flipping the jeans inside out as she went, inspecting the holes and planning her strategy.

She tore open the emery cloth and began fitting and pinning, aligning the cloth to the jeans, the sand-side in, a patchwork of patches that reinforced the stability and breathed in abrasive new life.

When the holes were all filled, the patches in place, she stitched them together, creating a strange and mottled pattern that she knew would make Sylvester appear far more hip than he'd know what to do with.

And finally, as an added surprise, she folded them nicely and wrapped them in a box, with some feminine paper and a feminine bow.

She smirked to herself with a little bit of pride, her soft side shining through with its faint glimmer of motherly potential. She had a good and loving streak in her, buried deep, and she occasionally let it sniff the fresh air around the holidays.

*****

Sylvester's birthday mornings were often a time of joy and pain that always ended decidedly one-sided against him.

Felicia would buy Sylvester injurious gifts that would always find their way into her hands, the rest of the morning spent sharpening their dull edges and trying them out.

But this year was different from the get-go; Felicia had made sure of it.

"Open this one first," she told him, offering up the box wrapped in paper from another holiday.

Sylvester looked down at his assortment of gift opening tools, his favorite part of the holiday; scissors, knives, and pliers all were available in triplicate, settled beside a letter opener, a box cutter, and even a rather large hatchet on the off chance his gift had come wrapped in a tree trunk.

He settled on an overly sharp letter opener and sliced into the wrapping paper smoothly, being sure to let the tip dip briefly into his finger with each swipe. Underneath the paper was a roll's worth of tape, tightly strapped around the box, as if the contents had tried to escape and were being punished for their crime.

Sylvester switched to the box cutter and began slicing incisions, a swashbuckling enthusiast who enjoyed the bad angles and clipped fingers more than discovering the mystery gift hidden within.

When he finally cut off the top he saw the blue jeans, punched through with holes and gashes, bad stitching visible like a gift from Grandma Scissorhands.

He looked on curiously at first, recognizing them from the year before, but since Felicia refused to re-gift, he knew he was missing something.

"Try them on," she encouraged.

He gave her an odd look, but was happy to obey, stripping off his pants, somewhat unsure what he'd find.

When his toe hit the inseam he started to smile, a long-teased thought now finally made real, and he dove in thigh deep, embracing his first ever pair of sandpaper pants.

He slid in his second leg and hopped them on, zippering and buttoning as he felt sandy spots scratch angrily against his legs, causing him to once again regret the societal bondage of underwear.

They felt amazingly rough, coarse and grating, causing Sylvester to grin broadly and happily before putting them to use, an impulsive bit of exercise that combined jogging, stretching, and lunging.

"They're perfect! I love 'em!" he finally said as he enjoyed the world's most abrasive wedgie and peppered Felicia with grateful hugs and kisses.

"Great," smiled Felicia, her good side taking the rare bow. "I wanted to get something for *you* for once! These're guaranteed to remove all the hair from your legs and at least a layer or two of skin!"

Sylvester couldn't stop beaming as he began to dance in place, slow-grinding into his own body.

Felicia smiled even wider, knowing the hook was barely baited. "OK, one more. You ready?"

"I get two presents this year?" he sang. "Sure, bring it on! But I'm not sure you can top this."

"We'll see…"

And with that, Felicia stood up and wordlessly left the apartment, Sylvester looking after her, his hips still gyrating, unsure if he was meant to follow or wait.

Minutes ticked by as he played with his pants and admired her stitchwork. He amused himself with the box cutter and the scissors, teasing new holes in his barely stable pants, before finally committing to removing his boxers and properly enjoying the gift.

Felicia finally returned 15 minutes later, Sylvester now splayed comfortably on the couch, his pants hiked up to his navel. He sat up immediately, curious about the pet carrier she was shielding with her body, certain that Tasmanian devils were still not capable of being housebroken.

"What is it? A new dog? Better not be a cat…" he began, already envisioning litter box duty and wondering how that could possibly beat sandpaper pants.

Felicia settled the carrier in the corner and squeezed open the door, swinging it wide, before settling behind Sylvester and wrapping her arms around him.

"You're gonna love this…" she whispered in his ear as her nails traced white lines in his neck.

And then they watched. And they waited.

But nothing came out.

Sylvester tried to adjust his seat and get a better view, but Felicia held him down. "You need to let him get comfortable first," she said in a soft voice completely unlike her own.

"What is it?" asked Sylvester, getting a sense of curious excitement as his nerves started to flutter.

"It's your perfect pet."

From the shadows of the cage dark eyes blinked awake and peered out, a small nose poking its way past the cage edge, sniffing the air, before disappearing again. And then, a tentative step. Then another. And finally, Sylvester could make out what it was that was nervously inching its way out of the carrier. His voice was soft at first, rising in pitch as the excitement took over.

"Is that a porcupine?! You got me a pet porcupine??"

The poor creature's quills poofed like a blowfish at the loud voice as its eyes went wide and small and it tried desperately to scamper backwards into its carrier, its inflated posterior blocking the way like an open umbrella.

Sylvester slid to his knees and dropped his voice to a whisper and gingerly held out his hand towards the frightened creature as he smiled broadly.

"Hey, fella…I'm sorry…shhhh….it's ok…"

Felicia smiled at him. "I heard they make pretty swell pets once they get used to you."

Sylvester's voice was barely above a fly's whisper now, "I didn't even know you could get one! Where? How? Oh man, I always wanted to pet these things at zoos, but they wouldn't let me…"

"A friend of a friend who lives outside the city. Fluke kinda thing, but when I heard about him needing a home I knew he was perfect for you."

The porcupine inched its way out again, sniffing and pawing and taking in the surroundings, its quills still up, nervous and on guard, slowly but curiously making its way towards Sylvester's still outstretched hand.

It took all of Sylvester's restraint not to rush in with a bear hug and pepper it with unexpected kisses, vibrating goosebumps of excitement quietly forcing their way through him.

The porcupine had begun testing the carpeting, deciding whether the strange alien surface could bare his weight, seeming to dance and hop between legs as he learned to enjoy the squishiness of Berber.

They watched as their new roommate circled and sniffed, exploring his new territory, taking in his new home, and wondering about the awkward smell of ointment and bandages that surrounded him.

Sylvester slowly leaned over and gave Felicia a kiss. "This is *the* best birthday ever. Sandpaper pants and a porcupine. Do you know me or what?"

"Glad you like them. Gotta pick out a good name for him now."

"Yeah, but first I gotta pet him…"

But before he could pet him, the porcupine suddenly fell forward, face-planting on the carpet, stone cold asleep.

It was then that Sylvester discovered that porcupines could have narcolepsy.

CHAPTER 8
THE BIG BOX BOOKSHOP

Long ago, Sylvester learned that there were many different types of pain in the world, all of which had their time and their place. There was physical pain. There was emotional pain. There was psychological pain. There was even the pain of being patient, which Sylvester would often tease and tickle by going through airport security lines during the holiday season.

The list was endless, and Sylvester had long ago learned to indulge the urges that bubbled to the surface, which was how one night he found himself with an itch and an urge to inflict something painful and literary.

The only thing open was the big box bookshop, coffee hooked late-nighters being squeezed of their final pennies. The store wasn't busy, employees restocking shelves and capturing escaped magazines, allowing Sylvester an easy wander to the coffee counter where he bought a cup of their hottest and blackest, plucking off the lid and tossing it aside as he carelessly splashed himself with fun.

As he sipped and spilled his paper-cupped coffee he pondered his options, his mind craving a good read bent with personality and oddness and a splash of painful prose. Maybe something he could sneak at work when Carl wasn't looking, stoically perched on his register, a vultured owl on prey for customers.

He wandered into paperback fiction, seeking out something quirky and thick and painful if he could find it; even literature could be painful if you found the right thing. He owned six different books by Gertrude Stein.

Destiny hit him hard when he saw Chuck Palahniuk's *Fight Club* on an endcap and knew it to be an instant classic. He dove in headfirst, burning through the first dozen pages while standing in place, his coffee cold and forgotten.

And then Natalie made her entrance.

It started as the flutter of a book being dropped before proceeding to a cascade. One by two by four by ten by twenty. It sounded like the entire bookstore had just fallen off the shelf.

And muffled under the sound of flapping and folding books, was a slight and feminine, "*Ugh*".

Sylvester stepped around the corner to see a pile of unhappy books with an arm poking out, still grasping whatever had started the avalanche. The arm may as well have been waving a Swiss flag for how much it reminded him of St. Bernards and their whiskey-barrels racing to the rescue.

Sylvester reached down and took the flailing hand as he gently pulled the body to its feet, books falling off like quagmired dust mites.

Natalie was dressed in a long skirt that touched the floor, this one green and gold and looking like something from a Jane Austen novel, but immediately contrasted by the thick down jacket of a fighter pilot. Her glasses hung crooked on her face, somehow flipped over and perched upside-down, her dark hair pulled back into a tail with a few wisps waving about as if gasping for air or hailing a cab, and bumbled on top, tilted off to one side, a beaten old football helmet, ancient and leather-born, its earflaps arm-wrestling the hair twists.

She glanced up at her savior and immediately blushed.

"You again?" she asked.

"Maybe it's kismet?" he said.

"Maybe you're a stalker. I'm almost sure of it now."

"Don't you own your own bookstore? I think it's you that's stalking me?" Sylvester asked as his eyebrow arched in a smirk.

"Oh shush."

"Isn't this cavorting with the enemy?"

"My grandparents would pitch a fit if they saw me here, but that's their loss for playing shuffleboard. As much as I love my little store, we don't carry paperbacks...or romance novels." She said the last bit with almost muffled embarrassment, as if immediately realizing she'd said too much and hoping to will it back in.

Sylvester looked down at the pile surrounding them, for the first time noticing the array of torn-shirt libidoed men staring up at him.

"You're a voracious reader of them it would appear."

She blushed and bent down, gathering them up, Sylvester watching as she expertly and unconsciously alphabetized in her arms as she went, before finally bending down to join her.

"Keep your distance if you value your eyes. I've been known to flail when I fall," she offered.

Sylvester glanced at her for a moment and then shifted forward a step.

"I like being poked in the eyes," he said.

Natalie gave him a crooked look and then fell backwards over the book pile.

"See?" she pointed out.

"You didn't flail, though. Total letdown."

"No, my hands were too full."

"Why not let the big box minions clean this up..." he glanced around before quietly adding, "...think of it as payback for 30% off the best sellers."

She smiled and took the hand he was again offering.

As if on cue, a clerk suddenly rounded the corner, taking in the situation and somehow deciding it was the fault of the books, which he profusely apologized for before shooing the humans away and beginning to stack and alphabetize. Sylvester swore he heard the clerk berating the books as they left.

"So, romance novels..." Sylvester began.

"Yeah...guilty pleasure. I think all women suffer from it."

"Not written in ancient Greek, are they?"

"No. I don't think they make them that way."

"In Greece they probably do," he said.

"I don't think they speak ancient Greek even in Greece these days..."

They walked to the checkout counter together and she paid for her two books and he paid for his one.

He watched as she slipped them into her handbag after refusing a bag or receipt, as if wiping away all evidence of her illicit purchase and any trail she may've left behind.

They walked out the door together, still quietly saying nothing, and when they got to the curb, she promptly fell off it.

Sylvester helped her up and over to a bench, where she rubbed her bruised and scraped knee for a moment before digging into her bag and producing a large piece of moleskin that she covered it with.

"I guess you do buy in bulk," he said.

"Yeah. Moleskin solves everything. Universal bandage."

"It is," Sylvester agreed as he opened his wallet and slid out a piece from between the bills.

She giggled.

"Two strangers, both walking around carrying moleskin. Can't imagine that's common," he said.

"It's probably common for moles," she smirked.

He smirked back. "Yeah, it probably is."

They sat in silence for a minute looking out on the darkened parking lot, a few café stragglers weaving their way to their cars, drunk on the caffeine of a good book pressed to their noses.

"I have a girlfriend," he finally said.

"Oh," she paused. "I thought so."

He could hear some sadness in her voice.

"But if I didn't…" he dangled as he searched for the right words. "You…intrigue me."

"Thanks…" she mumbled. "Guess it's nice to be intriguing to a guy with a girlfriend."

"Hey, c'mon now. I meant that as a nice thing."

Natalie looked out at the parking lot for a moment, and then back at him. "I know."

She got up and started to walk away, before turning one last time and smiling at him, "You intrigue me, too."

It was a nice smile, full of hope.

Then she tripped over a shopping cart.

CHAPTER 9

INTRIGUING

Socket laid down a deep orange edge of ink before adjusting the light and leaning back to admire his handiwork, Sylvester once again planted in Socket's canyonous living room listening to squirrel feet pitter-patter in the ceiling above.

"You ever meet a girl that downright intrigues you?" asked Sylvester.

Socket squinted at his work, then pulled back, continuing to dip in and out to gauge the impact. "Intrigues me? As in, 'I want to see them naked and dancing around my living room?'. Yeah, a course, every day. I'd go so far as to say all of 'em intrigues me. Even the funny ones who don't dress themselves right and smell like cantaloupe."

"No, I meant 'intrigues' as in…makes you curious…on a deeper level. How they tick. And why."

"Deep level? No. Not really. Either naked or nothing. But I'm a shallow guy. Not really looking for stimulating conversation. Who're you talking about? The Leash? The only deep thoughts that girl has are how deep the knife'll go…"

Sylvester laughed. It was a funny comment, and strangely accurate. "No, not Felicia…a girl I ran into a couple of times. We keep crossing paths. At the market, at a bookstore…at another bookstore. Probably nothing, but she's…intriguing. Makes me curious."

"Really liking that word, aren't you? In-treeg-ing." Socket shook his head in mocking humor, as if Sylvester was using big words to impress him. "Ya know what else crosses paths? Black cats. Ya know what that might be? Sign you're unhappy."

"Nah, I don't think so. Never been happier…" Sylvester paused, realizing he'd spoken automatically. Apparently, there were some thoughts you avoided following, fearful of where they'd lead.

"Did I tell you she got me a porcupine for my birthday? How cool is that?"

"Didn't even know you could get those as pets."

"Me neither, but she found one."

"Think she tried the little guy out first? Ya know, ran around stabbing folks with its butt?"

"Entirely possible, but not something I want to think about," said Sylvester, his eyes dilating as he realized how likely that scenario was.

"Shows commitment is what it shows. Longevity. Desire for sturdy babies…" continued Socket as he leaned back and held out his thumb, a sad impression of a stereotyped French painter. He only needed a beret and a little mustache.

"It's probably the best gift I ever got. Someone who knows you that well? You can't beat that. Ya know how many neckties I got from old flames? What am I gonna do with a necktie?"

"Use it as a tourniquet?"

Sylvester paused, looking down at Socket's inkwork before his mind wandered back. "But this girl…she keeps popping to mind. I can't get her out."

"What's so special 'bout her? Big chest? Nice ink? Mohawk?"

"Nope, polar opposite. Flat-chest, no ink, hair in a bun."

"She got a nice tummy? I love nice tummies. Or money? You lookin' for a sugar momma? Get yourself outta the french fried oil fields?"

"No money that I know of, although she does look like she'd have a nice tummy…but it's more this…vibe. This pain vibe I can't shake."

"She like Felicia? Pushes kitty cats down wells and kick cripples in the crotch?"

"No, not like Felicia. Very different. She…attracts it? Like flies on fruit. Some kinda magnet. The hurt just comes at her."

"A pain magnet?"

"Yeah. Sure…" said Sylvester as he absently scratched his head, as if this concept was only now dawning on him properly. "I can't think of any better way to phrase it than that? A pain magnet…"

"Do you mean she makes folks want to smack her? Cuz I've known plenty of people like that, and they ain't nothing special…"

"Naw man, nothing like that," said Sylvester as he sat up, his hands bouncing to life to help illustrate. "OK, so I met her at the supermarket and she just kept falling down. Shit kept falling on her. It was like gravity hit her sideways or something. Cans and displays just tumbling towards her when she walked too close. Sometimes, even when she didn't walk too close. Same thing in her own bookstore. In stocking feet! Couldn't stay upright."

Socket paused and leaned back, eyeing his friend skeptically. "And you find this…attractive? An accident-prone noodle-knob who can't keep her balance?"

Sylvester paused, cocking his head before looking down at his feet, as if this thought had also only just arrived. "Yeah…I guess I do?"

"You are a strange and bizarre dude."

Sylvester gave him a cockeyed look, "Just picking up on this now, are we?"

Socket shrugged. Either the thought never crossed his mind, or he'd never paid it much attention. Then he smiled. "But ya know, this totally opens you up to chasing one-legged blind girls. Probably the same kinda vertically-challenged dynamic…"

Sylvester snorted and settled back into the chair, letting his gaze shut down and his lack of response answer for him.

After a long pause Socket asked, "So what're you going to do about her?" There was an air of curiosity and hope in his voice, as if he'd be happy to take whichever girl was left over.

"Nothing. You think Felicia'd like me chatting up some other girl? She'd run her down in the street and back over her twice just to make sure," said Sylvester, mostly doubting (but half-believing) his assessment.

CHAPTER 10
FELICIA PARADES AROUND

Felicia beamed at her reflection as she approached the door, her smile fixed at an angle, her fingers crossed, before kicking it hard, promptly being rewarded with a sudden stop and a yarking yelp from the other side.

"Oh, I'm so sorry!" Felicia began as she rounded the door, her apologetic attacks now practiced expertise. "I didn't know anyone was there!" There was a slight pause before she said the second part, experience telling her it sounded more believable if she made eye contact first.

A bumbled man sat sprawled on the ground, his hand on a sore forehead, an array of papers and pears spilled around him, a torn paper bag blowing off down the sidewalk. "Oh, it's...it's ok...accidents happen..." he said as he vigorously rubbed his head, before glancing up at the emerging figure. He smiled when he saw Felicia, falsely beautiful in the way well-dressed women seem to unkempt men, a playful smile teasing her face as she hooked her prey.

Felicia reached down and offered him her hand, which he graciously accepted as he tried to pull himself to his feet...but he quickly found himself sprawled on the ground once more, his bottom now doubly sore from the second sudden cushioning it'd been forced to experience. He glanced up at Felicia, confused.

"I'm sorry!" she smirked, fakely innocent, shrugging her shoulders as if to explain away her second unprovoked injury in the last minute. "I lost my grip. Total butterfingers!"

The man glared more crookedly now, seeing her for the succubus she was, a dark shadow cackling on the wall behind her.

"It's ok..." he said slowly, ignoring her again-offered hand as he used his own to push himself to his feet, one eye tracking her as he collected his papers and pears, scuttling off toward the doorway and salvation.

Felicia nodded after him and smiled, waving happily. She had long ago mastered the art of the accidental injury. She knew how to time the releasing of a door, the kicking of a rock, the requisite pause needed to ensure a backhanded compliment a chance to land.

She skipped around the corner, a jolly mood engulfing her as she glanced at her watch, noting it was barely noon. Felicia loved her lunch breaks. Mid-day was an active time, the workforce folk bustling and rustling to jobs and gyms, lunches and brunches, and all the other parts of life people stuffed into their few free minutes. For Felicia, she was stuffing in playtime.

Her next appointment was a sallow 2pm with a colorful bloke who seemed interested in nothing but the boring, sadly ignoring the spike-chained chirapsia she excelled at.

But that was a lifetime away, and for now she had a backpack full of dangerous toys to litter about town, their crinkling contents akin to a Santa Clausian satchel of gifts, yet with far less joyful intent nestled within.

Her walks and meanderings were no doubt a mirror image to Sylvester's, the lone difference being who was on the receiving end of the injury, their ticks and tacts sharing one mind.

"Where to begin, where to begin…" she mumbled to herself, shiny objects abounding around her as she wandered aimlessly, hailing taxis as she went and refusing them when they stopped. She flat-tired people's shoes and cut past the elderly in bathroom lines, jostling sidewalk crowds with elbows of impatience while catcalling curse words near the ears of passing toddlers. Where the line was between 'sadist' and 'asshole' she was never sure, but it seemed indistinguishable.

The echo of a murmuring crowd eventually drifted through the canyoned alleyways, inveigling her curiosity. Gathered groups offered opportunities seldom found in the solitary wanderings of her misanthropic-parasitic self.

She took the noise as a guide, continuing through the alleys and side streets, dropping caltropped rocks on well-worn pathways while gluing cactus spines to crosswalk signals, finally emerging on a shadowed overpass with a glimpse down into the pinpricked masses gathered far below.

Felicia smiled as she ogled the common cattle, a parade winding through their midst. She wasn't sure what the parade was for, nor did it matter, simply a well-timed visit to a well-trod location.

"Oh, this looks to be blissfully fun!" she exclaimed as she clapped.

Small family crowds sat in lawn chairs on sidewalks, beer and bubblegum in hand as they thrilled at the procession of town cults, cheering the elderly arthritics and their angry mob mentalities. A local scout troop was currently marching beneath her, banners and flags hoisted high on sore shoulders, the look of teenage embarrassment chiseled on their faces. Felicia's eyes followed their trail into the distance, the next half mile of targets slowly winding down the street and into her crosshairs, the forced drawl of an ant's pace.

"So many tasty choices marching right past my window, what to use, what to use..." she mumbled to herself as she rummaged through her backpack, trying to match her targets to her tantrums.

She pulled out a paper bag, one of a dozen stuffed inside, hefting it and joggling it until she had a good sense of what it contained, before throwing it back and grabbing another, this one with a rubber glove stapled to the outside.

She smirked deliciously as she snapped on the glove and shoved her hand in, her fingertips drifting through a mess of itching powder and crinkled fiberglass before grabbing a hefty handful. She took a happy breath to steady her excitement, and then reached over the banister and let the itching armageddon dapple down on the gaggle of high school cheerleaders dance-marching under the overpass below her.

"Some cliques you can't help but have fun with," she chuckled as she closed her eyes and listened as giggly girl voices turned to horror as the scratching began and the panic spread, their painted attempts at perfection unable to cover the fingernail scars they inflicted.

She proceeded slowly through the rest of her bags, pacing her placements as she drizzled injury and irritation on the unsuspecting swarms below, the afternoon air dancing freshly through her lungs, the shifting shadows conspiring to hide her playtime as a never-ending stream of innocuous objects fell from above. She laughed at the masses, so focused on the traveling spectacle that they never thought to look for the puppet master far above.

She felt like an invisible pope, ennoculating prayers to the huddled flock with her righteous wisdom of wounding.

And soon enough there was only one thing left, her favorite flavor saved for last, and she looked out on the tail of the swarm in search of a fun final target.

"Who's it gonna be...who's it gonna be...where're the unhinged ignorati when you need 'em..."

And then she found them, sensing their hatred as they approached, angry arms and echoing voices, a religious horde marching in goose-step, shouting hate-faith opinions against everything that scared them.

She smiled fondly as she looked at her final shoebox, a motherly moment, paused to perfection, before shaking it violently and tossing it over the edge, a tufted fall that fluttered on the wind, doing her the service of removing the top.

The contents drifted out, a murmuration of green specks swarming and dancing on the wind as they caught the currents. It had taken her weeks of weekends to corral the contents, shredded nettles and burdock burrs and specks and flecks of poison ivy and oak, all mixed together in a salad of tickling fun.

The box and the breeze pierced the chanting and angry parade mob, beaning off heads in an explosion of grumpy mesclun.

Felicia smiled as she leaned into her cradling hands and looked down, watching the spectacle as the miasma attacked, poking and poisoning unmercifully, coughs and fits and scratches erupting out. She laughed as their confusion disrupted their bigotry, chants and screams mixing with swats and barks as the group dissolved into self-inflicted violence and fled through the watching crowd, their callous cause dispersed.

"Best lunch break in weeks!" she exclaimed proudly to herself, happy to have hurt the hurtful, careless about her loud voice or the brazenly discarded shoebox, her own hubristic success ballooning her arrogance.

Felicia smiled as she wandered off, a skip in her step, another hour of her long lunch still remaining, her thoughts weeviling about in cheerful exuberance as a final idea flit through her head for the cherry on top of her desserted day of fun.

The city's subway system was notoriously old and unsupervised, a commuter playground she'd long dabbled in and grown fond of. She skittered through the turnstile (leaving a piece of chewed gum on the bar as she went) and bought a cheap newspaper, experience telling her it never hurt to have something to hide behind.

She took in the toteboard, searching for an outbound train with an inbound bounceback, finally finding it in a 4-stop jaunt to the dairy farms, an overlooked line to rurality where the people would dwindle and fade into the past the further they went.

She searched for the loneliest car with the loneliest people and wedged herself into a seat when she found it, her protective prophylactic paper propped in front of her, her eyes hidden behind sunglasses as she shiftily scanned the game board.

A good number of nobodies still shared the car, but they all wore expectant looks of pending departure, none seeming likely to tarry for the turnaround.

She glanced at her journal, noting her past accomplishments. "Thirty-one would be a new record…" she mumbled to herself, a giddy feeling of anticipation rushing through her as liberal nibbles and personal records poked her conscience and convinced it of the merits.

The outbound train trickled past stop after stop, small crowds of commuters detaching at each one, before finally grinding to a halt at the end of the line, a two-minute hesitation before it returned to town for its next payload of passengers.

As soon as the doors shushed closed, the final stream of people now emptied out of her way, Felicia smiled and reached into her bag for her final, favorite plaything: thumbtacks.

Felicia took her tacks seriously, these being flat-bottomed and disc-based, with a 1/4" point that could pierce through denim, color-matched to perfection to blend into the seats.

Clearly, she'd done this before.

She wasted no time in skipping around the train car, depositing fresh tacks on empty seats, sharp side always up. If there was a hole in the fabric she infiltrated it. If there was a handstrap she spiked it. She knew how people sat and which seats were likely to be used and even which angles they'd fall at when the train hit the turns. There was an order and an expectation to humanity.

Thirty tacks were placed by the time she hit the poles, a dab of gorilla glue holding another dozen in place, pointed anger on display.

By the time the train left the station her trap had been set and her record recorded, and when they reached the first stop she'd already meandered a few cars away to safety, taking a random seat in a random space, hoping to be ignored and overlooked while she giggled her satisfaction.

Few people seemed to trek inbound from cow country at lunchtime, so she bided her time as the train plucked along, a few folks jumping on at every stop, but none bothering to walk the distance to her trap car.

Eventually the train began to slow as they finally approached the downtown station, third-shift crowds jostling outside the windows begging to head home.

Most of her enjoyment came from watching her trap sprung, the greed of temptation too much to ignore, so when her fellow passengers began to shuffle, and the doors juddered open, Felicia found herself mixing and matching her way back down the platform towards her theater, a virus blending into the bloodstream, a circular escape to rejoin the festivities.

She made it in record time, skirting herself back inside and weaseling into a corner, a plastered grin on her face as she turned to watch her game unfurl.

Today's match was particularly exciting, a warm weather day enticing skirts and thin clothing, shorts and shaved legs.

Three different yelps erupted almost at once, the thin and frail business-barker women with their tight-bunned heads and over-glossed lips angrily jumping to their feet during the opening ceremony. The slow-witted ones, now turned towards the sounds, soon joined them, causing the cascade effect Felicia so loved, yip after yap, all down the line, cruel shocks from an unexpecting audience.

She knew the round was finally over when a tinkling of scattered tacks battered the floor as the quick-witted ones, now forewarned, swiped their seats to safety. She'd counted seventeen total yelps, including the dense girl who did a double after sitting on the same tack twice, each of which she recorded in her journal, another record happily set.

Felicia stifled a giggle and a smirk as pride bellowed inside, her paper held over her mouth, excitement and happiness risking her anonymity, the last thing she needed being attention and guilt.

But in this case, it had already happened, attention and guilt clearly assigned, as a hand came down on her shoulder with a policeman's firm grip, and a low and gruffled voice spoke to her with the unmistakable air of authority that anxiety recognizes and fears, "I'll need you to come with me, Miss."

CHAPTER 11
THE INFAMOUS TRAIN TACKER

Sylvester was sitting cross-legged on the couch juggling skewers when Felicia arrived home, Poke the Porcupine nestled beside him, happily bathing himself as his butt-quills rubbed into Sylvester's thigh.

Sylvester had been going for hours now, his hands pricked and poked a dozen times over, the never-ending joy of amicable injury.

Skewers had been an amazing find. For years he'd juggled knives, a temptation that still called to him, but after catching one wrong he moved on to less damaging toys (the eleven stitches themselves he was fine with, and quite enjoyed, but he regretted missing two weeks of work and the paychecks that went with them).

"Hey 'Licia, you're home early. No fetishists this afternoon?" he asked with a chuckle as a skewer landed point down, puncturing a small hole in his palm.

When she said nothing he looked up, expecting her constant snarky banter, and was surprised to see her long face and crushed expression. Her eyes, normally devoid of all moisture, looked ready to erupt. He leapt to his feet, flipping Poke onto his back and causing him to defensively bristle and curl himself into an angry pillow.

"What's wrong?" Sylvester asked as he held her by the shoulders, massaging them as he dipped his head down, trying to look up into her floor gazing eyes.

She sniffed a few times, as if trying to suck up enough snot to power speech. "I...I was arrested," she finally got out.

Sylvester's eyes lit up as his jaw popped. "Arrested? For what?" he asked, alarm and expectation rising in his voice as his mind flipped through a rolodex of her likely crimes.

Felicia shuddered a bit now that the words were out. She seemed to be in that state of shock where time doesn't quite work right and you view yourself from the outside. There was silence. And then, after a few seconds, a torrent of breath exploded out as she explained her train-tacking game and the trip to the police station and the anxious realization that she may not get away with it, finally pausing to sniff and snortle and take in some air.

Sylvester's mind raced around the gameboard, trying to plug in all the pieces and the potential outcomes. To be honest with himself, he wasn't all that surprised. She'd been inching further towards the reckless side with him recently, and who knew what trouble she got into on her own.

"And what was the...errr...charge? Or the...penalty? Is this something like a fine? Community service? Or something more...serious?"

"They said I'd find out at my arraignment! Arraignment! Vest, I can't go to jail..." she said as she rested her cheek on his shoulder, her fingers scratching across the fabric of his shirt as her voice dropped to a whisper. "I'm not a criminal...I was just an addict having fun...I don't belong in jail..."

Sylvester pulled her close and gave her a hug. She was weeping openly now, tears streaming through his shirt leaving Rorschach designs, the scared little girl inside the tough turtle shell peeking her way out.

"Don't worry 'Licia, it'll be something small, like a fine," he said. "They'll yell at you, glare a little, you pay some money...you don't go to jail for thumbtacks..."

"Yeah...only a fine..." she said without a trace of hope. She knew she'd gone too far, playing the game to the point of routine. She wasn't being honest with Sylvester; this wasn't something she only did once. This was something she did weekly, on Tuesdays, and had for months. It might even be a year now, she'd lost track.

"You don't have a record, do you? First offense, right?" Sylvester asked, realizing this was the kind of thing you may want to know about your girlfriend.

She shook her head no.

"No to a record or no to a first offense?" he thought silently as he tried to stay comforting.

"Don't worry. It'll be a slap on the wrist. I'm jealous! I love slaps on the wrist!" He smiled down at her. "Worst case you'll be picking up garbage on the highway in a jumpsuit. Maybe you'll even get one of those poking sticks! Bring it home, we'll have some fun with it..."

She laughed, her first giggle of the afternoon.

"Take the afternoon off and relax. Take a bath. I'll order Chinese. Or burritos. Your choice."

"Burritos," she smiled.

Sylvester pulled her close and let her bury her face in his chest, the tears still streaming out, miraculously unequipped for the outside world and taking their chance to make a break for it. For once he was happy to be wearing a clean shirt.

She took her bath and ate her burrito before crashing to sleep, her entire body exhausted from the experience, even brushing aside Sylvester's offer of a meat tenderizer and his lower back, instead simply rolling over and gesturing to kill the lights on his way out.

And so he returned to the living room and began clipping his toenails too close, wondering how their lives may be about to change, and whether that was a good thing or a bad thing.

*****

For once, the justice system moved quickly. The arraignment was the next day and the trial two weeks later. It didn't go well.

It turned out that there had been a long string of complaints about *The Infamous Train Tacker*, including three newspaper articles, two evening news segments, and one fundraiser for the victims (which netted $87 and two cans of creamed corn), none of which Sylvester or Felicia had known about, but which the local newswoman had droned on about for twenty minutes the night of Felicia's arrest, endlessly shrieking about the vile and seedy underbelly of society that produced "such sadistic satanic sickos".

It quickly became clear that the torrent of opinionated media attention meant the hammer had to come down, and while Felicia tried to smile her most charismatic innocence, her charms fell on deaf stares and angry ears while jurors on wooden chairs creaked their uncomfortable silence against her.

The police had enough evidence to make it an open and shut case, an obvious trail leading straight to her door, a litany of videos and fingerprints sprinkled amongst the crime scenes, a variety of witnesses recognizing her sharpened features and serrated grin. Apparently, Felicia wasn't quite the diabolical mastermind she envisioned herself.

Sylvester attended every day of the court proceedings, clasping forkroaches and sitting on keys while the evidence was shown, and the verdict was read. He offered to testify on Felicia's behalf but her public defender was skeptical, certain it wouldn't help that he encouraged such behavior in her. In fact, when the prosecutor saw Sylvester's scar-arm she even handed him a business card and suggested a private consultation about his rights as the victim of domestic abuse.

The trial lasted less than a week. In the end the court accepted a plea deal where Felicia admitted responsibility and went to county jail for a year, with parole eligibility teetering around six months. Two days later Felica was locked up. The entire ordeal, from train ride to jail, had lasted less than a month.

And for the first time in a long while, Sylvester realized that he was left with the itch of his strange addiction and no accomplice to help scratch it.

Unless you count a narcoleptic porcupine.

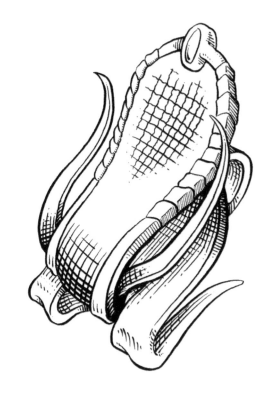

Part 2
Natalie

CHAPTER 12
SYLVESTER'S SOLITARY

The weeks passed as Sylvester tried desperately to occupy himself without the aid of his punishing and punchy playmate of pain. It was a welcome change at first, a breathy airment of freshness putting his bachelor life back into circulation, pants being optional, the sink only emptied when its contents threatened to topple and shatter, his attention focused solely on whatever tickled his temperamental tastes.

But it'd been a long recess since he'd been made to manage his own tendencies, and he soon found he wasn't up to the tasks he once was, age underscoring its time-consuming nature and the constant itching he now had only himself to rely on. He'd grown fallow in his appreciation for what Felicia had done, her never-ending poking and prodding that had allowed him to inhabit the rest of life a little bit more.

Now his focus often rested with the little things he'd grown accustomed to. An alarm clock that needed to be set. Waking up early to put your keys in the oven. Filling your pockets with salad forks and cocktail knives and the small toys someone else had always found space for. The bits of life that sped it up and greased it along.

So he sadly spun on without her, a part of him beginning to wonder if it was her he truly missed or simply her usefulness, as he tried to distract himself away from knowing.

His first target was Poke, who he inundated with attention, their relationship growing to include bedtime snuggling and pillow-cased wrestling matches. They learned each other's rhythms and moods, enticements and derelictions, but soon even Poke's attention wore down from his inability to fill Felicia's void.

Apartment life became a chore of boredom and complacency, living amongst Chinese takeout containers and sniffing them for freshness.

He read books and watched movies, *Fight Club* being his new favorite after reading the novel a dozen times over. He thought about going to self-help groups to occupy and distract himself.

His boredom had taken its toll on his body as much as his mind, distracting him to greater risks and further reaches for a fix he didn't need, as if the injury would fill the emotional gap Felicia had somehow provided.

He soon found that self-control was his enemy as much as his boredom, his clutch uncontrolled, his obsessions magnified. He scratched before he itched. He injured without desire. He gratified instantly. Soon even sleeves of cookies and boxes of donuts were grasping with the inequity of short life spans.

He tried to drown himself in his work, mundane and moribund as it was, taking extra shifts and working daylight hours with grin-faced sunny vampires that giggled at commonalities. After a few weeks he even began to identify with Carl in a bothersome and soul-swallowing way, finding himself arriving early for work and no longer counting down the minutes until he could leave.

It was a boring life on hold; a life of distraction.

He wrote letters to Felicia, branched soliloquies of adolescent banter, and visited her on weekends with cheery pies and broad sappy smiles, but it wasn't the same. The spark wasn't there without the pain, for either of them.

They would sit behind glassy walls and make unfulfilling small talk, staring off the spoiled time and going through the motions, surrounded by far better examples of appreciative families and lovesick conversations. They always came back to their relationship weakness, the conversation most relationships were built on, and found it worse without the hurt to lace it together.

Felicia struggled doubly with her own predicament, a constant desire to injure and impugn, riddled with temptations surrounded by bountiful risks. Prison was not a place to press buttons; not a place to incite people and make enemies. It was another world from the casual-Friday workforce she was used to preying upon.

Her hands wandered loosely the first few days, trying their best to find her footing, the fix for her addiction, but she soon found that a simple poke or a prod could result in retaliation, a cafeteria tray to the face, an earth-sharpened edge against the throat, held by those with loose-string tempers and long-term sentences, and she quickly soured on tempting the fates for the fun of it.

She settled back into her routines of traps and unwatched irritations, the small satisfactions from knowing someone would eventually get zapped or poked were snacks, not entrees, and filled little of her hunger.

And with Sylvester, her outlet, her dream canvas, she was separated by glass, a zoo exhibit restrained from the populace. As much as she dreamed of hurting him, she was denied that.

And so, their relationship waddled and wavered, their spine of pain severed, and as more time passed, they slowly lost the feeling between their fingertips and saw their relationship for the pain-filled morass it was.

CHAPTER 13

MOVING DAY

The other unavoidable outcome of Felicia's fugitive vacation was that, along with her clawed talons and penchant for turbulence, also went her rather substantial portion of the rent, the core financial reason Sylvester had been able to live where he did. They held no savings, no rainy-day egg fund for an uncertain future, but were instead, like most people, accustomed to life on a bi-weekly pay cycle.

For the first month Sylvester simply ignored the piling bills, letting the more important thoughts rascalling around his head have the room they deserved, but when notices turned to voicemails and thudding fists on the door, he knew the issue was pressing more keenly than he'd given it credit, and so he did the only thing he could think of and moved out, crawling back to the affordable safety of friendship and electricity.

Light Socket arrived that Friday wearing the cross-bred look of an electrician who fancied himself Indiana Jones, a curled hat perched on his head, a toolbelt clipped to his waist, and a coil of cable wire slung over one shoulder. He was in the midst of chewing on a plastic wiring cap as if it were gum, and in his hand he carried a car battery, which he handed to Sylvester like a housewarming gift the way most people hand over wine.

"Don't want anyone stealing it," he explained as he gave Sylvester a nod, and without another word began wandering the apartment like a dog in new territory, inspecting the electrical outlets and instinctively bending any metal object in reach, as if his central focus was more on the electrical systems of the apartment than the long and heavy move that lay in front of them.

After his full circuit and inspection, which included curious and uninvited trips to the bathroom and the bedroom, he finally plopped himself on the couch, no offer being needed for him to kick off his boots and wiggle his toes out through his sock holes.

"You realize you'll probably want to keep those on since, ya know, we're supposed to be moving," offered Sylvester.

"Yeah, yeah, in good time. So, the end of your temporary bachelor pad, huh? Hope you got some use out of it. Sorry to hear about Felicia," said Socket with an air of honesty as he began to thumb through the TV guide, inspecting its spine for collectability. "Can't say it surprised me much; you knew she was due. Crushed too many ants to not finally step on a wasp, am I right? Girl was vindictive something fierce."

"Yeah, a part of me's been expecting this, just didn't think it'd really happen. Doesn't mean I'm happy about it." Sylvester paused, his mind wandering briefly, realizing deep down that there was a part of him that *was* happy about it, a part that dipped briefly and subconsciously into thoughts of hardbound novels and wooden gargoyles. "But you're not here to talk about her. Moving help, remember?"

"Yes, yes, but that's not to say we can't chitchat about other things to boggle the mind and distract the loins, right? Fun and games and electrical currents?"

"Yes, I see you've brought the current," Sylvester said as he pointed toward the car battery.

"Yup. DieHard Platinum, best they make. Not gonna leave that around for folks to eyeball and pocket!" Socket added with clear pride in his voice. He smiled and picked up a forkroach from the end table and began obsessively curving its antennae. "So how long's this gonna take? I can see you haven't packed much."

And the truth was he hadn't. Some unfolded boxes sat in a corner, a few duffle bags of dirty laundry, but for the most part the apartment still sat in its Feliciaesque state, a living monument to criminality.

"Shouldn't take too long. Not that much stuff is mine. Mostly hers," said Sylvester as he grabbed a cactus by the needles and righted it, an unlucky bystander of Socket's wandering path of destructive curiosity. "Talked to the landlord. I'll come back next week and put her stuff in storage. He said it'll help to show the place off furnished. Just have to throw 'Licia's personals down into the basement before he comes by snooping and collecting. Are landlords all strange and creepy?"

"Most are," began Socket, as he landlordishly sniffed the TV Guide still in his hand. "Think we got time for a stroll in the park first? Weather's lookin' a bit overcast..."

Like mad paupers planning a rich man's heist, whenever the two friends got together they would scheme around the off-chance of lightning, both fantasizing about running through open fields to see who'd get struck first, their Christmas exchanges often involving steel rods and golf clubs.

"Nah, we gotta be out by five. Landlord's got a cleaning crew coming by to Windex the place down, sorry."

"Bummer yet again," said Socket, dejected, clearly running out of distractions to waste away the time. "So hey, where's this porcupine of yours?"

"Oh right, you haven't met him yet have you? Probably fitting for the new roommates to meet..."

Sylvester made a clicking noise with the side of his mouth and clapped his hands. After a moment there was a rustling from the bedroom and out walked a tired and inconvenienced looking porcupine with sleepy, drooping eyes that strangely seemed to imply a late-night bender. The porcupine looked at them both for a moment before yawning widely and doing a double stretch, indicating the pecking order of apartment life and the low importance of their calling.

"Whoa!" said Socket.

"This, is Poke, my porcupine."

"Now that is a manly pet, cute as it is. Can I pet it?"

"Sure. Friendly but prickly, so you may get stuck."

Light Socket reached down toward the awakening porcupine, who immediately inflated his quills in excited happiness and stepped forward expecting a hug. Socket did his best to safely scratch the outskirts of his face, which Poke seemed to enjoy.

"That's a great mate for you."

"Thought so. Friendly, painful, huggable, and a little bit odd."

Sylvester collapsed in the chair and Poke hopped on his lap, circling around and nuzzling in for an apparently long overdue nap. Sylvester patted him on the back, sticking himself with a few quills he didn't bother removing.

Socket put down his properly curved forkroach and began on another, absently keeping himself busy. "OK, so you'll get the dining room. Best I could do. I cleared some stuff into the corner. Mostly habitable. Could be a few bats still in there but they shouldn't bother you much. Night critters and all."

"Thanks man, I appreciate it."

"It'll be good times. There's a junkyard I want to visit, some high-tension wires we can camp by, and there's even an Edison exhibit coming through the science museum I'd love to take a gander at."

"Sounds good. Let's do 'em all."

"We were planning on it," said Socket with a broad smile, clearly indicating that the exchange rate for a free room was accompaniment during electrical excursions.

"Ready to pack?" asked Sylvester, chomping at the bit.

"I'm getting there. Need another few while I rest my feets." Socket paused for a moment, clearly another nagging topic tickling the back of his mind, before ignoring the off-limits territory, "When's she get out?"

"Four months, three weeks, two days, assuming she makes parole."

"Exacting, aren't we? And what's the plan when she gets loose? You gonna wait or move on?"

Sylvester looked at him crookedly, uncertain himself, before realizing he'd do best to not let the topic drag on unspoken. "Not sure. Probably wait. We get along, generally. She puts up with my eccentricities."

"Yeah, I've seen quite a few women not be able to get past those eccentricities," Socket said with a chuckle. "Tough to find the slightly nutty ones you need."

"Thanks man."

"Buds!" said Socket, as if he were being incredibly supportive. "Ya know...a lotta guys would look at this as a free pass. A few months with no lady around...the relationship on hold...oat-sowing time, ya know?"

"I'm not much of a farmer."

"Don't gotta be with a story like that. 'Woe is me, my lady was sent up the river and I got months and months all by my lonesome waiting for her to get out…if only I had someone to spend some quality time with…'. Chicks dig a taken man."

"You watch too many bad TV shows."

"Could be," Socket said with a shrug as he picked up a third forkroach, his artistic OCD insisting he fill the need to fiddle. Sylvester noticed the impressive forkroaches now littering the end table, majestic antennae curling up to the heavens like the headdresses of high-Elven priests.

"Hey, what about that clumsy one you kept talking about?" offered Socket, bad acted as if the memory had just whispered into his ear. "The one you couldn't get out of your mind? Where's she at?"

Sylvester crinkled his brow as the thought suddenly struck him. "Ya know, I haven't thought about her much since all this started with Felicia. Been too distracted…"

And just like that, she flickered back into focus in Sylvester's thirsty mind, a mirage of distraction.

"Well now's the time! Bump into her. Let some of the story slip. Test the waters. See if that 'intrigue' is still running strong, ya know?"

"Yeah, we'll see. C'mon, enough talk, let's pack!" said Sylvester as he hopped to his feet, clapping his hands together and changing the topic. Poke leapt down and meandered away like an indifferent cat, a look of mild skepticism at the both of them for having awakened him for such a short scratch.

"OK, fine, fine," said Socket as he pulled himself to his feet, wiggling his half-socked toes into his well-worn boots. "Will be good to get you back to my place. Did I mention I set up the bug zapper in your room? Things a blast. You're gonna love being a bug."

CHAPTER 14
SOCKET'S HOUSE

Acclimating oneself to the live-in world of Light Socket on a more permanent basis was akin to acclimating oneself to life inside an amusement park, which, in effect, was what Socket's house was, albeit an amusement park designed specifically around a single individual who had more than a passing penchant for electrocution.

Just as Sylvester poked and Felicia prodded, Socket lived a life measured by electric jolts and kilowatt hours. Where Sylvester had a porcupine, Socket had eels. Where Sylvester had vices, Socket had habits. And where Sylvester had rough wooden edges and sharp metal corners, Socket had electricity running rampant and unexpected throughout the house and property.

This is not to be taken for its more conventional connotation that he had outlets and plugs and lightbulbs that needed changing, but above and beyond that, Socket had wired his house to shock and surprise. Doorknobs and fixtures, bedboards and picture frames, refrigerator magnets and pickle jars, Socket had found a way to make anything and everything give you a shock.

As a visitor and past resident Sylvester had long since learned to be careful of what he touched, weaving his way clear of anything made of metal or in sight of a plug, often restricting himself to the living room and the backyard that somehow seemed off limits and electricity-free.

Moving back in meant coming to terms with the constant risk of a shocking surprise. This was especially funny since Sylvester, while having no problem with the pain of electricity, was never a fan of fright, which meant the sudden and jarring jolts would unnerve him far more so than any of Felicia's more violent, but expected, attacks.

And what made Socket's own deviance so diabolical was that there was no consistency to the timing, the house wired to randomness; you could open the refrigerator door a hundred times before it finally decided you were due, electrifying you to unconsciousness.

This uncertainty was exactly what Socket so enjoyed about it. "You don't want to *know* when! That takes away all the fun of it! You want it to be a surprise!" he'd say with an innocent grin, as if trying to explain to a child the simple things in life and how to do them properly.

In the long dead past Socket had been simple with his fun, obvious wires running from outlets and batteries, making them easy to spot and avoid, but experience and expertise had long since adapted his approach to something more devilish and sneaky, acidic attempts to fool even himself.

Now you could never tell.

And it wasn't only the metal objects that had the tease and the tickle, but the things you'd least expect; wood and cardboard and plastic were all known to mysteriously jiggle your arm hairs when you touched them, and once Sylvester swore he saw tendrils of blue electricity arcing between the aloe plants.

For Poke's benefit Socket agreed to disconnect Sylvester's room, lest the poor creature live in a state of perpetual fear and urine confusion, being unwilling to move or leave the safety of his bed, but the broader parts of the house were still Socket's domain, and Sylvester soon developed a fearfully quick touch to anything he had to deal with.

"And this," explained Socket as he finished the welcome tour, "is a non-Sylvester area. I don't want you borrowing my tools for your weird deviant activities." He said the last bit with a mocking tease, seemingly challenging whose deviancy was likely to corrupt the other.

They were standing in the basement, a boxed and bordered corner workshop Socket had finagled as part of his rent, and as overwhelming as the upstairs appeared, it didn't hold a candle to what lay beneath.

The ceiling rafters dangled and dripped with exposed wires that snaked into the walls, an unlabeled cacophony of jumbled, twisting confusion. How the entire house had not simply decided it had had enough and burned itself down Sylvester could only imagine, but the sheer enormity of the wiring and its still-standing nature underlaid the skill with which Socket had worked.

Beneath the danglings and precarious piles sat the workbench itself, littered with wires and plugs, batteries and bulbs, and accentuated with odd looking bowling pins that seemed made of metal and sparked quite regularly.

Sylvester absently picked up a small fossilized transformer and flicked the switch, half expecting a shock but receiving none.

"Ok, so the rules of living here are threefold..." continued Socket as he plucked the transformer out of Sylvester's inexperienced hands, coddling it like a baby bird.

"Oh, this'll be good..."

"First! Any electrical equipment that falls off a truck while driving by the property belongs to me. We clear?"

"Does that happen often enough to require a rule about it?" asked Sylvester as he picked up another fuzzled oddity and began to fiddle with it.

"You'd be surprised."

"Fine, all yours."

"Second! If there is a power failure you do NOT call the utility company. You call me. I'll fix it. The electric company does not step foot on this property. Queso?"

"You're not likely to have much of a problem so far, and there's no need to bring cheese into it..."

"Third! Ya gotta be my guinea pig."

"Guinea pig for..."

"Same as always - tzzt tzzt - electricity stuff."

"I swear," began Sylvester as he shook his head, "it's like I moved right back in with Felicia, just without the sex..."

"And you'd best not be expecting any either!" Socket said with a glare, sizing up his friend, before adding, "Oh, and rule four..."

"You said there were three."

"I was home-schooled until I was eight and can't count. Sue me," he said as he plucked the fuzzled oddity from Sylvester's fumbling fingers. "And fourth, you gotta help out on Halloween with the trick-or-treaters."

"Giving out candy...? There must be some kind of a catch?" asked Sylvester.

"Nope, not really. No catch."

"Not really?"

"Not really."

"You're still doing it aren't you?"

"Doing what?"

"Tricks, not treats. The sizzling, jolting, silliness you did years ago when I lived here."

"Maybe…" said Socket as his eyes scissored the ceiling distractedly.

Sylvester smirked. "And the kids still come? Haven't learned their lessons or called the cops yet? No angry dads with billy clubs showing up to learn you some manners?"

"Kids line up early now! Sure, I had to raise the treat a few times to keep 'em coming and keep 'em quiet, but they still seem to enjoy it."

"How much ya up to now?"

"100 clams."

"Oh, well that's something…might have to give the course a try myself…"

"Age limit of 18 there pokey-proddy. And be serious, you'd just walk straight down the path without breaking stride. Little electric shocks won't stop you…"

"Too true… And what do they gotta do? Just make the porch?"

"And ring the doorbell."

"And do any ever…"

"Make it? A decade back I had five make the porch and three the doorbell. Most years it's none."

"And the two that didn't make it?"

"Touched the wrong doorbell."

"You have more than one?"

"Of course."

Sylvester shook his head and smirked again, "More rigged than politics, huh?"

"We all have our favorite holidays and traditions…. "

CHAPTER 15
THE BREAKUP

Felicia's life behind bars had been ridden like a roller coaster around a strange variety of unexpected twists and turns. For six weeks she'd been in jail, and for six weeks she'd been unable to injure, unable to inflict.

She'd been on the receiving end of her first few attempts, the quick and anxious eyes of the prison population far ahead in spotting what she was up to, and by the third week she'd been smacked around enough to know not to push her luck. Instead she'd fallen back further on Sylvester and his weekly visits, her small tunnel to society, still blocked by an invisible wall, only words capable of passing between them, her arrows down to slung insults and references to inadequacies.

"So? How's things?" began Sylvester as he sat down opposite her, the sunlight dappling his face as his eyes bounced around, taking in the cinder blocks and fluorescent lights and plaster-faced guards who seemed just as imprisoned as she was.

Felicia was bristling with excitable news, "Much better!"

"Oh? What happened? Did they update the dinner menu with something seasonal?" he continued. "Lobster bisque with fois gras? Stone crabs with bone marrow truffles?"

Felicia snorted, "Yeah, but it wasn't very good. The lobster was out of season."

They smiled at each other through the glass, a brief taste of the past flitting between them.

Felicia continued, leaning in and catching him in the eye, "No, it's better because I finally figured out how to scratch!"

"You did? Great! How?"

"I joined a gang!"

Sylvester blinked briefly, certain he'd heard her wrong.

"Seriously?"

"Completely! It's not the best gang, but it's a solid second tier one. Not quite the 'shivs and teardrop tattoo' crew, but a few steps above the 'knitters and library bimbos.'"

"What're your gang colors? Black and white striped?" asked Sylvester with a proud chuckle at his bad joke.

"Nah, no colors in prison. I may get a tattoo, though!" exclaimed Felicia, clearly enthused.

"I seem to recall you refusing to get a tattoo from Socket..." added Sylvester.

"Well, sure, but that's Socket. Not the most sanitary of options, now is he?"

"And prison is?"

Felicia shrugged. "It's a package deal. If I get one, they'll let me needle the next person!"

"But you have no artistic skill."

"Who cares? I just want to needle someone!"

"Hope you have fun," Sylvester said with a comedy head shake, his own love of tattoos long having been a gullious gap between them.

"Thanks, I plan to! The gang's really helped me know what I'm doing in here, and let me tell you, this place is great! It's like an adult summer camp! You'd love it."

"In arts and crafts do you make license plates?"

"Yes! We do actually! And if I play my cards right, I may even walk out with a master's degree in the criminal arts..."

"And that's what you need, too. Serious resume builder there. 'Criminal Mastermind, Minors in Extortion Science and Pottery Making'."

Felicia rolled her eyes, "Like they'd let us play with sharp bits of pottery..."

A brief image of a broken sake cup danced through Sylvester's mind.

"I'm starting to think six months isn't going to be enough time," Felicia continued. "I may need to blow off best behavior and aim for the full term..."

"Enough time for what?"

"To play of course, silly! There're too many toys and too much to learn in here!"

"A week ago you were scratching through the glass trying to impale me, and now you want to book an extended stay?"

Felicia smirked and smiled, an unexpected shade of happiness bubbling through her. "Oh sure, at first it stunk, but I didn't realize the potential! I was playing an obsolete game without learning the rules. Do you know how many people are in here for things like embezzlement? Insurance fraud? Come on, it's like surrounding me with kittens!"

Sylvester rolled his eyes, incredulous. Only Felicia would go to prison and enjoy it.

"Outside, ya always gotta be nervous," she continued. "Look over your shoulder, watch out for cops and cameras. In here, you keep an eye out for the inmates, not the law. The law barely exists in here. Nobody cares. As long as you don't shiv a guard or try to escape, anything goes!"

"You are a very odd woman," said Sylvester with a complimentary air and an indulgent smile as he clenched a pocketed forkroach.

"Thank you!"

"So you really want to stay longer?"

"Totally! You know what I can do in here? Punch people. Flat out. Just *wham*, right in the kisser! And you know who cares? Nobody!! Well, maybe the person I punched, but the guards, the law, they could care less! It's like the wild, wild west o' fun!"

"So you're punching people now? Isn't that a bit...uncivilized? Doesn't seem the kinda challenge you're normally up to..."

"It's not about the challenge, it's about the freedom! I can finally chase those weird whims we never get to scratch! Seriously, go try it yourself. Punch that guy sitting at the next seat over. See what happens. You'll get arrested! You'll get sent here! But me? Here, watch..."

And with that Felicia leaned over and slugged the woman sitting at the next seat over, a boggle-eyed white collar who fell off her seat, coweringly crawling two seats to safety and forcing her guest to follow her.

"See? It's that easy! Guard probably saw it, didn't care a lick!" said

Felicia as she turned, glancing at the guard, who simply smiled and nodded back, a look of amusement on her face.

Sylvester shook his head, unbelieving.

"I'm telling you Vest, you'd dig it on this side."

"I think I'm good over here, what with wearing my own socks and not having to pee in front of anyone…" he said as he smirked, hoping for a giggle.

Instead, Felicia scowled and looked away as a dark cloud of nervousness settled over her. She clawed at the glass briefly, confirming to herself it still existed, a sad tiger in its habitat hoping for a weakness. Her eyes squirmed and wandered as they followed her evaporating thoughts, until it became clear that the moment she'd been dreading was now waiting politely at the door.

"Listen Vest, I can't be myself in here with you out there. Can you get that? Don't get me wrong, I still love you. I mean, I think I do. But I may love this more…this freedom. It's addictive something fierce, like some magical Christmasland! In here, I can be anything. But the glass…the glass between us is killing whatever we had…".

She paused, nibbling her lip in some strange form of embarrassed admission, "You can understand that, right?"

"It sounds like you want to break up with me so you can have more fun in prison?"

"Well, yeah. Basically."

Sylvester looked at her crookedly, unsure if this was another verbal attack meant to injure him through the glass. A week before she'd scratched her itch by bemoaning his career choices, calling him *'a slack-jawed broomer and fry oil pussy-wussy'*, before giggling and taking it back.

This seemed different.

"C'mon Vest, why is this such a big deal? We have our thing, but it's an outside thing. A physical thing. In here, it doesn't fly. There's an inside me and an outside me, and in a few months when they let me go, outside me'll be back. Seems simple and straightforward, right?"

"And what am I supposed to do?"

"I don't care. Wait, wander, whatever."

"Whatever? Seriously? After all we've built, all we've been through, this is how you wanna end it? On a weird whim?"

"It's not a whim. I've thought about this a lot! Come on Vest, give me some credit. Think this through!"

Sylvester scowled at her. She rolled her eyes, as if the obvious needed to be explained.

"Fine, let's say we stay together. You come here every week, we chat through glass, we never touch, I tell you how miserable I am, you tell me how miserable you are, then we both leave and go back to our bubbleworlds where that conversation didn't matter. You know the one rule of the big house? Only the big house exists. The outside world's not real in here. Now, you wanna go hotwire a car and join me in here? Then maybe we can keep the flame alive. But otherwise, we need to cut this off, for both our sakes. I need to be who I need to be to get through this, and that's not latched onto someone on the outside who moans about his tough life of itchy freedom. Six months is a long time Vest. I'm not convinced what we have survives six months without the violence."

Sylvester looked off, his chin wobbling as he refused to let the angry and confused tears dribble out.

"And in six months?" he gritted.

"Who knows? For all I know they keep me here for another twenty. I'll face freedom when it greets me at the door. Until then, now is now."

Sylvester looked down at his hands as they pressed white against the forkroach he was unknowingly fumbling with, a moment of lost memory he didn't know how to process.

"C'mon Vest, don't make this so strange," she said as her fingers tapped sadly on the glass. In her mind she'd clearly expected him to be excited about this idea. "Maybe a break is what we need? Recharge the brutality batteries and recalibrate the defibrillator?"

Sylvester shook his head in disbelief, "This is too weird! You're breaking up with me so you can have more fun terrorizing people in prison. Who the hell breaks up with *that* as the reason?"

Felicia smiled at him, genuine pride brimming at the thought. "Us! That's what makes us unique! We're a couple that can't be replicated!"

Sylvester continued to shake his head, the disbelieving shock having a tough time finding its way into permanent memory.

Felicia tilted her head, her unused motherly side hoping he understood. She gave him a solid thirty seconds of head tilts before finally getting bored.

"OK, I gotta jet. Yard time's in thirty and I gotta be early to get the best beaning spot. Later!"

And with that Felicia stood up, waved goodbye with a smirk, and wandered off, high-fiving the guard as she went, a mild melodic humming following her into the distance as she sashayed out of sight, oblivious to the titanic disaster she'd left behind.

Sylvester sat in a daze, looking back and forth between his hands and her receding back, the shocking oddness of the moment adamantly refusing to settle in. He wasn't expecting this when he sat down minutes earlier.

The shock remained until someone with face tattoos and vibrant grillwork sat down opposite him and he took the hint, wandering off in confusion and leaving his forkroach perched on the counter, a lost lamb in a lost world.

CHAPTER 16
SYLVESTER DIVES INTO OIL

Carl was waiting in his usual three-point stance behind the register, a look of gameshow preparation plastered on his face, his hand on the buzzer. It didn't matter that customers rarely, if ever, sprinted into the restaurant and threw orders at him in seconds. It didn't matter that the average customer would meander and drawl and take minutes to order a cup of water. He was ready. He was set. In another occupation this was probably an admirable quality. Here, it seemed ridiculous.

"You're late..." Carl began as Sylvester's pinky toe passed the doorjamb.

"Yeah, sorry Carl, new bus schedule to get used to."

Carl gave him a skeptical look, as if doubting that anyone could possibly be so irresponsible as to not budget extra hours for a new commute.

Sylvester ignored him, walking behind the counter to his grill as he began his routine.

He checked the drawers of frozen meats and fries and overhead bins of buns, ensuring he had what he needed to last the night. He pressed his finger to the grill plate, testing for the skin sizzle at the right temperature, then dipped his pinky tip into the oil to ensure its blistering heat.

The first few hours were the same as always, with the drunks and the homeless and the all-night partiers cycling through in their usual way, demeaning the usefulness of his life in tiny increments.

Biggie Berwick and his non-existent entourage came through again, this time seating themselves at a large square table in the back. Sylvester enjoyed watching the craziness of Berwick as he shuffled himself from seat to seat, keeping the conversation going from different points of view. He wanted to sit down and join the crazy, if only to see if he'd be noticed, the three-dimensional player at the four-dimensional party, but a cheap busload of tourists diverted him back to frying food and scooping slaw, letting Berwick shift his peculiarity party elsewhere.

Sometime after the tourist train left Carl looked back at Sylvester over the divider and smiled. "Good day so far, huh?" he asked, as if they had some mutual vested interest in how busy it was.

"Sure. Always good to have a crowd. Makes the time go by," said Sylvester.

"You been quieter than normal lately. Working harder. I'm gonna mention that to Quentin when I see him next."

Carl had a habit of thinking his opinion mattered. The owner had franchised 11 locations and barely knew Carl's name. If anything, he likely equated his value to a step below that of a salt shaker. So when Carl spouted off employee reviews, Sylvester knew how well they were likely to be heeded.

Still, it was nice.

Sylvester scraped his brain trying to twist it into a teasing joke, but his heart wasn't in it. "Thanks," was all he eventually eeked out, which plastered a smile of success on Carl's face.

The door jingled again, and another giggly couple staggered in, instantly pulling Carl back to his Secret Service-like post. Sylvester heard them order and turned to get a head start, throwing a handful of frozen squid into the fish fryer and another of potatoes into the fishless one.

He watched as they paid, handing money back and forth, Carl following his perfect script of responses. Sylvester could recite them word for word, and often found himself doing just that when standing in line at other stores. "We thank you for your business and hope your taste buds remember us!" was one of his favorites. He also had an affinity for "and a quarter and a dime and a nickel makes a set", which came up surprisingly often with how things were priced.

But it was also more evidence of the boring consistency of his life.

Repetitive, identical, unchanging.

Whether he was here for a month or a year or a decade, those lines wouldn't change. Carl wasn't likely to start up a new catchphrase any more than the menu was to add a deep-fried salad. This world was established and would stay that way until the end of time, regardless of who wandered through it.

And at that moment Sylvester's life changed.

In retrospect it was one of those seminal moments where something inside either burns out or breaks or simply decides to work differently. At the time he didn't know it, but for whatever reason it happened, Sylvester decided right then and there that maybe this wasn't the place for him. Maybe he needed a life with a little more living in it.

And then as he turned, his attention became transfixed, as if staring into the eyes of a medusal Siren on the open ocean.

The golden oil was bubbling wildly now from the ice crystals, reminding him of filmic scenes where molten gold would bubble and flow, erupting up from the earth.

His hand started to reach towards it, almost instinctively.

He'd thought about the oil often, but had never given it much heed; the magical bubbling basket of burns.

But somehow it now seemed to make more sense. It clicked.

The warning lights in the back of his head dimmed and turned off and he could almost feel his eyes dilating to pinpricks of focus as sound began to escape him.

His mind stepped out of itself as he saw the fryer from the inside, looking out, like a lost child trapped at the bottom of a well.

He looked up through the yellow bubbling liquid and saw a finger and then a hand slide into the oil like an Olympic diver splitting the pool water.

It was crisp.

Clean.

Greg Louganis would certainly approve of his form and rate him well.

But his hand only made it past the wrist before it stopped, pausing, quavering, afraid of the depth and running out of air, before some otherworldly sensation pulled it back.

Maybe his conscience. Maybe Carl. Maybe gravity.

He didn't know, but he watched as the hand slipped back out of the frying oil and vanished from sight.

Then his senses came back and his eyesight returned.

His hand screamed. A deadly, piercing internal scream he felt certain he could only hear inside his head. Or at least it seemed in his head. Maybe it wasn't.

He guessed he knew how a lobster must feel when it was cooked. This might be worse. Lobsters generally weren't deep fried.

He looked down at his hand and watched as it registered in his racing mind. It was not looking well. It looked like a suntan gone horribly wrong. He should have used a much higher SPF. His mom was going to yell at him. He may miss some school. He'd have to go to the doctor and get a big needle shot and some medicine he'd have to slather on his hand again and again and again. He'd have to clear-cut every aloe plant in his house. Blisters were already forming as his skin was cracking like a baked desert riverbed. And then he thought about how he wouldn't really want to eat those fries. The ones that would taste a bit like skin and arm hair. He hoped the customers would be given a fresh batch or at least a coupon. And he heard that screaming noise again, and this time realized it was coming from him, through his ears, not his mind.

And then he passed out.

*****

The ambulance ride was a blur of forgotten memories and flashes of concerned looks. He could have been transported in a school bus or on a flying squirrel for all he knew.

He seemed to recall hearing himself tell the EMT that he didn't want pain medication because he was quite enjoying the sensation. The EMT told him he was in shock. Sylvester tried to shake his head and insisted he had a high tolerance to pain. He tried to wave his hand briefly and swore for a moment that it was the wrong color.

He then started to wonder if he'd filled out the race question on the forms wrong all these years and should have chosen Black instead of White. But isn't it usually for your entire body and not just one appendage? And why hadn't he seen more people with mismatched appendages? It seemed completely logical to him that a person with a black parent and a white parent would have a white arm and a black arm, as well as a white leg and a black leg.

How else could it possibly be?
And then he passed out again.

CHAPTER 17
THE HOSPITAL

Sylvester awoke to the smell of aloe and ointment.

He was in a dark room with the curtains drawn, small slivers of light dancing on the ceiling and floor as the air conditioning shook and rattled what it could. As his eyes adjusted he realized he was strapped comfortably into a hospital bed, his hand wrapped in a bulbous glove of liquid that looked like an incredibly expensive pool toy, which in turn was tied to tubes and wires that ran into a compressor that cycled the liquid in and out.

His hand still throbbed, but it was a dull throb now, far less painful than his last lucid moments had been, and he gave ample credit to the almost certain mountain of medication vigorously pumping through his system.

His first task was to get a sense of time, the dark and clockless atmosphere giving no indication, and after a few minutes of fumbling with a remote, discovered that it was Thursday, which seemed a long time since he last remembered working on Tuesday, leading him to conclude that it must've been a bad burn and a powerful narcotic.

He looked down happily on his hand with renewed appreciation for its two-day vacation-inducing dormancy and tried to wiggle his fingers, which he swore caused part of his skin to flake off and float about, reminding him of a piece of burnt chicken in a bag, which made him laugh, knowing that Fry Daddy's had a rule about marinating all their meat.

His eyes traced the wires and the tubes circling around him to see where they went, a few dedicated to his hand-bag of goo, orange and obvious, while another set seemed to drip him his meds and a third measured his vitals.

He felt like an awkward science project, trussed up and tied down, awaiting a spark of thunderous lightning to bring him back to life.

And it was then that he finally felt the pain, a slow but constant throbbing hurt that seemed to wave and smile louder with every twitch and flex of his arm. The coolness of the pool glove did little to slow it, and within minutes his hand began to hum on a level he'd never before experienced, far worse than skewers or lighters or door slams.

It was also a hurt he wasn't sure he enjoyed?

The chronic aspect was certainly appealing, every wiggle of his pinky shooting knives through his nerves, but he was also a right-handed realist, thinking perilous thoughts of daily tasks that now presented unexpected challenges and unpleasant repercussions.

He was undecided whether he should smile or frown, but before he could decide, he heard a noise and a whirr and a nurse wandered in, smiling and cheery with her hair in a hive and a skip to her step.

"Finally awake, are we? Gimme a minute and I'll help get you out of that bed," she said, both motherly and wardenly as she pulled open the curtains. "You right-handed or left?"

"Right."

"That's too bad. You won't be able to use it for at least a week, and even then, it's gonna be crusty for a while. Did you take a look? It's not pretty."

Sylvester tried to look closer, but there were still too many wires in play to get a good view.

"You're a lucky man," she continued. "Lotta people get a burn like that go into shock. Don't know where they are. Don't even pull their hand out, just let it sit there, bubblin' away like a pot roast. Had me a coupla patients come in, they sit here for weeks and weeks not realizing they don't got no hand no more."

"Guess I'm a lucky one, huh?" asked Sylvester.

"Luck, divine providence, all depends on your point a view."

"Or maybe just the inevitability of gravity."

She gave him a look that conveyed he was either stupid or a wiseass, neither of which she appreciated.

"Now you best be careful with that," she said as she pointed towards his hand. "I'm not gonna be in the mood to truss you up again, so if you unplug yourself or pop a leak, you're on your own until I feel like it."

Sylvester nodded, getting the sense that incurring her wrath would be something he'd regret allowing to happen. She helped him out of his bed and showed him how to move, sliding his glove and its wired and wheeled contraption along in short steps, as well as how to operate the control that managed his meds, a mental hurdle he struggled with on a fundamental level, pain-relief being the antithesis of his life's goal.

He'd burned himself many times in his painful past, but this was the first time he'd reached the third degree, a memorable occasion which he felt called for a plaque to commemorate it. His nurse was of a different opinion, box-earing him for stupidity and informing him that another degree could've meant amputation, which immediately soured him on the plaque.

Sylvester had been lucky enough to land on a quiet week, when the beds weren't needed and the staff's curiosity was at his disposal, an unexpected calm between summertime fishhooks and holiday explosions, so he spent his next few days being prodded and monitored while they ensured the feeling in his fingers returned and the outer layers of skin started to regrow.

Socket came by early Friday, genuinely concerned about his well-being, delivering him a change of clothes and some books, a sharpened forkroach and a sneaky place to hide it, plus the news that he'd been feeding Poke and taking him for walks, which Sylvester thanked him for profusely.

Socket also explained that Quentin, the owner of Fry Daddy's, had generously offered Sylvester three weeks of paid leave (minus the cost of the contaminated oil that had to be thrown out), followed by an immediate layoff and the gift of unemployment, under the agreement that Sylvester not come back or try to sue them.

Carl, who was clearly scarred and bothered by the whole fiasco, was in counseling. He was flamboyantly reenacted by Socket, as he related the story of Sylvester's scream and Carl's reaction to rounding the corner, Sylvester convulsing blindly as he fell to the ground, grasping at his charbroiled hand, while the basket timer went off in the background and confused Carl's priorities.

He did finally dial 911, closing down the restaurant for the first time ever, completely at a loss as to what to do since he certainly didn't want to serve any more fries that night. The straggling customers were, in fact, given coupons.

The news stream continued, the gaps were filled, and soon Socket departed, a firm and grateful left-handed handshake and an appreciative 'thanks' for his continued porcupine daycare, and with no job and no insurance and no money to speak of, Sylvester laid back and enjoyed the first real vacation he'd had in years.

CHAPTER 18
RUN-IN & REHAB

By Saturday Sylvester had been given the freedom to move, dragging his tubing machine down the corridors and alleyways of the ICU like a roving gypsy. He discovered a small lounge with some tables and vending machines, more likely for the nurses and doctors than the patients, but it was a nice change of scenery that possessed far more painful quirks than his small, sterilized room.

The tables were old and metal edged, providing comforting sharp corners for Sylvester to play with and explore, the splintering undersides giving him something to sand. There was even a bulletin board off to one side, overflowing with insurance notices and medication information that slowly lost track of its staples over the course of his stay.

He played cards with other guests, often chittering away with the maintenance staff and the interns he felt more kinship towards. He read old magazines and studied ingredients on vending machine food, while he memorized side effects on strange drugs he never knew existed and hoped he was never prescribed. He smuggled plastic forks under hospital gowns to occupy his late-night fidgeting, knowing full well he'd need to stay on his best behavior, hiding his poking and prodding lest they begin to suspect the intentionality of his accident.

But on this point even his mind was unclear, the memory fuzzy.

He had given it a lot of thought as he sat alone in the darkness, counting ceiling tiles and forking his fingers, tapping Morse code messages into his chest with stolen staples. Did he dive into oil as just another game for himself? Boredom dangling teases in his mind? Or was it something else? Even a cry for help? He had no clue. His mind seemed to have blocked out the incident and all webs of thought connected to it.

The whole experience was made doubly difficult since a hospital, by its very nature, was akin to a circus of fun for fans of the sharp and pointy. At every turn was a scalpel, a needle, or a mallet, often resting on a tray of instruments Sylvester didn't recognize and had no idea how to use (but was drawn to all the same). A few times he even felt himself reaching for one subconsciously, only stopping when he realized he had nowhere pleasant to hide it.

He made a point of adding a few of the more enjoyable looking items to his Christmas list, even going so far as to slip in curious questions as he tried to identify what some of the stranger implements were for. "Oh, an 'Artificial Leech' you say? It looks so expensive...is it? How much do you think...? Oh no, just curious chitchat, what use could I possibly have for *that*? ... I don't suppose Walmart would carry it, would they?"

And so it went for a couple of days, mindless banter and chitchat punctuated by changes of goo and doctoral inspections, while his bored mind would often daydream of Felicia and chuckle at the thought of their reciprocal forms of lockdown as he began to wonder if there were hospital gangs he could join.

*****

So it was that on the third morning Sylvester found himself in the lounge reading the ingredients on a candy bar when a cacophonous crash from the hallway drew his attention, a metal tray of instruments skittering past the doorway.

At first he thought little of it, the common happenings of a busy hospital, but when he heard a follow-up crash a moment later, followed immediately by a third, his curiosity pulled him along to investigate.

He suspected that a dervish of a patient had broken loose, Tasmanian-deviling their way down the hallway, and sure enough, sprawled on the floor, three different nurses trying to help her up, sat Natalie, her leg in a cast, a variety of bent and broken surgical tools littering the ground, a few still trying valiantly to penetrate her cast.

It seemed clear that the staff was familiar with her, passing hand signals between one another and trying to avoid getting too close.

She glanced up and caught Sylvester's eye and widened her own as he crooked his head to the side in puggish curiosity.

"Our fates seem to be magnetic," he said.

"I still think you're stalking me."

"Yeah, ya know, I decided to hang out in the hospital on the off chance you'd swing through. Good place to meet the ladies."

The nurses managed to get Natalie to her feet without knocking anything else down and handed her back her crutches while they did their best to guide her to the lounge, her body still trying valiantly to flail and fall and attract things to it.

Despite her body's best efforts she managed to stay upright, finally sinking into a chair with a stabilizing thud, far from anything that offered the potential for a collision or a crash.

When she was settled and steady, nothing else at imminent risk of falling, the nurses left, backing away slowly as if from a lion, until they were out of the room, at which time the fast echo of running steps filtered back in.

Sylvester and Natalie remained alone now in the lounge, only the whir of the vending machine fans and the crashing of the ice machine breaking the silence.

"So…" she began, unsure of where to start a conversation.

"Your leg…" Sylvester chimed in helpfully, "…broken?"

She looked down at her cast, a full length one that went from ankle to hip, completely immobilizing it.

"Yeah…" she said with a hint of sadness. "In five places."

"Five places? How did you do that? Parachute not open? Weekend motocross? It wasn't just canned fish again was it?"

"I fell off the couch reaching for the remote."

Sylvester looked at her, dumbfounded. "Off the…couch?"

"The couch."

"Is your couch…particularly tall?" he asked, scratching his head.

"Nope. Fairly normal couch. Fairly normal remote. Fairly normal Natalie."

"You said that before. You, uh, have a problem with that?"

"Gravity?" she asked.

"Yeah. And falling. You seem to fall a lot. I think this is now…four times you've fallen around me? Four for four. Maybe I'm unlucky?"

"You should see how many times I fall when you're not around," she smirked.

Sylvester smiled inside and out. He liked how she didn't let it get her down. Klutzy or poorly coordinated or simply born with bad luck, whatever it was, she was somehow OK with it.

"And is it only a problem with a strong pull of gravity or do you have…other…strange issues?" he asked as he pulled up a chair and climbed onto its back, his arms draping the rest.

"Such as?"

"I don't know…do you attract knives? Bees? Do you electrocute yourself? Do buses career off the road trying to run you down? Do satellites crash in your backyard? Do the laws of physics break in their attempt to destroy you?"

"Yes, yes, yes, not often, not sure, possibly, and that would explain a lot. The 'not sure' was because something did crash in my backyard, but it was too mangled to know what it was. Mighta just been a meteorite."

She said the last bit with a wry grin that twisted it enough that Sylvester couldn't tell if she was joking.

"So your hand," she began, pointing to it.

Sylvester tried to lift it, pulling his wheeled contraption along.

"Work accident."

"Do you have a lot of work accidents?" she asked, remembering his scar-marked arm.

"Oh yeah, plenty. But honestly most are self-inflicted."

"Was that one?"

Sylvester looked at his hand for a moment, still trying to decide. It wiggled at him in greeting.

The boiling oiling moment was vivid in his mind, but in the grainy way old movies are, and he viewed it more objectively, outside of himself.

"Jury's still out."

"Hmph," said Natalie, clearly hinting that she doubted his honesty.

"I'm just…not sure, in either direction," said Sylvester, feeling on the defensive. "I remember being at work, I remember it happening…but I don't remember *willing* it to happen. So I don't know?"

"Maybe we share some distant relative. Do you fall a lot? Do you have a lot of bumps and bruises that you don't recall the source of?"

"No, I remember where all these came from," he said, looking down at his scarred arm with a grin.

"Is this going to be that obligatory scene where Quint, Hooper, and Brody start comparing scars?" she asked.

"Huh?"

"*Jaws*. Did you ever see *Jaws*?"

"Oh...yeah. I think I saw the...fifth one?"

"There wasn't a fifth one," she said. "There were four of them. And only the first two were any good, although the third was in 80s 3D and had Dennis Quaid and the guy from *Manimal.*"

"*Manimal*...where's that remake..."

"But it was the first one I was talking about. They're all sitting on the boat together comparing shark bites. It's a classic scene," she said with filmic authority.

"So you're a movie buff?"

"Not really. Book buff, yes. Movie buff, unintentionally. I don't get out a lot. But I like Jaws," she said. "Rare case where the movie tops the book."

"OK, let's do it then," he said.

"Do what?"

"Compare scars."

"You have no chance," she said.

Sylvester cocked his head at her in a Harrison Ford kinda way, then rolled up his sleeve. "I was gonna say the same thing."

He started pointing to different spots on his arm. "This one is from a grapefruit spoon when I was 13, this one a Zippo when I was 15 and tried to give myself a Batman brand, this one was a heated pastry wheel that I ran racetracks around my arm with, and this one was from a sharp piece of bamboo that broke off while I was battle golfing. And that's just the first few I noticed."

He stared at her proudly, mocking her competitive gesture, certain she couldn't match him, let alone top him.

She smiled back and slid the sleeve of her own gown up. He immediately knew he'd met his match.

"This one," she began, pointing towards her elbow, "was from when I fell off a skateboard when I was 12. The bone snapped and went through the skin. I never skateboarded again." She smirked. "This one (pointing towards her forearm) was when I fell running for a bus in college. I landed on a cyclist and my arm got stuck in the chain. The large discoloration running down my whole arm was from when I fell off my stool eating dinner and went through the plate glass patio window. It changes colors in the cold."

"I got one of those color changers, too!" interjected Sylvester with the giddy excitement of commonality.

"...and this one," she said as she held up her middle finger towards him, "was when I got my hand caught in a door and the finger popped right off." The scar looked like an unfinished whittling job that spanned two bones that were not actually connected.

Sylvester was duly impressed, but undaunted. The game extended past the arm.

"I stabbed my leg once with a kitchen knife and snapped the tip off inside," he began. "I broke three toes in my right foot kicking it into a bulldozer's blade. I broke all five metacarpals in my left hand trying to knock down traffic barrels barehanded while driving by at 40 miles per hour. My ear was detached once because I was machete fighting someone and deflected him at a weird angle. And I chipped four teeth after biting down too hard on a screwdriver."

Natalie nodded her respect back at him but kept going.

"I'm not even going to address why you had any reason to bite down on a screwdriver," she said with a smirk. "My right leg has been broken seven times and has more pins and screws in it than your typical Italian automobile. I fractured my skull twice in the same week doing two entirely different things, one of which was while lying in a hospital bed recovering from the first, when a TV fell on me. I had a detached retina in each eye at two different times because I blinked too fast while reading. And once, while I was sleeping, I somehow popped a vertebra out of place that required me sitting in a harness for a month waiting for it to heal."

"Yeah, but those last few don't leave scars," Sylvester added.

"They still count!"

"This wasn't a 'pain competition', it was a 'scar competition'!"

"You *just* mentioned broken toes and chipped teeth! You don't get scars from chipped teeth, pal."

He smirked at her. She glared at him. Then they both laughed.

"How about we just agree we're both a mess."

"Agreed!"

They smiled at each other.

Then somehow, from a sitting position, she fell out of her chair and knocked over the water cooler.

CHAPTER 19
HOSPITAL FRIENDS

To be clear, Natalie wasn't accident prone. It was a diagnosis far more elusive than that.

She'd been tested for every possible affliction under the sun including (but not limited to) inner ear imbalances, dizzy spells, spasms, blackouts, seizures, poor eyesight, voodoo incantations, and even family curses.

At the end of the day, she was simply told that she was clumsy. No other explanation was needed. She fell over. A lot.

It didn't seem to matter what she was doing or where she was doing it, she'd fall. Standing alone in the middle of an empty field she'd somehow lose her balance and find herself on the ground.

And in many ways this lifestyle extended beyond just gravity.

She took her driving test four times. She got into four accidents. She decided not to get a car. The driving instructor sent her a thank you note.

When she moved into her first apartment she was excited about the large kitchen and her opportunity to cook. After two weeks she listed her set of knives and frying pans online and got $50 for them. Even boxed macaroni & cheese posed injury risks. Now she subsisted on TV dinners, cold vegetables, and pre-sliced deli meats.

For a while she tried to explain it to people, doctors and such, but people only knew what they knew and couldn't see the world through her eyes no matter how confidently they thought they could.

If aisles of soda pop didn't spontaneously erupt on you regularly, you didn't understand what it was like.

If you've never twisted your ankle sitting on the toilet, you didn't understand what it was like.

If you went through days or weeks or months of your life without a scratch or a stubbed toe, you didn't understand what it was like to face a constant barrage of injuries no matter how little you moved or how much you strove to avoid situations and obstacles that encouraged it.

Accident prone didn't even begin to describe her.

All of this came out in conversation over the next few days as Natalie and Sylvester met often, joking and bantering and enjoying each other's stories of accidental and intentional pain while trapped in the hospital prison of the fourth floor.

They were a strange pair; Natalie pestered him about why he'd subject himself to pain for the fun of it, while he questioned her endlessly about how she could achieve it all so easily.

"Do you know how much effort I have to go through?" he once said. "It's not easy to spend all your time seeking it out! The idea of just living my life and knowing I'd be buffeted by pain? What a relief that'd be!"

She looked at him with wide eyes, unbelieving, her head shaking back and forth on its own, as if even her skull didn't believe what it heard coming from his mouth.

"Do you know what I'd do to live pain free? To live a normal life? To walk down the street without getting hurt? To drive a car to the corner store for milk? To use stairs? I don't even leave my house most days! All my furniture is padded. I haven't gone on a vacation since I was a child for fear of the things I haven't even discovered that could hurt me! I got poked in the eye once by a moth. *A MOTH.* I had to wear an eye-patch for two weeks!"

Sylvester stared at her, his focus set on maintaining a straight face, a vision of support and sadness...but he couldn't do it, a deep guttural laugh peppered with smiles erupting from his belly, every fiber of his being disbelieving her amazingly bad luck.

"I never thought of injuring myself with a moth before. Did it hurt?" he asked as the giggles bubbled between words.

Her eyes were both incredulous and laughing at once, knowing how absurd it was. "It only hurt when it tried to fly out. It got stuck."

"Stuck? It's a moth! And an eyeball! How does that even work?" Sylvester was rolling now, his body bent in two, tears streaming.

Natalie shook her head, unsure herself how it worked, before leaning in and closing her eye and pointing toward it. "See?" she asked, and Sylvester, strangely enough, could see small scars on her eyelid, as if a tiny moth warrior with a sword had tried to cut its way out from the inside.

"Wow," he said. "I'm impressed."

He avoided hurting his eyes. It was one of his few rules; his senses were off limits. Eyes and ears were big no-nos, and his tongue and nose were only allowed limited abuse. He changed the subject.

"So what happens to your bookstore when you're gone all this time? Does it stay closed? Aren't you worried about going out of business, paying rent, all of that?" he asked.

"My grandmother came up from Florida to watch it. She's old and senile but loves her books. Told me she was happy for a break from my grandfather. Seems he's intent on carving a magazine rack for the bathroom and she's all aflutter about it. Can you imagine that? Wooden gargoyles in the bathroom staring at you, guarding the toilet paper?"

She laughed at the thought of it.

"If she's in town why doesn't she visit you?" Sylvester asked.

"She does. Every day."

Sylvester looked around the room, as if expecting her to be hiding behind the ice machine or popping out from the recycling.

"Why haven't I met her yet? Bring her by, let me say hello. I love that bookstore."

"Well, she's 80. She wakes up at 4am and comes by at 5am. She's off to work by 6:15. Are you even up that early?"

Sylvester laughed to himself. "Oddly enough, I usually am. I worked the late shift. My brain doesn't understand sleeping in darkness."

"OK, we'll swing by and pester you tomorrow morning. She's quite the hoot, especially before breakfast."

*****

At 5:30am the next morning Sylvester heard a light knock at the door and looked up from his latest rereading of *Fight Club* to see Natalie leading her grandmother into the room.

His first thought was to hide his aggressively dog-eared book before he was reprimanded by the both of them, quickly shoving it under his pillow, a rough elephant-ear now saving his place.

"Hi there, this is my Grandma Norris," said Natalie.

"Hello Mrs…" began Sylvester, only to be cut off by Grandma Norris as she noticed him sitting on the bed.

"This is the one? The strange man you spend your days chittering away with and who likes to poke himself with scissors? He's not even attractive! Big nose, unshaven. Can he even read? I doubt it. What's your story sonny, you trying to get in my Natalie's pants?"

Sylvester was taken aback, both by the amount of information she knew and her comically forward manner. He wasn't even allowed time to process and respond before she changed direction and kept going, her eyeline pulled to the window.

"Oh, what a view this room's got! Ya see all those air conditioners out there? Oh, how we'd love to have chilly air in our condo. Your grandfather keeps insisting that he's gonna build one, and I keep telling him *'Ya can't build an air cooler from wood, ya billiken!'*, but I'm sure he's gonna try! That man will be the death of me as much as he's the life of me."

Natalie looked over to Sylvester with wide, smiling eyes, hoping he was enjoying her strange, senile charm.

She was already off on another tangent though, trying her best to kick the other empty bed in the room (although she could barely lift her foot off the floor). "And look at this empty bed! How'd you get a private room when my Natalie is sharing with some muttonhead of a woman who snores loudly? It's awful! Snorers should be stoned to death. My husband snored once 50 years ago and ya know what I did? Held his nose closed until he stopped. Learned his lesson right, he did, and he ain't snored again since!"

Both Sylvester and Natalie were now giggling, thoroughly enjoying her sporadic and entertaining one-sided conversation.

"Guy came into the bookstore yesterday Natalie, young man, must've been just past 70. He called me a dish. A dish! Haven't heard that one for a while. But I knew his game…he wasn't going to sweet talk me into giving him a discount! He wanted that first edition of Uncle Tom. That thing's old! Old I tell him. That's the retirement fund for when we get infirm and need the money. He looked at me and said *'Miss, you ARE old'*. Well I don't take that kinda lip, so I booted him right outta the store then and there! Ingrateful young hooligan..."

She didn't seem to pause to take a breath before leaping in another direction, as if she'd mastered circular breathing simply to avoid anyone interrupting her train of thought.

"Did you know he's building a magazine rack in the toilet? A magazine rack! Who reads magazines? Trash I say! Now if he wanted to build a BOOK rack I'd be all for it, although I don't think I'd want to leave anything in there. Too moist. Maybe some of those trashy romance paperbacks you used to read. Remember we found those under your bed one time, Natalie? Threw them in the burner and set you straight with Steinbeck and Hemingway! You ain't never read one since, have you?" She squint-eyed Natalie like a psychic cyclops, trying to reach into her soul and pluck the information out.

"No grandma, I stay off the romance paperbacks," she said as she shot Sylvester a look and visibly crossed two sets of her fingers behind her back.

"Good, good, horrible trash that is. If you want to be naughty read some good Jane Austen and Henry James! That'll wake the nethers better than any of that softcover fluff! Oh look, jello!"

And she dove at it, a small container sitting on Sylvester's food tray, still unopened and untouched, jiggling green in the morning sunlight. They watched as her old fingers fumbled for a moment and then ripped off the plastic covering, far more dexterous for 80 than Sylvester would have expected.

In seconds the jello was drained and her fingers were a sticky green and she'd moved on to other thoughts, not even concerned that it hadn't belonged to her and she hadn't asked permission.

"He made a stand for the TV box, did I tell you? Huge thing, heavy oak. Tiny TV. Two-bedroom condo. That man never stops building! Nonstop! I get sick of it. Doesn't even pause to breathe right..."

And then she stopped.

Done.

Quiet and silent and unblinking.

She licked her lips, happily content now to keep quiet, her eyes fluttering off, as if her whole mind had run out of power and shut down while it recharged its batteries. The room filled with silence and quiet as early morning hospital sounds drifted in from the hallway.

Natalie smiled at Sylvester and put her arm around her grandmother and started to head towards the door, hobbling along on her crutched leg, her grandmother's presence seeming to offset her curse.

"It was nice seeing you, young man!" Grandma Norris suddenly exclaimed as she was led out of the room, recharged and apparently distracted by the nurse's station in the hallway. "Look at that shoddy construction. Your grandfather would be so ashamed. Gotta use oak for nurse's stations. Oak! Everyone knows that. What time is it? It must almost be time to be opening. Can't be late. Hate having lines."

Natalie waved goodbye as she left the room, smirking and cocking her head as she went. Sylvester waved back, smiling, and after a minute carefully slid his buckled and beaten book out of its hiding place and found his page.

*****

The next morning Sylvester was released.

His burns had started to heal, and his bed had become valuable, so he was sent home with a prescription for ointment and a stack of gauze pads and bandages, as well as their best wishes and a follow-up appointment. He would be leaving his pool toy behind.

Natalie met him briefly for a goodbye laugh in the lounge, his hand now freed and breathing fresh air and smarting from the breezes that passed over it.

"So when do you get out?" he asked her as he clenched and stretched it, faint creaking cracks and clicks mumbling from his hand.

"Tomorrow I think. Maybe the next day. They know me here and said they'd rather keep me an extra day or two than risk me falling in the parking lot and being stuck here for months. They must get sick of me."

"Well, when you're out and on your feet, maybe we could continue these chats."

She smiled at him curiously. "I thought you had a girlfriend?"

"It didn't...work out?" he said after a pause. "I don't think."

She looked at him, searching for clues. She saw only sadness and confusion in his eyes that told her he probably had similar questions and wasn't the one who ended it. She wasn't sure it would have mattered to her either way.

"You know where to find me. Come by sometime. I'll probably be hiding under the floorboards with a good novel. Can't let the world get its hands on me again." She said this last part with a strange mix of humor and apathy, as if she was resigned to a fate of indoor living.

Sylvester held up his wrinkled and beaten book and gave it an eyeful, "I do need to find something new to read. I'm starting to feel like one of those nuts who keep rereading *Catcher in the Rye*."

"We have first editions if you're looking," said Natalie.

"Of Fight Club?"

"No silly, of Catcher."

"Never read it. Seemed too serious."

"It's a good read, but if it's not your cup of cocoa I'm sure we have something that'd tickle you."

Sylvester smiled and leaned forward and gave her a soft and protective hug goodbye. She looked up at him with bright eyes full of hope, so he leaned down again and gave her a kiss on the forehead.

"I'll see you when you make bail," he said.

And as he turned to leave he immediately thought of Felicia. What a strange choice of words he'd chosen to leave with. Clearly his mind was still spinning pie plates.

CHAPTER 20
PORCH SPLINTERS

Sylvester sat on the deck watching the gloomy, guzzling, guttered rain gush down from the rafters above, a smattering of thump-thump-thumping overhead as small bits of hail plinked off the tin roof in waves, the first sign of winter dabbling ahead of its time. His arm was still sore, his attention unfocused, the dampness of autumn filtering in through his pores as his eyes unfocused ahead of him.

With the hospital behind him Sylvester had spent his first few days playing with Poke (who ploomed non-stop for days upon his return) and tubsitting in ice water, trying to recalibrate his thoughts on his overall life and the two women who seemed to be unintentionally jousting about with his affections. To wait? To pine? To rebound? No easy answer seemed to come, and after a few days it seemed clear that nobody else would emerge from his subconscious to make the decision for him.

Felicia had been a surprisingly good fit and a solid relationship. Strained and painful, sure, but nevertheless solid. Yet where things sat seemed closer to a ditch than a future.

Natalie was an enigma of entertainment, something to delve into and attempt to understand, an oddity to be ottered and enjoyed. But how long the intrigue would hold seemed the larger question, the dalliance always indebted to the lifespan of the curiosity.

It seemed to Sylvester that life was dictating he make some overall decision now, in this brief moment of relationship freedom when no voices or bits of feminine marketing were twisting his mind.

Deep down he knew this was simply his scared ego trying to convince itself of its own worth; the arrogance to believe he was in a position to make such a choice all on his own, as if two equally interesting and amazing women both desired and fawned over him. He would quickly fail his life's own Bechdel test.

And so he pondered and postulated, his mind wandering and distracting itself, determined not to decide.

The screen door whined as Socket meandered out, a hung cigarette dangling from his lips embracing its death, a small dribbled tendril of smoke dancing as it chased him into the mist.

"Half rain, half hail…sure is some shanky weather for early October…" said Socket as he half-dragged on his cigarette, pivoting it on lip leverage before collapsing into the empty chair beside Sylvester, a screwdriver and busted lightsocket in hand. "How're you feeling?"

Sylvester lifted his arm weakly, hints of pain vibrating through the gauze as he looked at it, twisting it toward the past. "Generally fine. Arm's not too bad. Might be more the mind that's slow to heal."

"Oh? From the oil? Or did The Leash swing some long-distance whip lashes through the bars?"

"Neither. The klutzy girl was in there."

"The hospital?"

"Yeah…"

"Well that's kismety."

"If you go in for that kinda thing."

"Call it what you will, but your paths sure do cross a lot."

Sylvester nodded, still in thought, his hand absently picking at a splinter. They had crossed paths an absurd amount of times. Kismet or fate or unlikely coincidence, life had bumped them against each other like pebbles in the ocean, repeatedly blunting their edges and trying to soften them.

He looked out at the flickering hailstorm, the pellets pounding on the pavement, and reached his arm out, letting them plink off his palm before they turned to water and rivered down his wrist.

Socket interrupted the silence, "Did you talk to Carl? Still definitely canned?"

"Yeah…sounds like it."

"Too bad. Seemed a simple enough gig."

"I was thinkin' of leaving anyways. No big loss."

"You gonna look for the same kinda thing?"

"Who knows. Maybe. I need to see what's out there. Sorta burned out on the fry cook angle."

"Could probably get you something at my place driving a truck or something…" Socket offered.

"Thanks. Let me think on it for a few. Not in any rush. I get unemployment it sounds like. Or disability. Something. I have to look into it."

"Should be a nice vacation."

"Usually is. Probably not a bad thing to heal up right. Give me time to think on life for a bit."

"Life's sometimes not worth thinking about. Sometimes just worth doing and moving on. Focusing on the present always seems to make me drippy and sad. Same with the past. We know what those are. That's why we look forward to the future. The unknown. The dreams of how great it'll be, our lives lived through someone else's warped glass. Potential unrealized, all of that."

Sylvester smiled and looked at his friend. "You and your existential shit…"

Socket smiled back, clearly pleased to have his roommate returned.

"Thanks again for taking care of Poke for me."

"Not a problem. Fun and jumpy little critter."

"You didn't electrocute my porcupine did you…?"

"Not intentionally. We just hung out on the couch. Watched some TV. That sucker's into Twilight Zone something fierce!"

Sylvester eyed his friend, suspicious doubt and skepticism lacing his thoughts, before drawing his attention back to his splintered finger.

The splinter waved to Sylvester from deep under his skin, a treasure diver under glass, looking both preserved and in fear. Sylvester scratched at the finger, prodding and poking it with the end of his fingertip while Socket mumbled to himself, a screwdriver hung from his mouth as he fiddled and fobbled with a broken version of his namesake, its sprayed and flayed wires sprouting copper afros.

"It's not even about the job or the girl really," Socket continued, sensing his postulating was required, "as much as the novelty of 'em."

"I don't think most women would appreciate being called novelties…"

"Oh, like they view us any differently?"

Sylvester shrugged, slap-sliding his hand along the wooden armrest and embedding a dozen new splinters in his arm that he immediately started plucking out.

"What're you planning to do with that thing?" Sylvester asked with a nod toward the socket, visions of Felicia dancing about. "Another electrified toy to scare the trick-or-treating kiddies?"

Socket gave him a look and a smirk, before raising his eyes to the darkness above them.

"Just a busted light."

Sylvester glared at him before drawing his attention back to a particularly calligraphic splinter that seemed determined to burrow. Sylvester helped give it a push, nestling it deeper, readying it for hibernation, an act of personal vandalism.

But then his hands paused, unsure of themselves, as if realizing for the first time what they were doing, acting out of habit, not need, a pair of pickpocket hands that couldn't help but dance.

It was how he acted after Felicia left, his body moving on its own, jumping on the ride without asking if it wanted to.

He steadied his gaze, the buried splinters staring back, and he felt no urge. No true call to impugn, to injure. Emptiness met him, a desireless feeling that consumed him, teasing his past but refusing to satisfy it. He concentrated on a single splinter, the shard of wood buried and bleeding inside him. He could feel it. He could sense it. It hurt the way splinters hurt, but there was no satisfaction in it. No glory of pain and persecution. It just felt like a splinter.

He looked sadly on it, wondering why his bent had betrayed him.

And then it hit him – his hospital vacation had teased and tantalized him with something no longer in reach. Something which he desired more than pain.

And with that, his mind refocused itself on Natalie.

CHAPTER 21
TIME TO READ A BOOK

The weeks passed as weeks pass, faint memories and hungover laughs, mild regrets and trophy scars, and all the while Sylvester's mind continued to think back on the strange girl with the attraction to pavement.

So it was, with little surprise, that one day Sylvester's lonely boredom and confusion finally got the best of him, Socket's electrified house no longer occupying his interest, and he decided to take Natalie up on her invitation, a slim hope that it may put his brain's weeviling curiosity to rest.

It was early afternoon when he found himself standing outside Natalie's weathered old bookstore, an ice cold milkshake in hand, his nut allergy already palpitating, looking up at the gargoyles he hadn't noticed before and wondering what the odds were of them springing to life and carrying off courtesans.

He remembered a store in Northampton once, long ago, that had gargoyles perched on its crenels, beady eyes glowing red, looking down with a mischievous feeling of scribbled dreams and mythic turtles.

These gargoyles seemed to just glare and keep watch, intimidating him from entering, as if they looked angrily into his soul and knew he dog-eared books.

He wilted back, unsure of himself, and meandered toward the common, a triangular spate of grass with a small gazebo nestled within its borders, a staging ground for his wobbling confidence.

He tried to force himself to a proper mindset, extinguishing the waffling uncertainty dancing between his ears. He watched the darkened windows, trying his best to ensure he wouldn't be stuck chatting exclusively with Grandma Norris about bathroom cabinetry and homemade air conditioning.

After five minutes of anxiety his head hurt and his chest burned and he felt enough chistic confidence to try his bravery against the gargoyle-encrusted bookshop once again, certain that he'd spied a crutch-ridden shadow hobbling about inside.

He tightly gripped the forkroach that'd made its way into his pocket, a 3-tined amputee that, like a whiskey shot on a cold day, surged pain through him steadily, giving him confidence, overwhelming the foreboding feeling that the oaken darkness of the hibernating store gave off.

The bell jingled as he entered, announcing his presence loudly, an alarm that made him tuck his illicit brown paper bag further up under his arm. He gave a tentative glance around, pressing his ear into service, and then stepped into the bowels of the book cave.

The shop looked about the same, although somewhat reorganized. By the door now sat a variety of books on travel to Florida, as well as hard-backed editions by the 1920s authority on shuffleboard and canasta. The few chairs and benches he'd observed the last time through were all removed, with large open spaces to walk through instead of dodge around. The air had the scent of baby powder and turnips.

He headed toward the register, his eyes darting back and forth expecting a trap, nervous the elderly matron would be on the prowl for bargain hunters to berate. He could only imagine what she'd chat about if she was settled in for the day and had no excuse to leave.

He was thrilled when he cornered the bend and saw a cast-laden foot resting on the counter behind the register, the body it connected to sliding into a soft-hammocked chair where Natalie was sitting and reading. He put his paper bag down on the counter and made a fake coughing noise that always worked well in movies but seemed awkward in real life.

"Yes? Oh…it's you. The vanishing man who skirt-chases in hospitals," she said, her eyes flashing up briefly from her book.

He wasn't sure if she was mad or playing with him.

"I didn't mean to vanish…I just wanted to give you a chance to heal. Didn't want my attitudes and proclivities to be a bad influence. Ya know, convince you to go sky diving or bull fighting."

She tilted the book down long enough to give him a glaring and incredulous look, before turning back and muttering, "Be serious."

He felt undeservedly hurt and guilty, so he patted the brown paper bag he'd placed on the counter, plying his bribe into early service.

"These are for you. Library sale bargains. Figured you may appreciate some more subversive reading material while you're couch-ridden. Or do you avoid the couch now? Hammock ridden, maybe?" He glanced around, cautiously, before adding, "Might wanna keep 'em hidden from grandmothers, though…".

This piqued her interest and she reached for the bag, giving its contents a glance and smiling naughtily at the stack of used romance novels littering the inside.

"OK, bribery toll accepted," she mumbled, her mood softening as she gave a quick glance down the aisle before reaching under the counter to lift the bottom shelf, dumping the contents into a hidden trove of magazines, phone books, and comics, where they were promptly welcomed by their fellow contraband.

"So," she began, looking up to him cautiously, "you returned. Finally in the mood to try to get into my pants again without the orderlies looking on? My grandmother kept insisting she pegged you right."

Sylvester blushed immediately, caught off guard. "No, no, your pants can stay on as long as you'd like. I'm only here for the chitchat and camaraderie."

Natalie gave him a derisive look before going back to reading her book, "Hmph, too bad. They're made of Velcro."

Sylvester coughed and laughed at once, snorting air through his eyeballs. Natalie smirked as she fake-read. "So, did you have an eventful few weeks?" she asked, trying to sound distant and disinterested.

"No, not really. I went back to Socket's place - he's a friend I'm crashing with - and went through my mail, paid the one bill I could afford, tried to find a job, played with my porcupine…"

"Nice euphemism."

"Thanks! But I actually do have a porcupine."

"Well, that all but confirms I'm never visiting. How'd everything else go? Any luck?"

"Oh yes, paying a bill is very easy."

"I meant with the job," she snarked back.

"Most people tell me to wait until my hand is less icky and puss-filled," he said as he held up his hand, underscoring its sad state.

She shivered a bit, "Reminds me of what it looks like when they take the cast off, all shriveled and scared of the daylight."

"Yeah, it's not the most pleasant sight. Betcha vampires deal with it constantly. That and bloody morning breath."

She knuckled her cast, "My leg's not gonna look much better, but I've still got another week before they crack it. At least I can wear pants now."

"Not if I get them off," Sylvester added.

"We've already established you weren't gonna try. No changing your mind now. I want to collect on the bet I made with my grandmother."

"You made a bet about my intentions?"

"Oh sure. She's a gambler at heart. And she assumes everyone has the worst of intentions. I once saw her accuse a parking attendant of being fresh with her because he asked for her car keys. She's an entertaining old bird."

"Speaking of fowl, is she still around and about?" Sylvester asked as he craned his neck in circles.

"Oh yeah, she's back in the children's section reorganizing. I think she's color coding them or something?"

"Do children…buy books based on color?"

"No clue. This isn't the kind of place that attracts kids very often. All we have are hardback editions of *Grimm's Fairy Tales* and *Frankenstein* and Jules Verne; not exactly the pinnacle of trendy pop culture. It's her bookshop, though, so she can organize it however she wants. I stopped fighting her years ago…" Natalie gave a glance over her shoulder again before whispering, "…and once she leaves I'll put it back the way it was! She won't remember by her next visit. You know how many times I've had to pull those shuffleboard books? Haven't sold one since I was 15!"

"It may help if we had actual shuffleboard courts around, but I'm fairly certain they're restricted to the state of Florida and high schools built before 1960."

She smiled, happy to see him and his personality again.

Sylvester glanced around, suddenly noticing more gargoyled carvings buried in the ceiling. It had an awe-inspiring but unsettling feeling about it, as if he was surrounded by both protectors and predators.

"Does it bother you having all these creatures looking down at you?" he asked.

Natalie looked up at them, smiling. "When I was little they bothered me…but as I got older I named them all. Takes away the fear factor. No such thing as a mean and scary gargoyle named Nausicaa is there?"

"No, I suppose not," agreed Sylvester. "It's an amazing place. More personality than any other bookstore I've been to."

"Thanks. They tried to make it inspiring to the imagination."

"How's the customer service? I'm looking for something new to read, ideally less FBI-inducing than *Catcher in the Rye*. What've you got that would appeal to a guy like me with strange tastes and no talent for the Greek language?"

Natalie shifted and dropped her foot to the ground, bouncing it awkwardly off a few shelves on the way down, leaning her elbows on the counter and looking him in the eye. "Well, what're your interests? Romance? Adventure? Violence? Mystery? I could recommend a great book on shuffleboard…"

"Do you have anything with all of those combined?"

"Like a police caper about a lovelorn, serial-killing, shuffleboard player? Probably not, but to be honest, I doubt even Amazon could help you there," she said as she reached for her crutches and hobbled to her feet.

"I'm after something that makes me chuckle and flip pages. Not overly witty wordlery. No first editions that cost me a fortune. No bestsellers that everyone and their uncle has already read. I want something…me."

"Then help me understand what's 'you'. Do you want a story about broken bones and hospital beds and french fry machines?"

Sylvester shot her an arched eyebrow. She was quick and witty, this one. "Close, but I'm not really into french fry romance. I prefer books about people conquering challenges. I like books with some pain and violence in them, but not war books. I like books about art theft." He paused, scratching his chin and kicking his toe into the baseboard. "But I also like horrible, poorly written books that make me frustrated and angry."

"You do?" she asked, surprised.

"Well, yeah…it's a different kind of pain isn't it? Having to read something awful? A book that makes little sense, spends no time chasing facts, has plot holes that fit planets…there's something awkwardly fun and painful about reading stuff that bad."

"A bad and poorly written book we should have here somewhere…or a funny violent book about art theft…" Natalie's eyes light up. "Oh wait! I've got it! Something painful, right?"

"Yeah…"

"Have you read Irvine Welsh?"

"Doesn't ring any bells? What'd he do?"

"Trainspotting."

"Trainspotting…like the movie? Heroin? Toilet diving? I saw that once." He slipped into a fake Scottish accent, "Ursula Andress…THE quintessential Bond girl. Pussy Galore…what a misnomer."

"That's the one. And the book is written phonetically in that same Scottish brogue, so it's a bitch to read! You almost need to read out loud to understand what's being said, and even then…" she trailed off. "It took me a solid month to get through and it was a painful, albeit enjoyable, experience. And there's criminality involved, too."

"I'll give it a try. Lead on!"

They wandered down the aisles, Natalie hobbling them deeper into the depths, the walls growing thick with spider-webbed dust as Sylvester imagined tour groups of eight-legged travelers.

She finally stopped in a far corner with no shelving, huge stacks of books, piled high, teased against the ceiling in twenty-foot mountains. It had the look of a debris pile from a dam burst.

"Somewhere in here we have a copy," she said, indicating the morass. "This's the discount pile. All the mass-produced feeder store stuff that doesn't sell. You find it, you get 50% off."

Sylvester craned his neck up, "You are far less organized that I thought you'd be…"

"Don't let Grandma Norris hear you or she'll bean you with the annotated edition of Ulyssic," said Natalie with a serious and fearful expression on her face that gave the indication the 80-year old still managed a nasty curve. "Besides, the rest of the store is perfectly well organized!"

And so they dug in, delving deep, restacking and repiling their way through. Natalie instinctively organized by author and subject as she went, surrounding herself with stacks she'd shuffle books into. Sylvester simply migrated piles, blindly restacking them behind him as he went, papercutting himself lovingly on golden-edged pages, pinching his fingers between spines without thought. His addiction thrived in this atmosphere.

Only twice did large stacks topple and fall on them, and in both cases exclusively on Natalie, with nary a loose leaf fluttering near Sylvester.

"I once went to a bookstore in Saratoga like this," Sylvester began. "This shop in an old bank run by the Morlocks that just tunneled deeper and deeper into the Earth with books stacked everywhere." He paused, fondly remembering it. "They had a similar organizational system."

She smirked with sarcastic eyes and mock anger as she lifted up a copy of *Trainspotting* and waved it at him, "See? Easy to find. Only forty minutes of digging!"

Sylvester smiled and clapped his hands, palming them wide, encouraging her to toss it. Natalie shot him a crooked look of uncertainty. They were three feet apart; it seemed risky. Finally, she took the leap and tossed the book, regretting it immediately, the force of the throw toppling her into the organized stacks.

Sylvester, on the other hand, leaned in and took it off the chin.

As the stars and birds circled their heads they looked at each other strangely, rubbing matching chins for disparate reasons.

"You leaned in," Natalie remarked.

"You challenged gravity," Sylvester added.

"Strange..." they both said in unison.

Sylvester picked up his new book and reached over to pull her free from the detritus of scattered books, the destruction barely noticeable given the surroundings.

When they reached the register she settled back into her hammock and rang up his book, taking his few crumpled dollars and offering him back a pleasantly handled paper bag to carry it in.

"I hope you enjoy it," she offered. "Let me know what you think when you're done."

"Sure will..." he paused, not being particularly suave and unsure of the precedent in a boy-girl, buyer-buyee scenario (Felicia unsurprisingly having been the aggressor in his previous relationship). He looked Natalie in the eye, noticing the moth marks, before finally throwing out his weak attempt, "Would you like to do something? Ya know, outside of hospitals and supermarkets?"

She watched him curiously for a moment, weighing his intentions. This wasn't a game she got to play very often and she needed the practice. "So you *are* after my Velcro pants..." she began, "There goes my $10."

She pondered for another moment before setting expectations low so he knew what he was facing, "Hmmm, no...I'm much more of an 'inside' than an 'outside' person. But I will go somewhere inside with you."

"You don't like the outside?" he asked curiously, unsure of her meaning. "Which outside? Parks? Oceans? Car dealerships?"

"Sure, sure, all of them."

"You realize I'm only talking outside of the bookstore, right? This doesn't need to be a cross-country adventure..."

"Right. That's what I mean, too. I don't go out much. Apartment's attached out back," she said as she thumbed behind her, the act alone teasing her balance.

"What? Nahhh… I've met you outta here a buncha times. The market, the hospital, the enemy bookstore..."

"All emergencies I couldn't avoid. The supermarket, well, obviously I need to eat and buy bandages to live. But I only visit at night when nobody's around. And the hospital? Well, if you break something important you can't just sleep it off, right? Trust me, I'm more sedentary than a corpse."

"And the other bookstore? Are you telling me romance novels are life essentials?"

"Shhhh!!"

Sylvester quieted to a whisper. "Sorry…but that was outside, too!"

"Fine, three places in six months," she said with a huff. "Congratulations for being at all of them. You got a pocket full of kismet there."

"I just…" he stammered.

She glared at him. "Don't you get it? I do *not* go out. I am an inside person. I don't go for walks, I don't go to the movies, I don't hang out at malls or tan at the beach." Her voice was cracking, a mix of anger and sadness and tears mixing together. "I spend my time here, hidden away, where the world can't hurt me, OK? I'm sick of falling down and getting hurt, so if it's gonna happen anyways, I'd rather it happen in my own house. Look around! I buy cushions in bulk! I wear gloves in the summer! There're no sharp corners to be found anywhere in this building, and if you looked at my cutlery, you'd find a serious lack of serrated edges." She quieted a bit before letting slip, "It's a very well-padded life."

Sylvester looked at her, silently watching her eyes twitch and quiver. She'd given up a lot of herself there. It finally settled on him why she was available. She was buried. Hidden. Nobody knew she existed, like a forgotten princess trapped in a tower. Food may as well have been slid between the bars for how much she got out and interacted with people.

"Maybe…do you…do you need a copilot to help? Ya know, to avoid the pitfalls?" he asked, a slight air of nervous fear inching out, as if this girl may also suffer from the same flashes of pugilist anger he was used to from Felicia.

"Pitfalls? Pointy objects? Uneven surfaces? Meteorites? Seriously, the best protection I have is a roof over my head and a single floor dwelling."

"Aren't you blowing things out of proportion just a bit?"

"Nope."

"C'mon, let's go do something. Right here, right now, in the moment. It'll be good for you!"

"Why do men always need to be the hero? I've had too many failed heroes already in my life. At this point I'd do better settling down with the dragon that slayed them all."

Sylvester smiled at her, her swaggering wit peeking through even at her most exposed. He wasn't going to give in on gallantry now.

"Nope, not giving up!" he said with a roguish grin, teasing and tempting her, "I want to see you on the outside of this place! Let's go adventuring!"

"Adventuring? Are you daft? Sure, you wanna go on an adventure, fine. We can go to the supermarket. At midnight. Or give me six months to read your gift novels a dozen times over and I'll have enough reason to venture to the other bookshop, but that's only if I can't find a good selection online and lemme tell you, eBay rocks the used romance selection!"

Sylvester's eyes widened in warning as he nodded toward the aisle, and she quickly quieted down and shrank, unaware of how loudly she'd just announced herself.

"Natalie…I'm…I just want to spend time with you, OK? We don't have to go bungee jumping or shark riding or anything crazy. We can go for a walk, grab a slice, I don't care. How about ice cream? That's right next door. Whatdya say?"

"I freezer burn easily."

"OK, something else. There must be somewhere nearby you always wanted to visit? You haven't spent 30 years hiding in this bookstore without even looking in the phone book once, have you?"

"My grandmother was against them…"

Sylvester cocked his head and wrinkled his lips in a detestful way, trying to force-feed guilt into her brain.

"OK…fine…I'll consider it," she said with a pout. "Where do you have in mind? Gimme a realistic destination to aim for."

"I don't know, what do you like to do? Roller-skating?" he asked rather absently.

Her eyes widened and shattered and reformed in her head as she glared at him. "Are you mad? I fall down when standing still. I get cuts from soft objects. Roller-skating? Seriously? Why not just push me down an escalator and save us the time?"

"OK, OK, my bad…I wasn't thinking through your…proclivities."

"Yeah, and don't be thinking about my proclivities too much, cuz this isn't gonna get you anywhere fast….roller-skating…"

"OK, OK, wait…how about bowling? No wait…"

She glared at him, unamused.

Sylvester tapped the side of his head in thought, drumming SOS signals into his brain.

"Video games? Skee-Ball? Ball pit?" he asked, more hopeful.

"Carpal tunnel. Hard round projectiles. Death trap."

"Renaissance Faire?"

"Axe throwing."

"Circus?"

"Elephants."

"Walk on the beach?"

"Sharks."

"Sharks? On a beach? Come on, now you're just being impossible."

"Have you not seen the video of the shark bellysurfing onto the beach to swallow the seal?"

Sylvester rolled his eyes. "Walk in the woods?"

"Bears."

"Bears?"

"And bear traps."

"I think you're being paranoid now. Come on, give me something to work with. There must be something safe we can do at…," Sylvester paused at the clock, "…4 o'clock on a Monday afternoon?"

Natalie thought for a minute, pursing her lips as she held back her instinctive rejection.

"C'mon," said Sylvester, trying to tease it out.

"OK, OK…the common. I could do that… If you're up for such a weak adventure."

"The…common? Like, across the street 'the common'? As in, fifty feet away 'the common'?"

"Yeah. I haven't been there before."

He pointed in the direction of the door. "We're talking about that common? The grassy area across the street, yes? With the little gazebo?"

"Yup. That's the one."

"You're pulling my leg, aren't you?"

"Not when it involves crossing traffic. I've played *Frogger* before, ya know…"

"And you realize that's not a documentary, right?"

She glared at him.

"OK, baby steps it is!" he surrendered, defending himself with jazz hands. "A walk to the common it is! But beware, I may push for two whole laps around it!"

"Good. Finally. Takes forever to shut you up," she said with a playful smirk. "But first I have to notify my emergency contact."

And then she turned and hobbled down the aisle towards the kids' section, toppling only once and sideswiping a shelf of 1920s Italian cookbooks.

CHAPTER 22
THE COMMON WALK

It took them a surprisingly long time to cross the two lanes of traffic that sat between the bookshop and the common.

Natalie insisted on not only using the crosswalks, but also timing her crossing to when all three stoplights surrounding the common turned red at the same time, a confluence that happened only once every seven minutes. They missed their first opportunity when Natalie's crutch got stuck in a sewer grate, and their second when a gaggle of plastic bags decided to attack her.

When they did finally arrive, Sylvester realized the common was not much of a destination, spanning less than an acre of grass that was filled with a gazebo, some benches, a large pine tree festooned with Christmas ornaments, and a variety of plastic reindeer scattered about in such abundance that it seemed to indicate a breeding ground.

As they made their way Natalie explained her rules of walking in the 'perilous outside', which generally required keeping a safe distance between her and everything else, especially people and large unmoving objects (apparently signage had a habit of collapsing in on her like a black hole).

"Bit early in the season for reindeer isn't it?" Sylvester asked, looking up at the early autumn colors.

"I don't think they take the decorations down anymore. Too much effort and nowhere to store 'em. Around Thanksgiving they usually throw some hay on the ground and call 'em horses."

Sylvester smiled as Natalie kept her distance, walking a wide berth around a small herd in the midst of a meeting.

"I find reindeer dangerous," she conceded as they passed. "They attacked me in my own store once…"

"These ones did?" Sylvester asked jokingly, a smirk on his face as he flicked one in the nose with a loud *thunk*, "The plastic ones?"

"Right. The plastic ones."

Sylvester smiled back in curious amusement, egging her on, certain she couldn't be serious.

She was.

"A few years ago someone came into the shop carrying one. Really cold day out, wanted a place to warm up, ya know? We're a friendly shop, so we say 'sure'. And wouldn't you know it, somehow this thing gets kicked down the aisle, bumps off a bookcase, and *WHAM!*, bloody nose, three stitches to the chin."

"That sounds like a bad cartoon."

"I make Tom and Jerry look like inexperienced toddlers learning to walk."

Sylvester glanced suspiciously at the reindeer as they passed, the sun bleaching and mold more apparent up close. "Want to sit down on a bench? Safety in seating, right?"

"As long as it's not underneath anything precarious or close to the street. I've had more than my share of falling pines and out of control Cadillacs."

They found an empty bench, off to a corner, far from the pine trees, away from the reindeer, a good distance from the street, with only a few small shrubs nearby of such low and round stature that they were incapable of falling over. Even so, it took her three minutes of inspecting before she agreed to sit down, twice asking him to verify no insects or rodents made their homes in the bench.

Sylvester's curiosity continued to stare with uncertainly. Who was this girl that seemed entirely in contrast when moved outside the confines of four walls and a ceiling?

"You're a bit different when out in the air and exposed to sunlight ya know…" Sylvester began.

"You noticed that, huh? If you knew what I'd gone through thanks to strong breezes and bird attacks you'd totally understand where I'm coming from," she said as her eyes nervously skirted the skyline, as if expecting to be dive-bombed.

Sylvester shook his head, refusing to believe it could be as bad as her imagination was making it out to be.

"OK, so we're outside…," she began, "…how exciting." Her voice didn't seem convinced of the excitement. "Ready to head back in?"

"Oh, come on now, it's only been a few minutes! The tough part was getting here! No, I think you're required to enjoy some of it. Give it fifteen minutes."

"You're pushing my luck, buddy."

"How on earth do you make it to the supermarket? Or the bookstore? Is there some underground network of tunnels I don't know about?"

She eyed him sarcastically, "There is if you know where to find it."

Sylvester stared back, trying to read her humor. "You're a Morlock aren't you? That's it. Maybe that's the secret of all booksellers. You're all Morlocks…"

"Yup, you're on to us," she said as her hands sprung to life, waving in the air like a bad magician. "Every last one of us! Didn't my big round saucer eyes give it away??"

He laughed. She laughed. He'd won at least five minutes.

But before they could enjoy them she made a strange noise, and he looked up to see a dozen sets of wings now circling her.

She sat grudgingly, as if expecting this, her eyes rolled up in annoyance, waiting to be stung repeatedly and already bored of it. Sylvester was dumbstruck, certain that a moment before there wasn't a bumblebee in sight.

"At least I'm not allergic," she smiled happily as she watched one settle on her arm and sting her unmercifully. She didn't make a peep. She didn't try to run. She didn't try to swat. She didn't scream or curse or beg to leave. She just took it, sting after sting, as if she knew that any action on her part would only bring swift and painful karmic retribution.

Sylvester stared in awe and guilt, uncertain how to resolve the situation, yet curiously enthralled to watch it play out. "So…" he began, hoping that continuing the conversation and ignoring the bees might convince them to leave, "…do you have *any* allergies?"

"Strangely, I don't? Not sure why, really. Seems like I should be allergic to everything under the sun doesn't it? But no, I seem to be resilient there."

Sylvester nodded absently as his chest ballooned with envious jealousy as he watched the bumble-strafing continue. He tried offering up his arm as a target, but they ignored him. He tried swatting at them, but they ignored him. He tried calling them names and insulting their queen, but they ignored him. They were singularly focused on Natalie and nothing else, while in turn she was focused on him, her blinking eyes throwing guilt and "Now-do-you-believe-me?" messages.

Words began to tease on his tongue, a temptation flitting about that maybe they should retreat indoors, but he couldn't help but stay enthralled by her willpower and the odd scene playing out before him.

And then, as if to underscore the moment properly, the universe kicked up a sudden breeze, lifting a plastic reindeer into the air.

Natalie's eyes barely glanced up, knowing where it would land and not needing to follow its path. To the reindeer this was clearly personal.

"Watch this," she whispered as she swung her arms over her head and collapsed to the ground.

Sylvester could only stare, honestly unsure if he'd ever seen such a thing in his life, but before he could decide, the breeze shifted, and the reindeer attacked, nibbling its way through the sky before leaping at Natalie, razor sharp antlers extended.

A few moments later Natalie was nursing a bloody nose and a split lip as they slowly meandered their way back to the bookshop, expected defeat firmly within their grasp.

"OK, OK, fine, you've made your point!" shouted Sylvester to the sky gods as much as Natalie. "You're an inside person, I get it! Jeez…"

Strangely enough, with blood pouring down her face, Natalie smiled.

CHAPTER 23
SYLVESTER'S NEW JOB

Sylvester sat quietly in a wobbly old wooden chair, careful not to wiggle and squeak an echo that would bounce around the box-kneed room he found himself in. At least it seemed like an echo-friendly room, the kind with elastic walls with nothing hung on them to soften the sounds and quiet the march.

But he wasn't entirely sure; there were some assumptions at play here.

He was surrounded by piles of strange things and odd boxes that were stacked high and making random sounds all their own. Slithering and chirping and gnawing kinds of sounds. Sounds that bounced and amplified to a level of imagination-inducing hysterics.

Footsteps were approaching down a long hall, clip-clopping echoes of high heels or hard soles, and as they got louder Sylvester became curious what the mysterious Dr. Topus would look like and act like, and why a doctor would be interviewing someone for the job of a janitor.

The clip-clopping slowed and changed direction, disoriented and lost, before bursting into the room attached to a large and billowing man wearing twin lab coats of differing colors, a clipboard in his hand, and a pair of rubber gloves poking out of his pocket, one of which looked like the large yellow kind normally used for doing dishes. He had a half-combed head of hair and the squinting look of someone who should be wearing a monocle but was instead issued a full pair of spectacles.

He seemed to know his way around without looking, his head buried in his clipboard, mumbling to himself in small grunts and chirps as if he were speaking to the contents of the strange piles and odd boxes.

He flumped down in the chair opposite Sylvester behind a desk overflowing with emptiness. Either the doctor had only just started or was far more organized than Sylvester gave him credit for.

"So…Sylvester is it?" he asked with a scientific air that seemed to add an extra accent or syllable into his name.

"Yup."

"Nice to meet you," he said as he issued forth a hand to shake, his eyes still on the clipboard. "So you're here for the janitor job?"

"Yes sir, I have mastered the art of broom pushing and Windex spraying."

The doctor chuckled deeply as he glanced up at him, "I'm sure you have." He flipped back and forth on his clipboard, seeming to normalize what he found on different pages.

After a minute he looked up, curiously, as if he'd been asked a question. "Yes! You may be wondering why you're not being interviewed by the maintenance staff and the answer is that we don't have one. All been let go! Entire staff. Stealing our exhibits for a rival zoo. Strange business. Odd folk."

"What kinds of…?" Sylvester began to ask.

"Things did they steal? Oh just about everything. They started small with bugs and beetles, before moving on to bats and birds. We kept thinking animals were getting loose somehow. Finally caught 'em when they tried to smuggle a koala out in a baby stroller. Not the brightest lot, those ones. I'm doing the interviewing until we get things back up and running. Normally I'm responsible for the entomology lab here."

"Entomology…as in…bugs?"

"Yes, exactly! Oh, you're off to a good start. Far brighter than anyone on the old staff. Bugs, insects, arthropods, etcetera. I run what is affectionately called 'the bug house', which is probably why I was given the task of interviewing, the general consensus among my peers being that my charges are the quickest to feed since they have a nasty habit of eating one another, so therefore I must have endless free time." He gave Sylvester a glance over his glasses that seemed to indicate they were kindred souls, before adding, "They're totally right of course. I take a two hour nap every afternoon! Bloody easy job…"

Sylvester nodded in understanding as if he had vast experience with the day to day activities of beetles and bug houses.

"We have seven openings. The job's fairly simple; sweep the floors, empty the trash, and clean all the surfaces the sticky-fingered children touch. The goal is a spic-and-span environment that doesn't breed disease. And obviously don't steal the critters. How's that sound to you?"

"I don't like sticky fingerprints?"

"Exactly! The job doesn't pay too well, but you'll get free admission and all the peanuts and crickets you can eat."

"Crickets?"

"Old zoo joke. But seriously, don't eat the crickets. We need those." He nodded at Sylvester, an unspoken agreement about cricket snacks seemingly reached. "You can start tonight if you'd like; we have a week's worth of fingerprints to remove! We'll pay cash until you get the paperwork squared away. "

Sylvester smiled and extended an uncharred hand in agreement. "Lead me to the broom and the Windex."

CHAPTER 24
PANCAKE DATING

It had taken Sylvester the better part of two weeks, as well as embracing the concepts of bribery and guilt, coercion and charity, before Natalie finally agreed to go on a proper date.

The list of requirements was long and arduous, seemingly intent on doing nothing but avoiding the desired result. It must be within walking distance. It must be open after 8pm. It must serve cold food capable of being eaten with a spoon. It must not have stairs. It cannot be located beneath a train.

The list went on for three pages.

And so, one day, they found themselves wombling into Flappy Jacks, a local sidestreet pancake bar that Natalie would've never known existed, even if she'd wandered past with a homing pigeon and a tour guide.

Sylvester was a regular, walking and waving at the man behind the bar before pointing towards a familiar table and leading the way, snagging two menus as he went.

Natalie inched forward, swaddled in downy layers of thick winter clothing and steel-toed boots, her cast removed a few days before, a helmet strapped to her head, seemingly equal protection should she be shot out of a cannon or plunged into the ocean.

She glanced around and took in the restaurant's odd and unexpected look, appearing to have started out as a 70s era townie bar that was abruptly overtaken by a Japanese Steak House in the 80s, before settling into an IHOP knockoff.

The ceiling dripped rubber pancakes, dangling down like Dali paintings, while shelves nestled in the beamwork were littered with every manner of syrup bottle imaginable. There must've been thirty Butterworths, all with different shapes and designs (one appeared to be waving, possibly pulled live from the television), and an endless variety of brands ranging from the common to the obscure. It felt like a Hard Rock Café centered around pancakes.

A long wooden bar slid around the edge of the room, stools lined against it, but instead of its mirrored wall being fronted by bottles of booze and fishbowl tip cups, it was instead lined with jars of flour and batter.

The batter jars were nestled behind refrigerated doors, a misty cold steam frosting the glass, while the flour was housed in a set of mismatched cookie jars that strangely gave off the impression that this was the secret lair of the Cookie Monster.

Natalie could only glance at the contents as she walked by (her focus mostly on her feet), seeing simple staples like 'white', 'rye', and 'buttermilk', as well as more fiber-rich types like 'bran' and 'oatmeal', and finally outright oddities like 'fiddlechub' and 'charrup'.

She had no idea what to expect.

Apart from the jars, the other major oddity was the array of large flattop grills scattered around the room, all of different sizes and vintages, as if purchased from flea markets spread across the decades. A few had fry baskets latched on like sidecars, hastily bubbling away in pancake frying bliss. Natalie noticed Sylvester glancing briefly at them, smiling and nervous, before continuing on, while she gave the oil a wide and frightened berth, certain that some unwieldy act of god was likely to erupt the molten death upon her if she travelled within range.

Sylvester was already nestled in the corner seat and engrossed in the menu when Natalie distracted herself enough from the spectacle to catch up, tripping only twice on the carpeting as she fell into the booth.

"What a peculiar place this is!" she said as her eyes continued to wander, "I never knew pancakes were so popular."

"The people who love 'em, love 'em fiercely," he said, flipping the familiar pages as if he'd never been there before and was hoping they had soup. "Ever been to Amsterdam?"

She gave him a quizzical look and thought briefly about slapping him. "I haven't even left the city, let alone the state. A plane over the ocean? I'd be guppy food!"

Sylvester rolled his eyes, at him for his foolishness and her for her silliness, then smiled. "I went once and ran across a place that served only pancakes, but they were the strangest, weirdest, most amazing pancakes ever! They had pancakes with ice cream and whipped cream and chocolate syrup like a sundae, or pancakes with venison and bacon like a three-course meal, or even pancakes that made you drunk!"

Natalie's eyes lit up as she listened and her lips started to moisten, hopeful that this place's menu offered some of the stories he was selling.

"When I got back to the States I had a hunger, and after some searching, lo and behold, I found this place hidden away."

Natalie looked around at the somber appearance, the empty tables, and the feeling that they'd arrived after hours. "How does it stay in business? I've never heard of it. Doesn't look like anyone else has either…"

"The 'cake fanatics know…we can sense it! Come here on a weekend and you'll see a line out of the door and every seat taken. But 9 at night on a Tuesday? This's what ya get."

Natalie smiled softly at him, his mild teasing underscoring his willingness to fit into her life of avoidance and safety. She glanced down briefly, ensuring no silverware lived on the table before flipping open the menu and ogling the contents.

Strange concoctions with whipped cream proliferated the menu, even on things that didn't seem to deserve it, like Bacon and Egg Pancakes with Whipped Cream, or Watermelon and Arugula Salad with Whipped Cream.

As if to answer her curiosity Sylvester chimed in, "Their whipped cream is amazing, so be sure to add it if it's not included."

Natalie nodded, somehow expecting that wouldn't be a problem. In fact, as her eyes scanned the pages, she wondered if it was even possible to find something that *didn't* contain whipped cream.

"What are you getting?" she asked, hoping for guidance.

"I always get the Extra Bacon Pancakes."

"Then why are you looking through the menu?"

"Habit mostly, plus they papercut wonderfully!"

"Yes, I've noticed," Natalie explained, holding up her thrice-sliced hand. Sylvester held up his own hand, showing twice as many.

"And what comes on 'Extra Bacon Pancakes'?" she asked.

He gave her a deadpan expression as he held back the urge to let his jaw drop. "Bacon. Lots and lots of bacon. There's a pancake buried under it somewhere, I think…"

"That's it? Only bacon?"

"And whipped cream."

"Of course. Sounds super healthy," she snarked.

"It tastes delicious and gives me heartburn."

She paused, looking at him crookedly. "And you like heartburn, huh? You really do?"

He nodded.

"OK, you gotta explain this whole thing to me. Is your entire life hinged on being in constant pain and agony? Cuz it seems like it is."

"Just about."

"Just about?"

"Well…yes?" he asked, trying to discern where she was getting caught up and what was unclear.

She continued to look at him funny, as if he wasn't explaining himself well.

Sylvester decided visual aids would help and reached into his pocket and pulled out a forkroach, setting it on the table in front of her. Natalie looked at it crookedly, not sure what it was but fearing its pointy prongs. Sylvester kept going, reaching into different pockets and producing different things.

He pulled out some nail clippers, a variety of keys that didn't fit any of his locks, some corn cob holders, a second unfinished forkroach, a bent nail, a pointy rock, and a few Legos thrown in for good measure.

"You had all of that in your pockets? All day long?"

"Most of it, yeah. My day'd be too tame otherwise. Actually, the rock and the nail I found later," he added with toddler pride.

"Didn't I see you propelling yourself down slippery stairs in your stocking feet an hour ago? That was too tame??"

"Ya gotta challenge yourself!" he said with exuberance. "This's experience talking. The worst thing you can do in my condition is be bored and painless and reach too far to enhance the experience."

Natalie gave him a bent and crooked crazy person look, as if by turning her head she'd see the cracks in his skull. "You are downright strange," she said, shaking her head. "And you avoided the question of WHY you do this?"

"I don't know. Because I like it? It satisfies some urge. It scratches some scratch. Why do some people like anchovies on ice cream? There's just something about it that makes me happy."

"You LIKE it? How can you like it?? I spend my entire life trying to avoid it!"

"I know. That's why I find you fascinating."

"Because I don't like pain? The same as, say, the rest of the human race?"

"No…" he said, steadying as he looked at her. "I find you fascinating because you try so hard to avoid it, and it still comes straight at you, full force."

Natalie looked at him oddly, taking in what he said.

Sylvester continued, "Do you know how much time I spend *trying* to hurt myself? It's a full-time job! I'm obsessed with it! Did you know I spotted 23 different ways to injure myself between the door and this table, nine of which I took advantage of?"

"Seriously?"

Sylvester smirked, enjoying her disbelief. "When we walked in I made sure to grab the door by the splintered rough edge, not the smooth handle. Then I let it close on my fingers. I made sure to target the newest menus with the sharpest edges and papercut myself while grabbing them. I toe-stubbed myself on three pointy table corners and while you were eyeing the grills I finger-tapped two of them. The list goes on and on, all the time. I don't even notice I do it anymore. I'm an OCD addict touching everything I pass. My compulsion just hurts a bit more."

"Is it a…", began Natalie as she searched for a polite word, "…problem?"

"You mean something to rid myself of?"

She nodded cautiously, not wanting to offend.

He put on a thoughtful look, pondering what she said. "I don't think so? It's...me? I quite enjoy it, within reason at least. I've pushed it a few times...maybe high-fiving a passing car mirror wasn't the brightest idea...but I try to keep it in line. Know my physical limits. I only approve of pain that's not permanent."

"Is it about the scars? Are you a, uh, cutter? Do you like marking yourself up?"

"Nah, I try to be more creative than that! Scars are more accidental byproducts that come with the fun. If I could avoid em I would! Would certainly save me funny looks at the doctor. I swear those people must think I'm abused at home..."

"Howdy Vest," came a syrupy voice behind them, "Howdy Vest's guest."

Natalie turned to see a waiter sidling up, the same one who'd been behind the bar a minute before. He tossed down a basket of pancake sticks and syrup onto the table like dinner rolls. They reminded Natalie of what Burger King served in the morning and called French Toast.

"Howdy Werle," said Sylvester, giving him a head nod. "Any specials?"

"You kidding? We were closing up before you wandered your lazy ass in. You'll be lucky if we got half the menu left."

"You know what I want. Bacon me up, deep fried style. And a glass of milk. Throw it in the freezer for a few minutes if you could. Please."

"Bacon we got. Milk we got. And for the missus?"

Natalie looked at the menu intently, scrunching her lips in uncertainty. "How're the Tofu and Sprout Pancakes?"

"Horrible. Never been here before, have you?"

"Nope, first time."

"Lean toward the breakfast or dessert sounding ones. Anything else is a tourist trap. Beware, though, that the sugary ones are prone to causing addiction..."

"OK, I'll risk it! Gimme the Sugar Blitzkrieg Pancakes with whipped cream, please. And a milk."

"Freezer on the milk?"

"No, normal please, but in a plastic cup, not a glass. And let the pancakes cool off for five minutes before you bring them out, OK?"

"Ummm…ok. Sure thing. Cold pancakes. Excellent choice…" said Werle, scratching his head in confusion as he went to make their order.

Sylvester chimed in slyly, "They let me clean the grill plates and fryolators sometimes. Fringe benefits of being a good customer."

Natalie doubted anyone else would consider those 'perks', but let it slide as she let her eyes wander the walls.

Across the room she noticed what appeared to be a gift shop, a variety of emblazoned t-shirts, hats, and keychains for those out-of-towners who craved something to remember life by. She chuckled when she saw the large pancake blankets and could imagine throwing square yellow cushions on top to serve as butter.

Sylvester was busy bending the unfinished forkroach, distracting himself while she looked around. He had gotten it about halfway finished but was sweating too much and couldn't get a grip on the tines.

Natalie began to watch obsessively, trying to gain insight into his disease or addiction or whatever it was he called it. As expected, as soon as she looked, the fork immediately flew out of Sylvester's hands and stabbed her in the nose. Natalie simply picked up the projectile and returned it with a smile, a small dimpled bruise appearing behind it.

Sylvester shook his head, still getting used to her strange aura of calamity. She'd barely noticed, her eyes still fixed on his working hands.

She couldn't see anything at first, only a person playing with a fork, but then she started to notice the function of what he was doing. How his fingers turned white as he exerted pressure at strange angles, and how it stayed white, indicating he was pushing well past the point of irritation.

She was finding herself as fascinated by him as he was by her.

A few minutes later Werle appeared, ice cold beverages in hand (Sylvester's being quite a bit colder, an air of steamed frost billowing off the top like liquid nitrogen), as well as platefuls of pancakes.

Natalie looked down on hers in awe, the plate itself a work of art.

Huge, thin, crepe-like pancakes layered on the bottom, crisped sugar dappling the top and glistening in diabetic excitement, huge smiling dollops of whipped cream placed precisely and melting into rivulets, with not a twist of hot steam to be seen.

Sylvester waited and watched for her first bite, enjoying her reaction as she savored its rich and yummy goodness, before diving in and devouring his own.

His pancake meal was its own odd concoction of delicious, caloric death. It looked like a pouch, crisp around the edges, but bursting through the seams with craggled bits of bacon, as if erupting, syrup and butter dribbling out of the gaps and spreading onto the plate like lava.

She didn't want to know how many calories she was eating (certain it was a multiple of her daily allowance), but it was well worth the splurge.

Silence ensued for the next few minutes of bliss, unintentional moans escaping their mouths as they chewed.

Sylvester's plate had been cleaned of all bacon, only a few bits of soggy middle pancake left floating in the syrup. Natalie had finished half her plate (but all the whipped cream) and could see it bulging her stomach to capacity, a smile spreading across her face as a slow-moving belch worked its way up.

"That was quite good," she said with a burp.

"Glad you liked it! It's one of my favorite restaurants, and not just for the malleable forks."

Natalie laughed. She was enjoying the feeling of fullness mixed with the stationary lack of movement. She hadn't fallen down or tripped over anything major (besides carpeting) for an hour now. Maybe she was osmotically learning tips from Sylvester's behavior, an overcompensation on her part to keep the world in balance.

"How was your deep-fried bacon? Is your heart all aflutter now?"

"Yeah, I can feel the burn starting to kick in," he said with a smirk and a wink. "A few more minutes and I'll be riding the wave!"

"You are a sick, cholesterol-infused man," she smiled, before changing direction to something she'd wondered since they'd arrived,

"Did you used to come here with your ex?"

Sylvester was caught off-guard. "Felicia? Yeah, from time to time. She wasn't a huge pancake nut, but liked to bump people into the grill plates. She'd do laps when new people came in just to get the chance to hip-check them."

"She sounds…pleasant. Are you worried about running into her?"

"Nah. She's in jail."

"Oh." Another pause, this time by Natalie. A pause of surprise and confusion.

"Didn't I mention that?" he asked.

"No…"

Sylvester caught her eyes, painful and hurt, with a degree of fear present. Fear of Felicia? Or that she was only a rebound? He tried to compensate.

"She's the only girl I ever brought here if that's any consolation. I don't date around a lot. Not a lot of girls are into guys covered in scars and tattoos of forearms…" he smirked.

Natalie laughed, snorting a bit.

"So…can you tell me more about her?" asked Natalie.

"Felicia?"

"Yeah."

"I guess…" began Sylvester with a sense of curious confusion. "Ummm…we dated for a couple of years. Smart girl, little violent, did massage and acupuncture for a living. Seemed a good fit for me but got herself arrested. It didn't work out."

"But I mean, like…what's she like? Was she klutzy too?"

"Haha! Oh, I see why you're asking! No, she wasn't. I don't have a thing for klutzy girls," he said with a smile. "She liked to *cause* injury. To hurt other people. She liked to hurt me. We were two pieces of a sharp jigsaw puzzle that forcefully fit together. I gave her an easy target for her urges, and in return she helped me manage mine. Quid pro quo. For a while we were a perfect fit. Peas in a pod and all of that. Maybe a bit more violent than most peas, but peas all the same."

Natalie was quiet and sad, her eyes wandering to her hands as they played with the forkroach she'd somehow picked up. It was hard and firm and she respected what he'd done to create it. She would've needed pliers and three hospital visits. He did it in two minutes with his bare hands.

"We don't need to talk about her," he continued. "She's in the past. Gone, locked away, and doesn't want anything to do with me."

"And once she gets out?"

"I don't think anything will change."

Natalie thought she heard some sadness in his voice as he played with his soggy piece of pancake. He wasn't over her. Not yet.

"I'm sorry," she said finally.

"For what?"

"Bringing up sore spots."

"My life is all about sore spots," he said with a grin. "But it's not the soreness…it's the disappointment. I sorta viewed myself as her moral compass, so with how things went…I'm disappointed in both of us."

Natalie smiled softly at him, a wiggle of deep hurt visible, "Life's full of disappointments."

"Doesn't mean we have to like it."

"No…but there's always another disappointment waiting around the corner isn't there?"

"I suppose…", he said, lifting his eyes and smiling. "And here comes another one walking towards us right now…"

"Don't you be calling me a disappointment!" said Werle as he tossed the bill on the table with a smile. "I was ready to leave half an hour ago. You two were the disappointments. Be sure the tip isn't."

He wandered off again, laughing and shaking his head, flipping light switches and fryolator knobs and encouraging them to be on their way.

"I'm certainly never going to forget this place," she said, looking around one last time.

"It's pretty unforgettable. And we can always come back."

"Let's."

He looked at her smiling face, radiant with the power of sugary pancake goodness. If the conversation had bothered her she'd already forgotten it. He grabbed the bill and snagged the forkroach and offered her his hand.

"But let me get you one of those t-shirts just in case."

CHAPTER 25
ALL HALLOWS' ELECTROCUTION

The light flickered above the gate to the Shockhouse (as Socket's house had come to be known), a signal that the Halloween course was being attempted, and based on the amount of flickering, attempted poorly at that.

It was common knowledge that this house gave out $100 bills on Halloween - if you could reach the front door to knock. Legend had it only one kid ever managed it, paying his way through college with the money but never seeming the same again, stuttering his way through middle school with a strange twitch and a skunk of white hair.

Beyond the gate there was a moment of silence followed by a sharp, adolescent yelp, and a moment later the flickering stopped and a sullen shouldered Pikachu waddled out, a look of dejection on his face and a slight sizzle of hair in the air.

Pikachu glanced at the small line that had formed and nodded to the first in it, a silent fist bump between warriors. Batman nodded back, then glanced in, his senses attuned, his utility belt brimming with candy. This year he was going to make it; he had trained his whole life for this moment.

The flickering light turned steady and the gate unlocked itself. Batman pushed it open and slipped inside...

The yard itself did not seem too daunting to the uninitiated - a crooked gravel path to the front stoop, a variety of gnomes and beetles scattered about the property, a broken swingset off to a corner, a stack of garbage can lids strewn in a pile to one side. It had the look of a half-scavenged junkyard, or one in the midst of being collected and built out, but a junkyard all the same. And the more one looked, the more one realized that this was a junkyard that bartered solely in the currency of metal objects.

Batman took a step forward and immediately felt a current running up his leg. He glanced down and saw what looked to be blades of grass, swaying gently in the breeze, small blue arcs passing between them as they rubbed against his boots. Batman squinted, noticing they weren't made of leafy greenness, but springs and foil. Even the innocuous held a danger here.

He knew from last year that the gravel path was the dangling carrot, laced with traps. Barring a rubber ball suit (mental note for next year) it would be impossible. Instead, it was all about the edge cases.

He looked to the left and leapt lithely toward the fence, hoping to circumvent the traps he knew were waiting. He quickstepped off a tree stump (mild shock) and grabbed handholds of the pointy pickets, his feet planted firmly against the verticals, his cape billowing in the breeze, and started shimmying his way along the fence.

The unflickering light remained steady as he went, teasing his nerves as it built up its charge and awaited an unleashing.

An obvious and unoffending trash can leaned against the fence ahead and he knew not to touch it, a glaringly bright beacon of danger.

He reached into his utility belt and pulled out his sister's jump rope, wedging the handle between the slats before launching himself around the trash can, a twist in the rope spinning his arc to bounce him off his destination, his hands scrabbling for a handhold.

And then it happened, the slat unseen, perfectly positioned, painted a mottled brown to match the rest, but plunking differently when his boot hit, a metallic ting instead of a wooden thunk.

By the time he heard the sound he knew it was too late, a sparking blue current of electricity already whipping out from the metal fence post and through his body, his grip loosening as he fell backwards, his body twitching slightly.

Luckily his years of jungle gym training had honed his reflexes, and he spun, catlike, to land on all fours. A faint smell of melted Gummi Bears wafted from his utility belt and he knew whatever chocolate he'd earned was likely melted and destroyed.

But with $100 he could buy all the candy he wanted.

He refocused his attention and squinted at the porch, now a scant dozen feet away, as he crab-stepped slowly toward it, his eyes swiveling.

A large metal beetle loomed overhead, its eyes glowing and bobbling, a carnival barker inviting in the gullibles. Batman knew not to touch it, its poisonous and conductive exterior almost certain to end his endeavor.

He scooted past, ignoring the frog warrior that stood on its flank, the porch bursting into sight beyond the boxwoods. He could see the doorbell, or rather the three of them, glowing their pale yellow into the darkening eve. The steps looked wooden and simple and impossible to electrocute, but he knew that was unlikely. Everything here was a danger.

His body inched forward, still on all fours, his eyes searching for options…

And then it hit him, the unexpected burst of electricity that laid him out flat as his vision spun in dizziness. In the distance he saw the light flickering and knew his failure was sealed, finally raising an ungloved hand in defeat as the waves of electricity stopped and the flickering steadied.

Batman sat up and glanced around, trying to focus on where the attack had come from; he needed to plan for next year. But this close to the house there was a moat of nothingness. A nicely mown lawn, a friendly wooden stoop, inviting and welcoming, a wonderful place to sell cookies.

But something had gotten him. Something he hadn't seen that would get him again next year.

His hand slid in the gravel and he felt something pointy and something round, and he glanced down, realizing for the first time that up here, this close to the house, it wasn't gravel. It was nuts and washers and caps and lugs, bits and bobbins of metal, all mixed together.

The ground itself was electrified.

*****

Light Socket was howling with laughter as he watched the ten-year-old superhero crawl to his knees and head back to the gate, defeat firmly in his grasp.

"Did you see that one? Smartest kid yet. Insulated boots, quick reflexes, took the fence…he may beat me yet!"

Sylvester looked crooked at his friend, seeing a mix of blissful happiness and diabolical intentions. "Ya know, you really may challenge 'Licia on the sadistic quotient..."

"Nah, it's not sadism, as much as a desire to electrocute," said Socket.

"You realize that's the same thing, right?"

Socket ignored him as he turned back to his monitors, watching as the newest contestant entered the battlefield, a nervous Wookie with an orange plastic pumpkin basket in hand, a look of peer pressure visible through her quivering rubber eyes.

"Take this one for instance. Do I let her gain some firsthand experience or put her out of her misery early? A sadistic individual would clearly let her squirm on the hook. Really build up that anxiety."

Sylvester shook his head, trying not to think through Socket's perspective as he glanced around the room, amazed at the cockpit Socket had created for himself. There were boxes and buttons stacked all around, varying in size and approach, controlling everything from the fence slats and the mailbox to the battle beetle and the birdbath. Some were festooned with dimmers that wiggled the voltage, while others had levers normally found on space station lasers. There was even a long strip of flippable switches that appeared mail-ordered from the same catalog as the Mercury missions.

And finally, directly in front of Socket, was his favorite. It was small and modest, about the size of a pack of cards, with a lone purple button resting in the center that his hand now hovered over.

Socket grinned at Sylvester as his fingers pianoed over a button, "But me? Me likes to help the poor soul out."

And with that he slammed the button that had already dispatched The Batman, electrifying the walkway and sending the poor Wookie co-pilot crying and running for escape, happily making Sylvester's point for him.

"Life lessons I'm teaching that kid, life lessons..." said Socket as he smiled at himself.

Sylvester shook his head, wondering where he would move when Socket was also locked away.

"You realize that if the cops found out they'd probably throw you in jail, right? Child endangerment, all of that?"

Socket squiggled his mouth into a nervous frown, not liking the accusation. "Nah! These kids aren't being forced into anything. Money-grubbing little bastards is what they are. I'm just protecting private property. There's a 'Beware of Electrocution' sign out front. I can't stop stupidity."

"But you encourage it."

Socket shrugged, "Potato, potato."

Sylvester gave up and flopped into the seat beside him as he watched someone in a Hunter S. Thompson costume stumble drunkenly through the gate, a martini glass in one hand, a cigarette holder in the other, "So what d'you need me to do?"

Socket reshuffled his seat, squeaking a loud noise that awakened a drowsy porcupine who glared for a moment before circling and settling back down.

"Crew for me! I can't move for the next 6 hours. Gotta manage the line. I'm like a zippy, zappy Santa Skellington on All Hallows' Eve. I need a sandwich and a fresh beer every hour. A pee break every two. At three hours, a good stretch."

"Easy enough," smiled Sylvester, happy to get off so easy. He hadn't been looking forward to electrocuting people.

Socket grimaced as he shouted at the screen, "Come on kid! It's a costume, not a lifestyle!"

It was unclear whether the costumed gonzo journalist was method acting the role or had simply downed some long-expired candy, but he now appeared passed out on the lawn, his strapped-on alligator tail flopping back and forth in the breeze.

"Well, I'm not waiting. This ain't a kindergarten with naptime…" said Socket as his hand toggled two switches before pressing a button marked 'lawn'.

The tall grass of foil and springs burst into blue, arcs of electricity jumping between the fronds, erupting Hunter to awareness and chasing him back to the street, a well-voiced "Never trust a cop in a raincoat" following him as he went.

Sylvester couldn't help but clap, "I give him points for style."

"If style's all he's got he's playing the wrong game. How's that first sandwich coming?"

Sylvester let his arched eye linger for a moment before pulling himself to his feet and shuffling toward the kitchen, already nervous of the electrified peanut butter jar.

Outside, the gate opened again, and in scurried a small girl dressed as a squirrel, her chittering teeth seemingly dictating her costume choice. She walked nervously, clearly unsure what to expect, her eyes wide and wandering.

Socket smiled and leaned into his chair. The night was only just beginning.

CHAPTER 26
THE PUMPKIN ADVENTURE

The sun was barking down through the skylights high above, shafts of life piercing the quiet dusky dim of the early afternoon. Sylvester and Natalie sat cross-legged on the floor of the cave that was her bookstore, staring each other down, watching as slight twitches developed from the recycled air. Between them sat a pizza, half eaten, a dozen pepperoni grease spots stuck to the top of the box.

They'd spent the day playing 'book and seek', a game where a vast depth of literary knowledge was the only required skillset. After three matches Sylvester conceded to Natalie her dominance, and as penance was made to butler off and fetch a pizza, safely ordered far in advance to ensure no chance of a burned mouth from villainly melted cheese.

There was no cutlery, no glassware, and even the risk of a papercutting plate was avoided, leaving their places set with only napkins and bottled water.

"So…" began Sylvester, unsure where to lead the conversation with his tummy full and his wits exhausted, still confusingly noodling over how he'd been unable to come up with something as simple as *Huckleberry Finn* when the clues were as obvious as 'Mississippi' and 'raft'.

"Sew?" asked Natalie. "No, I avoid that entirely. Too many needles to prick yourself with. Too many inherent risks of death."

Sylvester took her thread and went with it, "From sewing?"

"Oh yeah."

"This makes me curious what your approach to sewing entails…"

"Come on, now. Sharp pointy needles? Easy to lose, tough to find? I've stepped on at least a dozen of them in my lifetime. One even popped out the other side!" she said as she pointed towards her foot, a clear unwillingness to get too close to her own appendage, lest it decide to injure her in retaliation for putting it on the spot like that.

"You're a bit batty, ya know?"

She smiled at him with embarrassed pride, as if he'd just called her the prettiest girl on earth, "Yeah, I know."

Sylvester looked at her fondly and inquisitively. It appeared filling moments of silence was amongst her skills. Always intriguing, this girl.

"So what would you like to do now?" she asked as she plucked a slice of pepperoni off the remaining pizza.

"Me? Oh, the normal. Play in traffic, chew glass, juggle porcupines. Any of those interest you?"

She guffawed loudly, knocking her head back, which immediately kinked. "Oh you and your crazy world." She gestured to the rest of the bookstore as her arena and playground. "Find something to do within the confines of this building. This is my world. I have a boatload of board games and card games and, ya know, there may even be a few books around to read."

"I don't want to stay in…its dark and gloomy! I want air that circulates and the chirps of birds and crickets. This is all radiator noise and stale musty breezes."

"Hey! I like my musty breezes and radiator noises! No making fun of my world Mr. Self-Inflicted-Stab-Wound!"

"You need to expand your world," he said with a smile, gently pushing on her phobias. "You may as well be in prison. You don't go out, you aren't very active, you're afraid of moths and shifting air currents... What's your life going to be like in 30 years?"

"The same as it is now, I imagine…" she trailed off with more than a hint of pain and regret.

Sylvester saw a sad echo behind her eyes, as if she'd tried many times to break free from this world but it never took. Something always got in the way, stopping the habit from being formed.

It seemed that life had locked her in, and her dreams and passions were powerless against the forces at work. It wasn't so dissimilar from how the pain locked him in. He clenched his nails into the palm of his hand as if to underscore his need for a fix.

"We are an interesting pair aren't we? Trapped in our self-made bubbles of oddity and pain."

"But I hope it's different!" she said suddenly, looking up with distant tears teasing her eyes and a crooked smile on her face. "I don't want it to be this way. I dream of being a very different person in 30 years."

"Oh?"

"Oh yes," she announced with a childhood air of celebrity confidence. "I'm going to run marathons and bake cookies and speak at public events. I'm going to swim in the ocean and dive under the water. I'm going to go to carnivals and spend hours on the bumper cars and those big slides with the burlap sacks. I'm going to build a house with my own bare hands, with hammers and nails and a table saw. And it's gonna have stairs! Big, sweeping, spiral staircases I'll run up and down. And all without injuring myself." She paused and looked at him closely, her attitude wavering. "At least that's what I like to tell myself…" she finished, her voice tailing off in the volume of doubt.

"I have confidence in you," offered Sylvester.

"It's not you that needs the confidence."

Sylvester reached down and plucked off a slice of pepperoni and popped it into his mouth, chewing slowly.

"We should do something then. We should go out more. Find more activities. Break you in like new shoes."

"New shoes? You have such a way with words." She looked up toward the ceiling, mockingly squinting and visoring her hand over her eyes. "Nope, try as I might, I can't see all the women you must've swept off their feet…"

He cocked his head at her as she smirked devilishly, the true Natalie, safe at home behind her bulwark of books, and for the first time, deep down, he knew he preferred her to Felicia.

"I'm terrible at sweeping," he added. "Much better at making a mess than cleaning it up, not that you'd know since we never leave the dungeon…"

"OK, OK, enough with the guilt! What would you like to do?" Natalie asked.

"What I like you probably wouldn't survive. I don't know if you've picked up on this, but you're a bit accident prone…" Sylvester said with a grin.

"I'm not saying I'll join in, but I'm not against standing on the sidelines watching from a safe distance, 'safe' being the dominant and important word there."

"Including outside?"

"Yeah," she said with a surprising air of confidence. "I'll even go...outside."

"Where the bees live? And the trees and cars and streetlights and spy satellites and all of that? That outside?"

"Yes, that outside. I'm in a brave mood! Pepperoni power!"

He sat back and pondered for a minute, flipping through his mental rolodex of activities and events hoping for something with a bordering sanctuary she might inhabit. He skipped past the obvious involving ninja stars and farm equipment, over things involving electricity and flames and fast spinning fan blades, and didn't even consider wild animals or tall heights or any risk of explosion, simply for fear that her own bad luck may hex something odd into happening.

"What's the date today?" he asked, suddenly excited.

Natalie glanced at the desk calendar on the table. "November 2nd," she announced. "It's National Deviled Egg Day."

"'Blech' to the Deviled Eggs but 'yay' on the date!" he said.

"'Blech' high-five on the eggs. Nasty things. What's 'yay' about November 2nd?"

"There's something fun I wanted to do tonight...so now you can come along!"

"What is it?" she asked, a quivering air of curious fear in her voice.

"Oh, it'll be a surprise! I think you'll get a kick out of it! Different from everything else you've seen in life, I'm sure of it!"

"What's my potential risk for injury?"

"If you stay away from the impact zone? Very safe! The key is not to wander too close for a photo op or anything..."

"I'm not sure I like the phrase 'impact zone'..."

"Oh shush! It's decided. You're coming! You need more sunlight in your life. Cure that orcish complexion of yours. We need to make a couple of stops first, so lock the doors and let's get a move on. We only have three hours to prepare!"

"Three hours of...prep time? This sounds serious..." she said, a creak of fear hinting in her voice. In an instant she had learned the valuable lesson of providing too much rope to hang oneself with.

"The time hinges on your turtle speed."

She eyed him with immediate regret as she reluctantly reached for her key and flipped off the lights, encouraging the books to sleep. After a moment's thought she grabbed her thick wool coat with the extra stuffing and threw her padded leather helmet on her head, intent at least on cushioning her experience.

She looked more than a little ridiculous, but Sylvester was too busy to notice, rubbing his hands together, his imagination roiling about. "We'll need to make two stops on the way, plus swing by my place so I can grab my gourd clothing..."

Natalie blinked at him a few times as she mouthed 'gourd clothing' to herself, and then followed him out the door and into the scary and strange world outside.

*****

Their first stop was the farmer's market which, at Natalie's plodding and protective pace, took an hour to reach, but came without serious incident beyond four falls, three stubbed toes, and one bird collision.

The sun was beginning to settle as they wandered between the dwindling carts, most in the midst of shutting down and packing up. Sylvester eyes searched for something specific he refused to mention, finally stopping beside an old beat up pickup piled high with wooden crates and flies.

An old man with a grizzled beard and a deep tan was busy stacking and sorting through some of his leftover produce, tossing the bits that wouldn't last to the next day.

"Hi there!" Sylvester announced, a sparkle of insanity in his voice. "I'm looking for really good, squishy pumpkins."

"Squishy?" asked the man.

"Squishy?" repeated Natalie.

"Squishy!" he replied to both of them with an eye of attention to each.

"They're not edible if yer thinking of makin' pies, ya know?" asked the old man nervously, envisioning a sick man lying in the hospital cursing out the farmer's market for selling him a moldy pumpkin.

"Nope, not for cooking."

"Vandalism? I don't cotton to vandals using my gourds for mischief!" he said with an authoritarian glare.

"There may be mischief in mind, but I swear it's not vandalistic in nature!" said Sylvester, holding his hands up, feigning innocence.

The man eyed them skeptically, seemingly noticing for the first time the strange girl in the leather helmet standing beside him, who in response to being spotted immediately fell out of sight.

The chin of the man's beard chewed in on itself as it pondered the decision for the both of them, finally nodding the man's head as he caved to commerce.

"How many ya want?" he finally asked.

"Two? Maybe three if they're on the small side?"

The old man turned and started rolling around his leftover pumpkins, looking for ones squishy to the touch. He dropped two of them on the table, a small splat emanating from beneath them as a drizzle of liquid seeped out and dribbled off the table.

"Here. These are squishy. Two bucks."

"Perfect!" Sylvester enthused, prodding them with his fingers to confirm. "Could you spare a bag? Don't want 'em opening early!"

"Sure..." said the old man as he fished out some plastic and double-bagged each pumpkin, turning the handles towards the exuberant customer with an outstretched grinning hand.

"Many thanks!" said Sylvester.

The old man eyed him again, certain that this mischief would come back to haunt him, but finally deciding he was too old to care. "Enjoy..." was all he finally uttered as he turned back to his eggplants.

Sylvester turned to Natalie, who had collapsed to the ground twice more since his conversation had begun and was in the midst of righting a table she'd knocked over. He offered her a hand before they made their way back through the sunset drenched rows of emptying tables.

As they emerged Sylvester paused, noticing a stack of old wooden trays, the sturdy and well-built kind used for grapefruit and oranges. He gave a quick look around and, when it seemed doubtful anyone would care, wedged one under his arm.

*****

It took another hour to swing past Socket's place, Sylvester changing into overalls and a long-sleeve flannel shirt and grabbing his mouthguard, before twisting back out the door with a quick toss of a treat to Poke. (Natalie waited outside the gate by the street, the consensus being that her safety was only assured at great distances from the premises.)

Sylvester loped along, Natalie curiously ambling in tow, lost as to what their destination was, but thoroughly puzzled and determined to see the adventure through. Thus far she had fallen eleven times, having tripped over three random objects (one was a dog) and walked into one open door, which by her standards was an almost error and pain-free day.

The thought had crossed her mind more than once that Sylvester may be functioning as a de facto good luck charm, offsetting her injuries by triggering them himself, and should the awkward situation present itself, his foot would make an amazing keychain.

They continued walking toward the small village that abutted theirs, a mile away up a gently rolling hill, a nestled New England town with a waterfall and a popcorn shop. A windy night had knocked the fall off the trees, leaving a floor of dazzling struzanic hues around them.

Natalie pestered him with questions as they went, but he stayed quiet-lipped, smirking aside her curiosities. She was safe for now it seemed, so she went along with it, enjoying the fresh air and the crunch of leaves as she lost her balance and toppled into them.

As they approached the town Sylvester paused and ducked his head into a hardware store (which she refused to enter for the all-encompassing risks it presented to her), but he bounced out a minute later with a sturdy stretch of rope tucked under his arm (which he made no mention of), and continued on, Natalie still in inquisitive trawl, her head cocking from side to side as if glancing into a flap to his brain that could reveal glimpses of his game plan.

In the near distance she saw a hill, cresting to a peak before it dove down into the town proper, and from its descent she heard the emanating murmur of activity and voices, a coddling mix of drunken youth and raucous rebellion. The hill itself made her nervous as it advocated height, but her curiosity by this point had begun to overwhelm her fear.

"We're almost there; let's get you ready," he began, uncoiling the rope and starting to tie a knot around her waist.

"What's this for? You better not be strapping me to your kamikaze self..." she warned.

"Nope, just wanted to get you as protected as possible beforehand."

He tested the knot strength before looping in an easy to pull bow, an escape route in case of emergency, before handing her the remaining bundle of rope and indicating that she should follow the voices.

The sun was setting by now and an orange glow peeked over the hill towards them, as if waving them in for a landing. As they crested the hill Natalie's mouth dropped open at the sight and her knees began to buckle in abject fear and unexpected surprise.

Below them, spread across the steeply descending asphalt hill were the gut-spilled corpses of thousands of pumpkins, their seeds and entrails strewn everywhere as an orange slime coated the world. There was an odor too, like that of stale and moldy produce left in a closet, but it paled next to the extreme smell of pumpkin itself.

And as Natalie watched, her mouth agape, high school and college students of all shapes and sizes leapt into the mass of pumpkin flesh and seed sprouts.

Some simply dove into the morass, bodysurfing their way downhill while others rode lunch-line trays and snow sleds. One man was trying to maneuver his way down on skis while another raced him on a snowboard. There were skateboards and toboggans and donuts tubes and inflatable pool toys. In fact, almost anything that could be used as a makeshift conveyance was being put to that use.

Most of the participants wiped out near the top and tumbled the rest of the way down, often lying in pain for minutes before their bodies could be willed to move and crawl to safety. On rare occasions an entrant would make it to the bottom still standing and slide to a halt, offering up a quick bow to the accumulated audience that cheered the insanity, before beginning the trudge back up the hill to try again.

Natalie was still staring as she felt the rope being pulled on, looking up to see Sylvester tugging her toward a tree off to the side, safely out of the seed zone, where he'd already begun lashing the rope securely.

"This is SO not for me," she said nervously, her body beginning to shake.

"I know! That's why I'm strapping you down. Safety first! If you can't get close, you can't get hurt!" he said as he smiled protectively, trying to make her feel safe and comfortable, before adding, "You won't be in any danger of slipping and sliding and falling down the hill, unless you uproot the tree!"

Natalie glanced up at the tree, doubting its resiliency, before looking back over her shoulder, eyeing the bodies that were now climbing back up the hill and into sight, covered with pumpkin parts and scraped blood, smiles of honor brandished on their faces. It reminded her of stories of ski slopes long ago, before lifts existed and people had to leg their way back to the top.

Sylvester stepped back and admired his knotwork. She looked like she was about to be sacrificed on a pyre and burned as a witch, strapped securely to the large oak with little ability to get into trouble.

"Snug?" he asked.

"Yes…"

"Great! And how can you get a better view than from the top? Far better than those jokers at the bottom! Here you can see the knuckleheads launch themselves!" he said proudly, clearly identifying himself as one of them.

"So…you good? I'm gonna go join in now…" he said as he slowly backed away, his hands trying to be calming while his lower half seemed to be trying to break into a run.

"Yes, I should be fine. Hope you have fun," she answered back, seeing the excitement pouring out of him while her eyes gamboled through the tree limbs above, searching for hives and nests.

He gave her another smirk and a smile, before turning and sprinting toward the crest, his excited screams reminding her of a happy harlequin. He stopped just short and hurled his squishy pumpkins down the hill, watching them shatter and splatter as they landed, his admission now paid to the pumpkin gods.

Then he backed up, got a running start, and leapt into the air, his wooden citrus tray instantly underneath him. She wasn't sure if it was for protection or momentum, but he seemed to know what he was doing, and she suspected this wasn't his first time diving into pumpkins.

He touched down briefly before skidding to his side and being dumped unceremoniously into pumpkin bits, flopping along, arms flailing, as he made his way down the hill, spiraling to a rest to a raucous round of applause from the audience. He tried to stand up and take a bow, but found himself dizzy as he wombled off trying to get back up the hill, wandering first through the audience before recalibrating himself upwards.

His second dive was a little better, and his third made further improvements. By his fifth he'd nailed it, sliding to the base of the hill on his feet to whoops and whistles from the audience like a triumphant packed-powder wrangler.

The hill now won, he tossed aside his wooden tray and started over again using only his shodden feet as protection and guidance.

When he was finally done he'd gone down the hill fourteen times and had accumulated two concussions, four sprains, thirty-seven scratches, nine bruises, three twisted ankles, and one split lip that in total caused a broad smile to spread across his face as a sense of true accomplishment swept over him.

Natalie had watched with a mortified expression of disbelief, jealousy, and fear, but oddly seemed to be enjoying herself.

She had not been attacked by bees or dive-bombed by birds, no cars had careened towards her, and no passersby had pelted her with pumpkin parts. The worst were a few errant acorns bobbing down and beaning her on the head, which by her standards was no worse than a gentle breeze and barely to be noticed. She was safely at peace, under her tree, watching Sylvester make a strange pulped version of himself.

"So? Whatdya think? Wanna give it a try?" asked Sylvester, as he plopped down beside her

"Haha! You wouldn't get me down that hill if it was covered with soft bunnies and pillows," she laughed.

"Had to ask and be polite! It's a lot of fun."

"Does not look so, even remotely!" she said with a crazy laugh.

"You said you wanted to do something I liked. Mission accomplished."

"I suppose," she began. "I'm in awe anyone *other* than you enjoys this. How often does this happen? It can't be common?"

Sylvester shook his head, bits of pumpkin flying off and landing on her like snot spittle. "Nah, it's a yearly thing. After Halloween. Local kids collect all the old pumpkins they can find, pile 'em up, and toss 'em down the hill. Town tradition and all."

"I'm happy I didn't grow up in this town..." said Natalie.

"All good-natured fun. Couple twisted ankles, couple broken bones, lifetime of memories and distaste for pumpkin pie."

"I'm sure."

Sylvester slid his fingers through his hair, combing out the pumpkin seeds, a thick layer of orange gunk still coating his arms, as they watched the suicidal knuckleheads continue to launch themselves off the hill with yelps and howls.

"It's like watching a documentary about sharks from really, really close up."

"A different world?"

"A different world."

"Would you like to get something to eat?" he asked.

"Sure, but can it be delivery? I'd like to get back indoors before my luck runs out." Natalie smiled as she pulled the emergency knot release, her eyes trying to send hidden happy messages without using her voice.

Sylvester glommed on, leaning over to steal a brief kiss, and as his hands slid down his pumpkin crusted shirt, it reminded him that he may want to take a shower, too.

CHAPTER 27
BULLET ANTS

Sylvester paused, looking into the habitat, noticing the glistening black ants that seemed far larger than what he was used to. The habitat beside it had a sign about Asian Weaver Ants and claimed they could carry a hundred times their weight. These strange black ones were larger. Much larger. He wondered how much weight they could carry at that size. Ounces? Pounds? He envisioned cartoons with ants sneaking off with picnic baskets and refrigerators.

He glanced up at the empty space where the sign should've been, acknowledging them as mysteries.

"Bullet ants," came a voice behind him as Dr. Topus waffled up, one shoe apparently lost somewhere in the zoo, causing him to pitch to the side. He didn't seem to notice. "*Paraponera clavata* if you want to be accurate about it, but 'bullet ant' sounds more colorful, doesn't it?"

Sylvester nodded in agreement, immediately wondering how they'd earned such a name since their shape didn't convey it. His mouth twisted into a grin as he imagined someone loading the ants into a rifle and shooting them. Felicia would appreciate that.

"Ever heard of a bullet ant before?" Dr. Topus asked as he tapped on the glass, very unscientific-like. One of the ants gave him a glaring look, doubting the validity of his PhD.

Sylvester shook his head, his eyes watching the ants lift relative boulders and move them about with the ease of a forklift. He swore he saw one throw a large pebble across the habitat trying to break the glass.

"They get the name from the pain. Like being shot with a bullet. On the Schmidt Index these little buggers rank the highest on the planet; the most painful sting on earth!"

The words buffeted Sylvester like a slippery hook as he fell into shock, his mind transporting him into the ether of disconnected understanding. The. Most. Painful. Sting. On. Earth.

He stumbled words out, "Most…painful…?"

"…on the whole planet, yup. Typical bee sting? That's like a 1.

Those evil little red fire ants in the backyard you step on when you're not wearing shoes? Like a 1.5. Yellowjacket? Maybe they hit a 2. But a bullet ant? More than double that. Only critter on earth above a 4. They break the scale."

"You ever been bit by one?" Sylvester asked, his envious drooling voice barely hiding his excitement and curiosity as he leaned in closer, his fingertips brushing the glass.

"Only once. I had on the thick gloves, not the thick-thick gloves I was supposed to, and the bullet stung right through 'em. I screamed like a baby, buried my hand in ice for hours, and downed a whole bottle of Advil. I refused to feed 'em for a day out of spite," he said as he rubbed his hand in memory.

"Not the most professional scientist, was he?" thought Sylvester, before adding, out loud, "Are they poisonous?"

"Nah, just absurdly painful. Might make you go numb or twitch a little. Lasts for a day, then poof, don't even have a mark on you."

"Wow…" said Sylvester, his eyes glistening.

"The guy who made the index went all flowery with his write-up, describing it like 'firewalking with a rusty nail in your foot'."

Strangely enough, Sylvester was perfectly equipped to put that description into perspective, and it made him sweaty with excitement.

"Where do they come from?" he asked. "Around here?"

Dr. Topus was busy making faces at the ants through the glass, sticking his tongue out. "No, no, South America. That's where all the big beasties come from. Something magical in the water down there."

Sylvester only nodded, his eyes transfixed. He was spotting his Red Rider Carbine Action BB Gun through the glass storefront and dreaming about finding it under the tree.

"There's a whole tribe down there," Dr. Topus continued, lecturing, "that puts these guys in gloves and wears 'em around like a cocktail party. Ritual of some sort, becoming a man, all of that. Can't imagine what that must be like."

"Where do I join?" laughed Sylvester as he tried to restrain the exuberance eeking out of his voice, clearly wishing to find an application and wondering what a plane ticket to Brazil would cost.

Dr. Topus motioned across the hall to a set of enclosures filled with leaves and woodchips. "We have some Tarantula Hawk Wasps and Red Harvester Ants as well. They also make the list, but a few steps below the bullets. Same story, though. Get stung by any of em and you'll cry for your mommy and wet yourself twice over."

"How long've you had these?"

"Only just got em in! The bullets and wasps at least. The harvesters we've had for a year or two. Been trying to add some more interesting exhibits for the kids. Need the cool bugs to bring in the audiences," he said with some animosity, as if simple segmented worms and weevils were not considered exciting enough to appreciate.

Sylvester looked on, nodding absently in agreement, his eyes growing larger and wider as he scanned the leaves, watching the creatures wander about their enclosures, and for the first time he began to realize that his new job may be just as tempting as his old one.

Or more so.

CHAPTER 28
THE CARNIVAL SLIDE

Sylvester looked Natalie in the eye, locking her gaze and trying to force-feed his confidence into her soul. Her lip quivered a little.

"I've never done this before," she said.

Her eyes flitted about, looking down and around, unsure, then darting back up. She had the look of someone trapped and nervous and stimulated all at once. An excited curiosity.

She gripped the canvas sack tightly in her hands like a security blanket, channeling her inner Linus van Pelt.

Sylvester smiled at her. "It's going to be alright. It's fairly safe."

"Fairly? Fairly safe? You promised me *completely* safe," she said, a brief hint of hysterics mixed in.

"OK, I'll admit it!" Sylvester exclaimed, "It's a deathtrap! You could get…" he paused and glanced around, as if hiding this information from others, "…a rug burn!" He smiled. "But that's it. Seriously."

Natalie looked down, her eyes challenging their sense of depth perception. "It's so steep…"

He smiled and gave her shoulder a slight squeeze of assurance. "It only looks steep from up here. There's nothing sharp. There're no distances to fall. There's nobody else to run into. There aren't even mosquitoes to collide with. Aside from a sudden lightning storm striking you, you're safe, and I've already checked the weather reports and removed any metal zippers."

Her eyes darted down again towards her feet. Her knees were wobbling against her will. She felt a little silly. Kids did this. Little 5-year-olds that still fell out of bed did this. But she was afraid. Afraid or excited? It bordered on both.

But she also felt alive, and that was something.

Behind her a few people were mumbling, muttering to each other. If only they knew the enormity of what they were witnessing. He'd already let a dozen people pass them. Impatience could survive waiting a minute.

Sylvester waved his hand forward, a gesture of offering. "The course is yours."

Natalie loosened her arms and squatted down, laying the canvas sack on the ground before settling her butt squarely onto it, the heels of her feet propped in front of her.

She felt slippery.

Sylvester gave her a smile, "Now just hold on…and enjoy this."

She took a breath and flexed her fingers on the fiberglass below, coiling herself for release.

Then she wiggled and pushed and felt the earth begin to slide.

The wind rushed at her face, blowing her hair back from its bun, loosing it in a flurry of energy and whipping it around. Something that felt exceedingly like a mosquito brushed against her cheek but was too slow to bite her. She opened her eyes a smidge and saw the world flying towards her, a bump and a dip coming up fast, her equilibrium juddering, the butterflies in her stomach losing their lunches of leaves and tree sap.

The air moved in her lungs and she realized she had been holding it, but when her breath escaped it was with a scream of exhilaration, not fear, that passed her lips.

Another dip, another lurch, maybe even a little air, and then she was on the straightaway and gravity was begging her to slow down before it finally caught up and ground her to a halt, tipping her to one side.

A moment later Sylvester slid up beside her on his own canvas sack, smiling and grinning. "That wasn't so bad was it?" he asked.

"No," she admitted, "that wasn't so bad." She couldn't wipe the smile off her face, and then added, "It might've even been a little fun." She paused, smiling, before looking up and adding, "Let's do it again."

Sylvester smiled back as they grabbed their canvas sacks and began trekking up the hill to the top of the Carnival Slide.

"But there *was* a mosquito," she added.

CHAPTER 29

THE ZOO VISIT

Socket rapped on the window, drawing Sylvester's attention away from the obstinate fingerprint he'd been having a prolonged battle with. It was overcast and sleepy outside, the zoo attendance at its yearly low, Sylvester's work reduced to hidden naps and one-sided conversations with subspecies.

"Thanks for bringing him in!" said Sylvester as he took Poke from the carrier and snuggled him in a swaddle.

"No prob, man. I'll take any chance I can get to see how a zoo exhibit is wired..."

Sylvester looked nervously at his friend. "Please don't mess with anything, alright? I don't want to find out you disabled the tiger habitat and they went prowling for tourists..."

"You have no sense of fun about you," said Socket as he began sticking his fingers in cages.

"Come on, I'll introduce you to Dr. Topus."

They wandered through hallways and trapdoors, hidden zoo routes only the animals and their caretakers knew about, finally emerging in Dr. Topus's strange office of chirps and whistles.

"Oh, so this is the narcoleptic porcupine I heard so much about..." began the doctor as he emerged from behind his desk, briefly tripping over a small box that was busy shuffling itself across the floor. "Not really my field at all, just curiosity on my part. Narcolepsy is often misdiagnosed...folks're usually just sleepy...but in a pet porcupine...well, it's just a wonderful opportunity!"

Poke looked up at the doctor with curious distrust, his appearance giving the porcupine pause about his qualifications. It appeared Dr. Topus had gotten distracted that morning and only shaved one side of his face.

"Who does your electricity?" asked Socket, his eyes tracing the walls and the outlets.

Dr. Topus looked up and pondered, giving the topic far more curious thought than it warranted, finally arriving at, "The electric company I imagine, but I really don't know?", before turning his attention back to the porcupine. "Now, how often does this little guy fall asleep?"

"Few times a day that I've seen."

"Does anything seem to prompt it?"

"Nope. Mostly random. Sometimes I'll take him for a walk and he'll just flop down on the sidewalk."

Dr. Topus shined a penlight into Poke's eyes, which the porcupine immediately tried to eat. "What are you feeding him? I don't know where the zoo even gets its porcupine food..."

"Fruit, veggies, sushi. The basics."

Dr. Topus looked up, his mouth open, clearly about to ask how the small creature managed chopsticks, before realizing it was likely a joke.

Poke waddled out of his grip and started sniffing at some of the other critters in the room, a pattern emerging of brief sniffs followed by sudden plumes, finally ending in a face-planting nap after the third such experience.

"Well then..." began Dr. Topus as he unscientifically prodded the sleeping porcupine with his foot, "This certainly does seem like a porcupine with narcolepsy. Never heard of such a thing!"

"Should I be worried? Or is there anything I should do about it?"

"Oh no, there's nothing that can be done. Just a chronic issue. But incredibly fun to witness!"

"Thanks, doc."

"Always happy to help!" said Dr. Topus as he wandered off, his head back in his clipboard as he distractedly bumped into one of his boxes, catching it quickly as the contents shrieked and yodeled.

"That dude is awesome," said Socket as they wandered off, wildly waving goodbye to the oblivious doctor.

"That he is," Sylvester said as he led them down the corridor, Poke still asleep in his arms.

"Least doctor-like doctor I've ever met."

"He has a diploma on his wall that I swear was drawn in crayon."

The pair chuckled as they walked, sharing an appreciation for weirdness and four-flushing.

"So, you off the clock now?" asked Socket. "What say we hit the links for a quick 9 holes? There's a thunderstorm forecast and I got a new driver made of copper you could try..."

"Sorry, can't do it. Got plans with Natalie."

"The paraplegic in training?"

"The same."

"What're you doing that can possibly be more fun than waving golf clubs at storm clouds? Wait, let me guess...cushion shopping? Going on a tour of a cotton ball factory? No, sorry, clearly you're going to playtest bean bag chairs to make sure they're not too dangerous..."

Sylvester smirked at him, confident the truth was even more outrageous. "Nope, today we're going to go on an adventure...she's going to try stairs."

"And when you say 'stairs' you mean what now?"

"Ya know, stairs. A buncha steps? Climb from one floor up to the next? She's not a fan and avoids them."

"How can you avoid stairs? They're everywhere!"

"She avoids a lot of things. Stairs, curbs, hot foods, sharp blades of grass..."

"So you're taking her 'out for stairs'?" Socket continued, shaking his head, disbelieving. "A night on the town cruising for a stoop..."

"Something like that. We already picked out a place. Plush carpeting, big landings, close to the hospital..."

"Does it offer valet? All the best stair places offer valet..."

"Nah, this place is too trendy for that."

"And you're sure this's the best idea? Taking the accidental epileptic onto something vertical she prefers to avoid? Your glass slipper may shatter before you get to try it on."

"She's tougher than she thinks. We went to the pumpkin dive last week. She survived fine."

"What'd you do, leave her in a parked car?"

"Tied to a tree."

Socket shook his head, "And you give me shit for electrocuting the neighborhood kids…"

CHAPTER 30

STAIRS

Natalie looked up, craning her neck as she sucked huge gulps of air down to her feet, hoping to make herself float.

Above her cascaded a hundred floors and a thousand stairs, twisting back and forth on crisscrossing wells of elegant design, gasps of light shooting through slats from far away windows, stabbing the darkness and dust mites.

Sylvester stepped up and gave her shoulder a hug. "It's only twenty flights, and there's a landing every ten steps, so you can't fall more than one floor…" he began.

"Your naiveté is priceless," she mumbled as her body tried to paralyze itself into hibernation.

"…and the steps are all carpeted and made of wood, not concrete, so they have a little more give to them..."

"That's perilously comforting…"

"…and I'll be with you the whole time. Consider me your personal crash cushion."

Natalie nervously tried to smile, hopeful but skeptical.

Sylvester smiled back as he reached into his backpack, "And I came prepared!"

He started by handing Natalie a fluffy-flopped rabbit hat and telling her to, "Buckle this on for brain protection", before following it up with a flak jacket and a set of riot pants he'd borrowed from Carl, who gave no rationale for owning them, but insisted repeatedly they be washed before being returned.

An inflatable inner tube emerged next, which Sylvester immediately inflated, handing it to Natalie a minute later and insisting she position it around her waist. She couldn't help but snort and laugh.

"And finally, here's a rope to belay ourselves with," he said triumphantly as he pulled one out, tying it around his waist before parsing out a few feet and tying the other end to Natalie, giving them the strange appearance of alpine climbers escaping from a missile silo during a pool party. Natalie wished she'd brought a camera.

"How you feeling? Safe?"

"Kinda-sorta strangely yes?" she admitted as she tugged on the rope and straightened her inner tube. "But I feel like a jackass."

"Worst case, we make the papers and check 'comical mugshot' off our bucket lists," Sylvester said, grinning.

Natalie smiled back, trying to gather her wits and her strength, bouncing a few times as she jackhammered courage into herself, "I'm gonna do this, I'm gonna do this, I'm gonna do this".

She looked up the stairwell, counting as she talked to herself, "You don't do well with two floors, you know, let alone…infinity."

"That's why this is perfect," Sylvester whispered into her private conversation, "Be brave. Break new ground."

"A break is exactly what I'm afraid of!" she exclaimed, her head still shaking. "And understand, if I take a slinky-ride down this thing, I'm taking you with me."

"You'll be fine! You're wearing an inner tube!" he smiled as he took the first step. "We'll go slow, whatever pace you want. We can do a floor an hour if that's all you can manage, or we can sprint to the top right now if you're feeling adventurous."

"No sprinting!"

"Fair enough," Sylvester smiled, before bowing, his open hand gesturing toward the stairs, "You wanna take the lead?"

She shot him a look, trying to steal his recklessness. "Sure, then you're positioned properly to cushion me when I fall."

"*If* you fall. You're gonna be fine! Maybe a little embarrassed by the time today's over." Sylvester said as he slipped into a damsel-in-distress voice, "Oh, woe is me! I can't walk up stairs. Stairs are my mortal enemy," and then he burst into fits of laughter.

Natalie shot him a look full of daggers and stomped up the first couple steps, pausing briefly, before trudging up the next few, pulling him along when the rope tightened.

She wasn't sure what made her do it, the ideas of both trudging and leading not readily found in her day-to-day toolkit. Was she succumbing to some unexpected form of peer pressure? Some desire to impress that was letting her take an absurd risk? It certainly seemed a denial of her better instincts.

The first two flights inched forward without much trouble, taking only twenty minutes for twenty steps, her padded gear giving her imaginary confidence as images of elegant and graceful dancers pirouetted through her mind. Some part of her psyche began to see the stairwell as a kind of vision quest, as if by simply confronting her demons she could conquer them. She was skeptical of her psyche's intentions.

On the third flight she stumbled, toppling back into Sylvester's waiting arms, shaken from the stagger but still determined to do more. She fell twice more on the fourth, twisting an ankle that she bore more as a badge than a worry, each floor slowly growing her confidence.

They'd been climbing for an hour by the time they made it to the fifth landing, her eyes now looking down to the starting point, as if a slip and fall wouldn't end until the earth itself came up to meet her, and she began to wonder if there was a basement to fall into.

When they hit the sixth landing they took a break, collapsing to the ground as Sylvester offered her a bottle of water, which she gladly accepted, swigging down half its contents in a single gulp.

"Seems to be going well?" he asked.

"The day is young," she gasped between fitless breaths as her wobbly legs tried to stiffen.

"Any concerns?"

"Earthquakes, sinkholes, buffalo stampede…ya know, the normal stuff."

"How much farther do you wanna try?" he asked, looking up at the floors above them. "It's fourteen to the top, but that's probably pushing it."

"You think?"

"It's up to you, but I say we aim to end on a high note and a round number."

She looked from him to the stairs and then tossed him the water bottle. "OK, the sooner we reach ten, the sooner we take the elevator back down."

And then she was off, hoping to catch up to her momentum and confidence, plunging up the first two steps and pulling him along. Natalie wasn't used to conquering her fears, let alone with such regularity. There was something addictive about it.

When they passed the seventh landing she was downright ebullient, bounding along, a steady trot upward on a runner's high from the exercise she'd long avoided. Even the air was thinner this far up, her ground-floor lifestyle having limited her in unexpected ways.

At the eighth landing she unclasped her hat, letting her ears breathe free, an endorphined feeling of invincibility washing over her as the goal became the destination. Halfway to nine she felt a jarring jolt that wobbled her balance and stalled her momentum, an apologetic Sylvester waving from the landing below as he gasped, holding a stitch in his side.

"C'mon slowpoke!" she grinned as she crinkled her nose and tossed off the rope, the arrogance of success taking full control.

A path of breadcrumbs began to fall as they went, and when Sylvester passed nine she was already long gone, a wispy cloud of roadrunner dust still floating in the air as if she'd been sprinting, the inner tube casually rung around a banister like a carnival ring toss.

He wondered what'd come over her. Maybe excitement. Maybe adrenaline. Maybe lack of oxygen. But it was clear that her fear and trepidation had been left far below, which scared Sylvester more than it encouraged him.

When he finally turned the final twist and trudged into view, he was pleased to find Natalie still waiting, sitting safely on the tenth landing and panting, a grin reaching across her face and back past her ears.

She'd done it, conquering a demon so fearfully primal within her that she barely had words. "I did it...all of it...millions of stairs...maybe billions...".

She was ecstatic, a phoenix reborn, a life avoided suddenly experienced for the first time.

Sylvester smiled, sweat pouring off his face and dribbling in puddles around him as he collapsed into a pile beside her, his scar-pocked arm scraping sheets off his forehead. "I am way...more tired...than I thought I'd be," was all he could get out, his labored breath panting out like an overexerted dog gasping for sweat glands.

"Well, I've got plenty of energy still," Natalie said through her jokered grin.

"We need...to get you...an elliptical," Sylvester forced out.

"I'm gonna head back down."

Sylvester shot up immediately, a curious and fearful questioning glance staring her down. "We're taking the elevator down, remember?"

Natalie leered, her new confidence cackling at his weakness, as if he symbolized something so far below the person she now was. "I'll be fine," she said with a hubristic glance, taking a step off the landing to head down.

And then it happened.

After a hundred floors and a thousand steps, the karmic balance of the world righted itself, time slowing as Natalie fell, slipping on the sweat-drizzled step born from Sylvester's beaten brow, and she watched as her confidence broke off and flew away from her desperately grasping hands.

She hit the first step at an odd angle that knocked out a tooth, the word "Ouch" escaping her lips briefly, before she twisted into the second impact in a way that focused on her knee, while the third tumble detached part of her earlobe. The fourth knocked her unconscious, thankfully robbing her of the memories from the next few that followed, when bones broke and muscles tore, finally coming to rest two flights down, precariously perched on the eighth flight cliff.

Sylvester scrambled down after her, slipping in his own sweat and twisting an ankle on an oddly placed tooth, before finally pulling her back to safety on the landing and checking her pulse and her vitals, tears streaming down his cheeks as his hand dialed 911.

CHAPTER 31
FAILURE

Natalie was crying hysterically as the gurney bounced off the curb toward the ambulance, despondent bones and muscles competing for her attention as they screamed in agony. They felt betrayed, doubly so by the millions of stairs they'd been forced to climb prior to the unjust reward at the end. It wasn't like she promised. It wasn't like *he* promised. He didn't cushion her when she needed it.

Her eyes were soaked with tears and swizzled hair, blinding her to everything. She didn't notice they were outside, or that it was raining, or that Sylvester was crying hysterically beside her, endlessly mumbling "I'm so sorry". Shock had taken the wheel and held a stranglehold on her awareness.

Sylvester wasn't faring much better, his own sense of shock taking a similar tact. He'd kept it together enough to call 911, but from there memories and actions blended together in a dream he couldn't remember as time sped by. Lights had flashed, an ambulance had arrived, questions had been asked and answered, but they all faded into obscurity, his brain refusing to store them as he fell into a percolating stupor.

When awareness finally returned, Sylvester found himself sitting in the waiting room of a hospital, alone except for the few bits of newspaper and crumpled candy wrapper that were tumbling by on air-conditioned currents of sterility.

He was unexpectedly damp, his face streaked with dried tears and sorrow, while his hand held a death grip on a forkroach, burying it to the hilt in his palm.

"Sir? Sir??" said a distant voice as its hand shook his shoulder.

Sylvester blinked, shaking off the disco-dancing cobwebs as he looked up at the face of a sweetly concerned nurse who was wondering if he was OK. He could swear she wasn't there a moment before.

"Yes?"

"Your friend? If you wanted to see her, she's out of surgery. She'll be awake for a few minutes before the meds kick in."

"How long...?" he began, his eyes searching for a clock as his mouth tasted the minutes.

"You've been here almost 9 hours now."

Sylvester nodded, struggling to his feet, his one sleepy leg stumbling him briefly into a ficus as the nurse led the way.

He was truly petrified of what he would find.

*****

Natalie was propped against pillows in a hospital bed, strange bits of cast wrapped around different limbs and pulleyed together like some poorly constructed jigsaw puzzle. The leg may've connected to the neck, but it was also connected to the arm, which seemed like a mistake, as if the pieces fit together but weren't supposed to go there.

Her eyes stared at the ceiling, counting dots in the tiles, swollen red from pouring out her weight in tears. She was spent and tired and in pain and awake, but she didn't want sleep to come, certain her dreams would be filled with lacerated sadness and fevered memories. She pined for her soft couch and piles of books and riskless environment of stairless living.

Sylvester tapped lightly on the door and stepped in, his head hung low, his puffered eyes scared and hiding behind his brow. Natalie could barely move hers, which both welcomed him and avoided him, unsure of how they felt. After a moment they motioned to the chair beside her.

Sylvester sat down, his hands in his lap, his eyes staring at the floor, unwilling to appreciate his own disastrous handiwork. Felicia would've taken pride in a moment like this. Natalie was used to it.

Sylvester mumbled a sentence or two before realizing no sound had come out, hastily turning up his volume and starting again.

"I'm sorry," was the first thing he got out - the obvious part - before he stammered on into confusion. "I don't...I don't even know what...to say? It was just...steps? Steps. I...I didn't get it? How bad it could be? The risk..." His eyes went up to hers, searching for understanding, childish regret from being taught a lesson the hard way.

Natalie looked at him, unsure what to feel. Anger? Pity? Anguish?

Superiority? She didn't know. She loved him for challenging her. The moments before the fall she'd felt more alive and exhilarated than at any time in her strangely accursed life. But now here, lying in plaster, she regretted it all. It was everything she'd feared, the failure and the pain. All she needed now was for him to flee like the rest for the cycle to be complete. She hoped her eyes conveyed some of this.

Sylvester's own eyes had dipped down, wishing they had something to distract themselves with beyond tiger-striped floor tiles. A rubber band, a paper clip, a dust mote, anything.

"I don't even know how we got here…" he continued, "I don't…I don't remember the elevator…the ambulance…I think it might've rained…? It's been nine hours…it doesn't feel like nine hours."

He looked up again, hoping for something, but her eyes had rambled away, trying to force out more tears but not knowing where to find them. She knew it'd been nine hours and regretted every minute of it.

"It was all my fault…what happened…but I can't…I can't understand it? It was an accident…yet it wasn't, was it? You knew it would happen. You expected it. But…you didn't force it. It was something else…"

He didn't know why he was rambling like this. She was the one who was injured. This shouldn't be about him. It should be about her. But she wasn't saying anything. Maybe she couldn't.

"Should I have left you locked away in your nook of a castle? Encouraged you to hide away the years until old age surprised you? That feels just as morbid. I know it's not on me…it's your life, not mine…but I hoped…maybe together…I could help somehow?"

"But no, we're polar opposite people trying to balance against each other. It doesn't work that way, does it? Felicia and I…we somehow worked…we scratched each other's itches. But you and me? We're ricocheting off each other and flying into walls, and only one of us enjoys it."

"I can't imagine what it's like to live your life…a destiny of cuts and bruises and broken hips? I don't have much of a destiny; I'm destined not to make it. Too many risks, too little point in them. Probably why

I pushed you to be more reckless. More like me. Throw some of my broken pixie dust on you and try to trick you into coming along to Neverland."

And then Sylvester drifted off, realizing his rambling was going unchecked, Natalie's reflected silence only making him feel worse as it sat like a fog. It wasn't the same as the silences with Felicia, but it reminded him of them. With Felicia it was a silence of boredom. Of nothing to talk about. This was a silence of guilt. Of embarrassment. Of regret. It weighed for minutes as they sat in ponderous silence. Natalie blinked a lot, her fingers wiggling as they wished for freedom. Sylvester simply stared, as if by doing so the world outside would cease to exist.

"I don't know how to live in your world," he began again at some point. "I want to take useless risks. Throw myself in front of things. And I keep trying to take you with me…but that's not you, is it? You want to hide behind things, not be thrown in front of them."

Natalie was staring at him now, knowing where this was going. The same place they all went. Running away from the mess they made. Running away from her.

"I don't think I'm good for you," he finally said, keeping his head down, refusing to look up from his now dwindling speech. "You're a good person…who needs to be protected. Not protected in some manly-man way, but…by someone who puts your needs first. I take risks for fun. Too many, really." He paused, trying to find eloquent words that wouldn't come. "You'll always get hit by pieces of me."

Sylvester paused, looking up at her. Her eyes were watching him and quivering, unsure. Tears were behind them; tears of pain and anger and sadness and fear, all struggling for the right to come out first, yet fighting for the right to stay in.

Pain and fear were what ultimately escaped, speaking through her tightly wired jaw, "You're right."

Sylvester's lip quivered in acceptance as his head nodded in agreement, his feet pushing against the ground and standing his body up.

His hand reached down and slid briefly across her uninjured arm, softly saying goodbye. He couldn't bring himself to look at her eyes. If he had, he would've seen tears pouring from them silently, matching his own.

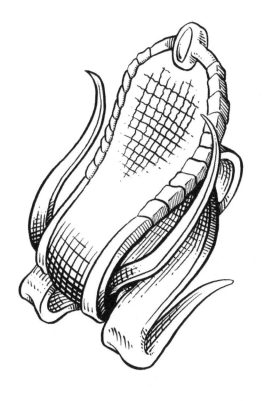

Part 3

Sylvester

CHAPTER 32
FELICIA RELEASED

Felicia smiled at the sunlight, somehow infinitely closer without the wire fence wedged between them. She glanced at the bus stop bench she sat on, waiting out her first five minutes of freedom. It was modest and wooden and peppered with mismatched rivets, as if underscoring the simple complexity of the moment.

Her parole had been granted, her sentence marked complete, and Felicia now found herself shuffled and processed and spat out to freedom, a papered checkmark to indicate her penance had been paid, her only currency an envelope of possessions from a previous life with which to begin again down the same path.

They'd given her a bit of money for her time, enough to get a room and a cab and a meal, as well as a long dead phone and a set of keys to an apartment she no longer lived in, usurped in the name of commerce, her belongings in moldy wet basement boxes being visited by uptown rats with downtown tastes.

At the opposite end of the bench sat another inmate, prison-crazed to confusion when the walls were removed, mumbling and rocking with a palpable fear of freedom.

There was no fear in Felicia, only uncertainty.

The prison experience hadn't worked out quite the way it was expected to. Felicia referred to it as her first stint in criminal summer camp, with a focus on gaming the system and riding the rails of the law. Experts and office hours, prison was full of the knowledge not found in books.

Intentional or not, six months inside a penal chrysalis had transformed Felicia from a crooked tooth to a polished stone. These days her eyes were shiftier, her skin was thicker, her strength more pronounced, and she'd learned subtlety, the thief's pause, the timing of moments that refined and improved the game. She still craved the rush of inflicting, but she knew the act more intimately now and saw the potential, both for casual subtlety and reckless violence.

All of which tempted her with a curious problem now – what

version of herself did she want to pursue?

At her feet she saw a rubber band, feeble and twizzled and tossed aside, and she snagged it, a fidget's toy of distraction while she pondered her futures.

She could certainly take the high road, forsaking her habit entirely in the name of personal growth, tossing aside her past in favor of a future. This would've been the smart play, the one without bars on the windows, where white picket fences teased a future of conservative boredom.

She tossed that one aside rather quickly.

Six months wasn't so long that you really changed; not so long that you didn't see the path back to who and what you were. Sylvester was still out there, a known commodity, elusively out of reach yet salvageable. That was a life of safe familiarity that she could snuggle back into rather easily.

But it held a degree of boredom, a step back from her true potential, a return to the days of train-tacking and parade drops that held only small sips of middling satisfaction.

The last option, though, was the most tempting - simply embracing it and letting loose the dark side of herself that she met in prison. She could pick her targets and her moments and run rampant for years, an expert unleashed on a sea of amateurs.

Her days could start by hip-checking her way through the coffee line, knocking people into lattes and endcaps, hot spills and scars her morning ritual. She could join a tennis club and spend her afternoons headhunting trophy-wives and their nosejobs, her nights spent online heckling teenage athletes and their acne. Felicia had an evil streak in her that saw all the fun ways to do bad things, a criminalistic second sight that came with her addiction.

She seemed perched on a polar point, one slant the simple slide back to her previous life, the other teasing the curious unknown, a fresh untouched wrapper crinkling before her. To be a good witch or a bad witch? To help Dorothy or to haunt her? Felicia glared back at the sun while she fidgeted, unsure its intent, sunbeams beating down useless warmth on a frozen January morning.

At its heart, the question was simple – was this even a habit she wanted to break?

She glanced down the bench again, the mumbling rambler still spastic, a nervous hesitancy that conveyed a ready expectation of being accosted and berated, the prison pecking order burned deep.

Felicia watched him for a moment, a palpable twitching fear ever present, before the teasing temptation of her addiction made the decision for her.

"Awww, who am I kidding…" she thought as butterflies hatched in her tummy, a cacophonous explosion of burst cocoons that had been lying in wait, and with a fluid move she launched the rubber band, snapping the rambler in the eye and sprawling him off the bench.

CHAPTER 33
SOCKET & POKE

Poke nuzzled Sylvester in the mouth, a reverse beard bristle that reminded the little fellow of a familiar familial scratch.

Sylvester hadn't noticed the porcupine, his tumbleweed dreams instead prompting him to roll over on top of him, triggering a spark of claustrophobia that immediately pierced the animal's quills through the sheets and evacuated Sylvester to his feet.

"Good morning!" he shouted as his senses came to him, his confused hands tracing the ceiling for shadows and support.

Poke gave him an angry glare before curling into the warm spot on the bed with a *snumph*.

"Fine, I'm up. Have the bed to yourself you gluttonous, slumbering, pincushion…"

Sylvester hopped off the bed, slid on some pants, and sidled into the next room, his toes stubbing themselves awake with quick jabs on exposed splinters while his fingernails dug wake-up grooves in his palms. He shuffled as he went, his fingertips touching what they could, feeble attempts to ground himself from the impending shock that undoubtedly awaited him. He wasn't sure he was awake enough yet for Socket's house.

The kitchen door loomed, bright and welcoming, sunlight streaming out as if the Queen herself was in the midst of afternoon tea. Sylvester knew better than to trust the elderly British. His foot pushed softly against the door, a silent swing as it opened, creakless, conveying utter safety. His arm followed slowly, reaching for the light, a nervous fear that was immediately met with a shock as his finger flipped the switch.

The flickering light slowly upped its confidence as it grew steady overhead, while Sylvester took a deep breath and glanced around, taking in the battlefield. A small wooden sign hung above the sink that identified it simply as "Normandy". It seemed accurate.

It took him 10 minutes to start the coffee, by which time he'd shocked himself 27 more times on everything from the metal coffee can to the plastic scoop used to measure it. He didn't understand how Socket had managed to electrify plastic, but he had, making even the certainty of non-conductive materials an uncertainty.

Coffee in hand, Sylvester meandered the gullious gauntlet through the canyoned living room of debris, finally crashing down on the electrified couch cushion he knew was broken. He didn't dare try the TV or the remote, Socket having rigged those with a variety of failsafes to stop himself from watching endless reruns of Tesla and Edison documentaries.

Instead, Sylvester sat in silence, sipping his coffee and pondering his life.

He didn't know what to do about Natalie. It'd been his idea to end things, some feeble, adolescent urge to protect her, and he'd regretted it ever since. He didn't want her out of his life, he wanted her in it.

But it'd now been weeks since the stair fall, and her ear-splitting silence was deafening.

He'd sent thornless flowers and nutless chocolates, three times to the hospital and twice to the bookstore, as well as a dozen hand-written notes he'd taken the time to file down the edges on. He'd even hired a singing telegram to bring her romance novels.

Thus far he'd heard nothing back and was nervously teetering on the border of full-fledged stalking.

As confident as he'd been in her ability to conquer her demons, it was clear now how clueless he'd been. He'd been trying to fix someone else's life without bothering to understand the engineering behind it. Her problems were not psychosomatic constructs designed to maintain an introverted life, but rather the result of an honest to goodness battle with the forces of nature. Gravity and bad luck were her sworn enemies, and they had mounted a fearsome attack on her life that could not be overcome with a few months of ego-stretching.

The responsibility for her accident fell fully on him for pushing her too far and too fast, only a small dollop on her shoulder from overconfidence and her limited experience wielding it. This left him in a constant state of guilt, both at the physical pain he'd caused, as well as the spirit he'd broken, a certainty in his mind that he'd wasted her final spit of courage on his foolish, arrogant theory.

All of which made him understand her silent brevity all the more; she'd taken his advice and was trying to protect herself.

A series of echoing shocks and cackles pulled his attention toward the bathroom, Socket evidently awake and about. He made a mental note to ask what he'd triggered. He may risk the toilet seat if the odds were in his favor; he wasn't in the mood to head to the safety of the library.

"Morning!" said Socket as he duck-footed into the room, the loose bathroom tile having clearly gotten him good.

"Hey Socket."

"Wanna help me test some wiring today? I need to redo the mailbox and the gutters."

"Sure," said Sylvester, his eyes still focused on his thoughts.

"What's with the mopes? Porcupine not giving you the prickly crotch love you need? I'm tellin' ya, if you wanna maximize things stop wearing underwear to bed."

"I'll keep it in mind."

"Only a small sliver of a chance you accidentally end up with porcupine-faced children…"

"You are a fount of wisdom and insanity."

"Why thank you!" said Socket.

A rustling, scratching sound drifted toward them through the piles of collectible garbage as Poke maneuvered his way through, his quills brushing dangerously against the perils that could topple and electrify.

They both watched curiously, Sylvester in fear for his little friend, while Socket rooted for the electricity.

A few moments passed before he emerged, unscathed, the omnipresent fear on his face being replaced by sheer ebullience as he spotted Sylvester and bobbled towards him, taking two attempts to hop awkwardly onto the couch and settle in beside him.

Sylvester scratched the little guy's neck, rewarding his bravery for making the trek and accidentally triggering a naroleptic collapse that left the porcupine's back half oddly perched between the couch and the floor as rodential snores filled the room, oblivious to their curiosities as his feet ran absent dreams in mid-air.

"I would love to fall asleep that easily," Socket mused as he began absently touching things within reach, curiosity and quality control manipulating his motives. "I always wonder if it's restful? Does he fall right into REM or does he get stuck on the fringes?"

"No idea," said Sylvester, his reflexes betraying him into catching the remote (and subsequent shock) Socket had thrown his way. "Oww, thanks."

"Just trying to get a rise out of you, buddy! Seriously, what's up? I left a fresh pack of mousetraps out and you didn't even crack the bag to steal one."

Sylvester squinted towards the table, surprised at himself as much as Socket was.

"I didn't even…wow. Sorry, I've been in a funk."

"Was it whatshername? Klutzy girl? Endless distraction and panty-twister that girl is. Want me to fetch the paddles? See if I can shock you back to promiscuity?"

Sylvester shrugged, uncertain what the fix was, but doubting there'd be any drawback to a fun game with the defibrillator.

"Sure, why not. Seems safer than trying to turn on the TV."

"Absolutely! TV's plugged into an outlet. The 'fibrillator works off a battery."

CHAPTER 34
SYLVESTER TALKS TO NATALIE

Sylvester looked up nervously at the bookstore gargoyles, Natalie's wooden wardens, fearful of their chiseled animosity. It was clear they knew more than they were letting on, but for now they stayed silent and watchful.

This was the fourth time he'd visited in the past few weeks (giving a lot of business to the shake shop next door), but the first that he found himself close enough to touch the door.

But still he hesitated, nerves shaking, eyelids blinking, frightened and scared.

A part of him wondered whether this was simply his body's normal reaction, enjoying the pain of the moment and the anticipation of what was awaiting him inside. He could tell the armored butterflies in his stomach were making ready to pelt his heart with sticks and arrows.

He took a long, slow drag of his ice cream shake, forcing an artic headache inside, then reached out and twisted the handle, kicking the doorplate and leading his momentum inside.

The door jingled its familiar ringle as the odor of wood and must filled the air. Almost immediately he noticed the Floridian travel books and shuffleboard rules littering his view and knew he would not have Natalie to himself.

He inched his way toward the register, eyes darting up and down the book alleys, fearful of being pounced upon at any moment. The store was silent, as if something in tall grass was in the midst of stalking its prey and even the crickets and muskrats held their breath as they watched the show.

He turned past the final bookcase and saw the register as he remembered it, piled high with books, but mere emptiness behind it.

His breath and his confidence left him.

He glanced and listened, up and down the alleyrows, hoping to catch a sign of her or the flutter of a page flip, but there was nothing but silence.

His eyes fell to the floor as his lips instinctively reached for the straw, determined to occupy his fidgeting while he decided his next move, but as soon as his skin touched the plastic an old beehive bun popped like toast from behind the register.

"No drinks! Can't you read??" shouted Grandma Norris, who had apparently just been plugged in. "Says so right on the sign outside! Same with shoes! You wearing shoes? You better be! I don't tolerate no cud-chewing Shoeless Joes in my establishment!"

She gave him the evil eye as he gawked at her, in shock at her sudden appearance and 1920s dialect. The evil eye continued to stare, briefly flickering towards the floor, as if trying to see through the countertop to determine whether he was, in fact, wearing shoes. She seemed to be waiting for something, frozen in place expectantly.

Sylvester stammered as he bunglingly looked for a place to deposit his drink.

"Oh! I'm so...so sorry about that. I missed the sign, really, I did. Totally distracted. I don't see a..."

But before he could finish the thought she thrust a garbage can in front of him, leaving no question as to her idea of what his response should be. He softly slipped the cup inside, hoping for leniency, but her guilty glare endured, her eye continuing to flicker to the floor. He quickly grabbed at his foot and lifted it into the air and across her line of vision, showing off the laced sneaker secured around it. "See? Shoes! I'm no...ummm...cud-chewing..."

"Yeah...maybe," she said as she slowly lowered the garbage, her one big eye still staring him down suspectantly. "So what're you after? We don't got no Stevie King novels here...no Jim Gristleham...only good old classics! Hardbacks. First editions. Got some books on circuses if you're interested...give you a good price..."

Sylvester smirked at the thought of her suggestive selling him circus books. Maybe in her youth, at the beginning of the last century, that would've been popular. A part of him figured he could offer her a dime and she'd be likely to take it, forgetting where inflation had gone since then.

"And no, I'm a married woman if that's what yer thinkin!" she blurted out, apparently reading into his smirk and paused silence of thought.

"No, no, I didn't mean to…I was just…" he flustered as he grasped for words. "No, I was looking for Natalie. Is she around?"

"Hmph," snorted the old woman, leering at him with a squinty eye that indicated pirate experience. "She's got today off. Come back tomorrow, maybe she'll be working."

"I just…I just wanted to talk with her…is she around? We're friends. I think. She may be up for seeing me?"

"Hrrrmmm," she guttered as she hocked up something from her lungs and made to spit it into the trash.

Sylvester tried to smile and present himself as friendly and honorable as could be, knowing he was being judged. He shifted uncomfortably from foot to foot, a mad temptation sidling through him that maybe he should roll down his sleeve and cover his tattoo arm.

She continued to stare through him, chewing her own cud, possibly stuck on pause, her eyes a mix of glaze and sleep. The stare drew on for a solid minute.

"Fine," she said suddenly, as if the processing had just completed, and before he could say *'thank you'*, she cracked open the side of her mouth and screamed "Natalie!" over her shoulder. "There. Good? Now leave me be if you're not here to buy anything," and before he could get a word out she vanished behind the register counter.

Sylvester had started to lean over to see where she went, remembering no staircase or depth for her to have vanished into, but as his nose breached the ledge he heard a squeaking noise approaching and straightened himself back up.

A moment later a rubber wheel appeared around a corner, followed by Natalie, nestled in a wheelchair, who immediately gave him a look that contained all the feelings of the world mixed together at once. Happiness, sadness, excitement, anger, love, hate, fear, hunger, and a dozen more he couldn't place but knew he recognized. Finally she settled on a frown full of curiosity.

Words left him, his teeth slowly nibbling his bottom lip.

"Hey," she said finally when it became clear his tongue was indisposed.

"Hey," he gubbered out. He was viewing himself from the outside again, like a moment of shock, a distant viewer, a non-participant.

Natalie was strapped into the chair, swaddled in casts, plaster wrapping her leg and arm and hip and finger. A neck brace looked to be all that was stopping her pumpkin head from falling off like the headless horseman and rolling across the floor. White tape crossed off hidden bruises and cuts on what little was still visible of her face and arms.

He didn't know what to say. Could he have caused all of this simply by encouraging her?

She seemed able to read him and helped out. "It's not all from the fall. Most of it is…the leg, the neck, the hip, the finger," which she made a point of lifting and flipping him off with, "but some of it came later. I had a couple of what they like to call 'cascades' at the hospital, where you sort of domino around like a pinball machine, falling into different things. Apparently my balance is really bad when I'm down a leg…"

"Oh, Natalie…I'm so…"

"Sorry?" she finished for him.

"Yeah…"

She looked at him sternly, a mother getting ready to reprimand a child. "It wasn't all you. I was the idiot who knew better. You were only being like the rest of them."

"The rest…?"

"Everyone else. Everyone who thinks they know better than me," she scowled, her voice growing full of malice and anger and emotion now. "*'Come on out Natalie, you'll be fine.' 'I'll catch you Natalie, you'll be safe with me.' 'C'mon Natalie, live a little.'*" Her lips quivered and her eyes filled with water as tears tried to pound their way out. "I should've known better. You think you were the first one to try to save me? I knew that couldn't happen. I can't be saved, but I wanted to believe, one more time. I still wanted the knight on horseback to ride in and save me, but by now I should've known it didn't work like that, right? That's not my lot in life. I was always destined to be allergic to horses…"

"Natalie…" he began.

"No. Stop. Seriously, this has happened to me time and time again and you know what always happens? They apologize and say, *'it won't happen the NEXT time'*, and then try to convince me to risk myself again. To leave my safety for some half-baked adventure. To make the same mistakes again." She was looking at him straight on now, the tears starting to spill out along with the words. "And then they leave. They don't want to deal with it and they leave me…"

She paused for a moment, trying to force the tears to stay in.

"I'm done. No more. I'm sick of spending my life being hurt and beat up and in casts. I don't want my heart broken along with my body. I'd rather be alone in life than be hurt again and again. I don't trust the world anymore. I'm sick of it. It's always had something against me and it's clearly not going to let me go until it kills me." She paused, panting, the words flooding out faster than she could speak them, "I'm staying here. Indoors. Where I'm safe. I'll read books and write poems and work my bookstore for the next 50 years if need be, without ever stepping outside again…"

Sylvester looked on, his eyes wide, his own set of tears dribbling out as the words stuck in his throat, blocked before he could speak them.

Natalie was gushing now, tears streaming down her face as her body started to convulse and shake. He took a step towards her to reach out - to hug her, to hold her, to be there for her - but she flinched and wheeled away, frightened of her own shadow.

"Fool me once…twice…a million times," she said on stuttering sobs before her voice quieted down to a whisper, "I can't do it anymore…I can't…I can't…"

"Nat…"

"No!" she screamed. "Stop! You're only trying to calm me down and make me forget. I don't want to forget! I don't want to be consoled! And I don't want to think about the happy times! They're too far between. This!" she said as she indicated the chair and her body, "This is what most of my life is about! It's pain and suffering and being miserable all the time! You're not here for this! You visit and barely understand it. I can't do it anymore. I can't. I can't keep taking risks; I can't keep going outside my comfort zone. I need to be safe…for me…"

Sylvester's tears were rivering down his cheeks as he struggled to say anything, his voice muted, his mind in pain, equally lost and scared and helpless.

He tasted a rare and strange kind of pain metastasizing through him, desperately trying to swap out his needs for hers. Maybe it was heartburn, maybe it was love, he didn't know, but it hurt.

Finally he got out a simple and stuttered, "OK," which seemed to be all Natalie had wanted to hear.

Then they looked at each other, tears flowing freely on their faces, both of them open wounds rubbed raw with salt. Their eyes were locked, silently talking to each other through only emotions now.

Finally, Natalie broke contact, her tears spent, and she wheeled her chair around and started moving away, mumbling softly, almost to herself, "I'm sorry…I'm so sorry…"

Sylvester watched her go, realizing there was nothing he could say or do.

Finally he turned back, about to leave, before he paused, his eyes on the floor where their tears had fallen. A small, crooked crinkle cracked the corner of his mouth as he reached down and dried the floor with his sleeve. At a minimum, he would do what he could to not hurt her again.

CHAPTER 35
JUNKYARD YARD SALE

The line outside Samantha's Salvage stretched a half mile behind them, bending and baying around fast food muffler shops and salty-eyed widow washers. Socket was first in line and had been since the night before.

Sylvester had only just arrived as Socket grabbed him by the shoulders and shook him, opening-night excitement vibes emanating through his hands. "Are you ready?? Any minute now! Junkyard yard sale! Junkyard yard sale!!"

"And you just need me to carry things, right?" asked Sylvester, his eyes taking in the crowd as his fingers fiddled with a forkroach.

"Yup! Push the cart and lift the heavy objects. Basic mulery."

"Always ready to packhorse myself for rent..."

"Quiet mule or it'll be the prod for you!"

Sylvester smirked, his friend in his element, Socket's Happy-Christmas-Birthday-versary about to erupt, "And you got here when?"

"4pm yesterday. First in line!"

"And the next person showed up at...?"

"Maybe 7?"

"Last night?"

"This morning."

Sylvester mockingly glanced at a non-existent watch, as if doing the math, before silently smirking.

"Shut up," said Socket, shaking his head in religious disbelief as if this heathen was doubting his ability to resurrect himself.

Sylvester shrugged his shoulders and leaned against the fence, letting his thoughts wander back to Natalie. Since their visit he'd recognized that her safety was best assured by his own absence, but he was having trouble breaking the news to himself. The truth was often difficult to absorb.

But for now it had to wait, as a siren sounded and the gate swung open, a mad dash underway as Socket and Sylvester scampered into a world of cacophonic discord.

All around them strange piles and mounds towered and dominated the skyline, pressing up against the slatted fence surrounding the property. A stack of school buses grabbed the most attention, five tall and fifty-five feet high, an OCD approach to organization that worked better with bricks than buses (albeit creating an iconic, eye-catching visual for highway kids to point at).

Socket grabbed a cart and pushed in, his eyes absorbing the festive air as mountains of miscellany loomed over them, organized by any variety of color, material, or use. The closest mound was full of purple 2lb dumbbells. The one beside it espresso machines. The next one car doors. In the distance was a stack of cracked open ATMs.

From there the piles dissipated into a strangely organized marketplace of randomness.

Thirty mismatched chairs circled an open space, strangely specific, as if some game of musical chairs among spirits was already underway. Beyond that a herd of snowblowers seemed to be facing off against an equally sedentary array of humidifiers, small warrior toasters perched about shouting orders across the battlefield. Against the far end of the yard stood a flat wall, a hundred different sized and shaped plungers stuck to it in comedic organization.

Sylvester shook his head in disbelief as they made a Black Friday beeline for the batteries and solar panels, Socket's reconnaissance run the week before identifying what treasures lay where.

"This place is crazy. It has everything!" said Sylvester, his eyes continuing to find new things to go wide for.

"It's the Spag's of junkyards."

"Apparently."

"Sammy once claimed she had a space shuttle buried in here somewhere..."

They continued to walk and wander, passing a forest of lamps nestled off to one side, their glittering branches enticing people in, a floor of plugs lying in wait to trip the unsuspecting.

"It's far more...organized...than I expected a junkyard to be. I was envisioning more of a tetanus factory…"

"Yeah, Sammy runs her yard a lot prettier than most folks. 'Organized with personality' she always likes to say."

The battery section was deserted when they arrived, plastering a smile of blistering success on Socket's face, absolute certainty on his part that a flood of competition was mere moments behind them. They worked quickly, snagging a dozen garden batteries and a pair of foldable solar panels before marching on, doorbusters in hand.

From there they wandered into the radio section, Socket pulling a beaten old Warbler from under the eight-track players, hidden the week before in a scuttle of devious intent. They snagged an old Blendtec from the kitchen area, and a cable-table full of cable from the wiring area, before a brief visit past the lickable taser display sidetracked them both for 15 minutes.

"Four more stops!" said Socket as he studied his shopping list, a zombilic Sylvester shuffling along behind him rolling the cable table as he waggled his swollen tongue against his teeth.

"Couldn't we have grabbed the table last then?"

"Nah, those go quick. Conduit-furniture hybrids are popular."

Socket paused, glancing up at aisles and locations trying to find his bearings. Sylvester busied himself inspecting an old spinning wheel, golden fabric still stuck in the spokes, his finger dancing brilliantly on the needle, a nervous feeling of ancient imp ownership making him question the purchase.

Socket folded up his list and started to move, "OK, let's grab some walkway mix next."

"And walkway mix is?"

"Washers, nuts, bolts, anchors, spacers, caps…whatever you can find that's small, cheap, conductive, and available in bulk. Oh, and ideally gravel in color."

Sylvester nodded, uncertain he could identify the color 'gravel' but content to fall in step behind Socket, the cable table bumbling along happily.

They wandered past a display of corn cob pipes organized into an

Elvis mural and paused briefly at a toddler-sized village that looked strikingly like 1830s London, before Socket led them on, eyeing aisle signs.

"Should be around here…" he began as he turned a corner, before stopping suddenly and instinctively scrambling away, running into Sylvester as he rounded the corner behind him.

"Oww, what's up Sock...oh," said Sylvester, his voice trailing off in understanding.

"Hi Vest!" said Felicia, a wry grin stretching across her face to create dimples where they didn't belong.

Felicia stood midway down the aisle, the unavoidable elephant blocking the path, a brimming cart beside her, a devious twinkle in her eye. Sylvester thought she looked different somehow, a more angular intent visible on her face, an aggressive passion he wasn't used to.

"Oh, hey 'Licia..." he said, caught off guard. "I didn't realize you'd gotten out…?"

"Yeah, they needed the cell for a real criminal," she said with surprising cheeriness as she bounded forward and embraced him in the strange hug of a graceless break-up.

"How long've you been out? Why didn't you call?" he asked as they broke apart, an awkwardness field seeming to bubble up between them.

"Couple weeks. Busy, busy, no time for the past, ya know?"

"I didn't realize I was known as 'the past'."

"You and the rest of it."

She said this last bit with a degree of animosity, as if the 'rest of it' was in on it together.

Sylvester changed direction, "Would've never expected to run into you here…"

"Oh, I love these sales! Always hobby hunting! Not many places a girl can shop and scratch," she said with a tilt toward her shopping cart.

Sylvester followed the nod, eyeing the cart filled to capacity with railroad spikes and barbed wire, broken toasters and circus gear. There was even a wireless dog fence perched on top beside a collection of collars.

"Thinking of getting a dog?" he asked.

"Sure," she said with a sarcastic delivery that indicated there would be no dog. "What about you? Big sale on forks and band-aids?"

"I'm on donkey duty for Socket," he said with a thumb to his friend, who in turn emerged from behind the corner waving and smiling goofily.

"Hey, Socket," nodded Felicia.

"Hey, Leash."

"Can you lean to your left for a sec, Sock?"

"Huh? Oh, sure," he said, angling away, a misplaced assumption that there was no criminal intent behind the request. Immediately he regretted it, his arm jabbing soundly into a handful of jutting tent poles that seemed awkwardly placed for such a well-organized junkyard.

"Thanks!" said Felicia with a smile.

Socket rubbed his sore elbow and glared at her, an uncertain certainty of her guilt.

"Nice to see you haven't changed," said Sylvester with a shake of his head, his eyes searching his surroundings for toppling jeopardy.

"Oh, don't be silly, Vest, I wouldn't set a trap *that* close to where I'm shopping..." she said, adding a wink back to Socket.

"You don't seem too nervous about getting caught again..."

"Nah! I'm gonna avoid obvious mistakes this time around and this kinda place is perfect! Low key, no cameras, minimal safety regulations..."

"So six months didn't slow you down, huh?"

Felicia gave him an eye and a smirk, "Might've sped me up."

"Oh shit..." Socket mumbled from behind him.

"I think some lessons life doesn't want us to learn, ya know? Contradict us too much on the inside," Felicia continued, dual-smirking them both. "I tried to play along. Fix the part you're told is broken, believe in the system, all of that. And you know what happens? You're miserable not being yourself. I gave it a shot, but it wasn't me. How about you Vest? Still frying away? Did you ever pull the..."

And then her voice trailed off, her familiar mocking tone silenced as he raised his arm, its crackled husk muting her with respect.

"Wow, I did not think you would ever actually do it."

"It's been a year full of surprises."

"Painful?"

"Very."

"Regrets?"

"Some."

"I'd offer to high five you, but I'd be nervous your skin would fall off."

"Probably a safe bet."

They smiled at each other, their past flirting to life, the flame still flickering deep down. Neither of them knew entirely what to do with it.

"How's Poke?" she continued, leaving the moment behind.

"He's good. A bit more anxious these days living with Socket, but he's learned where not to wander."

"I remember when you used to live there! Place was like an electrified rat cage."

"I prefer 'voltage-infused domicile'," Socket chimed in.

"Regardless of what you called it, I was always jealous I didn't think of it first!" said Felicia with a flirtatious grin to Socket, before turning back to Sylvester. "Well, if Poke ever needs a break from the anxiety, I'd love to see him."

"Sure, he'd love that," Sylvester began, before his lonely mouth kept going, "I might too, if you're up for it."

He blinked, confusion dawning on his face, uncertain why he'd just said that.

Felicia had a look of uncertainly as well, curious if he was a temptation or a reward.

She opened her mouth, about to speak, when their conversation was suddenly interrupted by a loud crash, a dishwasher toppling from far above into a compressive collision with the ground, frightening the bitter old biker browsing nearby, who instantly started swinging his arms and flapping his lips in sputtering-duck retaliation.

Felicia glanced over, nonplussed, as if expecting this. "Oh dear, I hope he's all right..."

Sylvester and Socket stared, wide eyes racketing from Felicia to the fallen dishwasher.

"Did you...?" Sylvester began.

"Did I...?" she led.

"Try to drop a dishwasher on someone?"

"Why would I do that?"

Sylvester stared, unsure how to read her.

Felicia turned back to them, a happy grin on her face as if nothing had just happened. "OK, I gotta jet. I need to get a few belt sanders before the good ones are picked through. Nice seeing you again Socket. Vest? Let's catchup sometime."

And with a wave Felicia was gone, her cart trailing a steady stream of broken glass and nails in its wake.

"Did you see that?!" said Socket. "She dropped a freaking dishwasher on someone! She's batshit loony-can!"

"She does seem a bit more...focused," said Sylvester, a mix of fear and curiosity shivering through him, arousing his goosebumps.

"Don't get any ideas! Stay away from the evil dudette. She's trouble. Be celibate. Take up meditation. Self-flagellate."

Sylvester barely heard him, continuing to stare after Felicia, his lonely mind pining for attention, until Socket grabbed it with a well-thrown hubcap beaned off his forehead.

CHAPTER 36
SYLVESTER TALKS TO FELICIA

Sylvester's mothlike self-control lasted all of three days before he caved to oblivion and called Felicia, Natalie's dismissal ripe in his mind and driving his lonely intentions toward the closest flame he could find.

"Hi Vest!" Felicia said as he slid easily into the seat across from her, a new diner table christening the event, even-sided and comfortable.

"Hi," he volleyed back, hoping she'd show her hand while he searched for traps, wondering how long she'd beaten him by.

They looked at each other, taking in what had changed, two anxious pawns curious about the unknown game they were about to play.

Finally, Felicia spoke, "You look good! A few more scars and grey hairs?"

He smiled weakly, "Yeah, a few of each. You look good, too. Little more buff. Prison was good to you? Survived it seems?"

"Well enough. It was a lot of fun. I can't wait to go back!"

"Did you end up getting that tattoo?"

"No…" she said in a huff as she flicked at the sugar packets. "They didn't trust me to follow their stupid design and not scar someone up, so I skipped it."

"Always a good sign when the inmates fear you."

"I try."

Sylvester smiled crooked, their jesting familiarity creeping back in, then waved his hand for coffee.

"So what're you doing for work now?" he asked. "Back to angry massages?"

"Nah, event planning."

Sylvester's head crooked automatically, unsure what he was missing.

Felicia smirked, "I booked a high school reunion today for octogenarians at a place called Ruby's Pavilion. I neglected to mention it was an ice rink."

Sylvester exhaled his awe, shaking his head in disbelief, "Another level Felicia, another level."

"Yup! But it's only temporary. I'm taking night classes to become a dental hygienist!"

Sylvester was still laughing when Mrs. Mosquit bustled over, coffee in hand, a pleasant smile tucked into the creases of her face.

"Ain't seen either of you in a while," she began as she poured. "We got pie now."

"I'll keep it in mind, thanks," said Sylvester with a warm smile.

Felicia's face quibbled with itself, a clear uncertainty about whether to mock or play nice as hints of a conscience poked through. Sylvester eyed her, watching the internal struggle before words finally emerged, "I'll have a piece of pie Mrs. Mosquit, thank you."

Mrs. Mosquit looked down at her and smiled, happy to hear her name said right, then wandered back off, her familiarity serving a nice bit of nostalgic ice-breaking for the table. Sylvester pondered the unexpected pleasantness of Felicia and immediately felt in danger, as if an anvil was about to fall from the sky. He checked the ceiling just in case.

But Felicia was busy staring at Sylvester's oil arm, her eyes wide with respect as she nodded towards it, "Tell me about the dip."

He looked at his arm, still strange and marbled after months. "Not much to tell. The oil kept calling to me and it finally made a good argument. Turned out to not be as fun as I was expecting."

"Did it hurt?"

Sylvester gave her a cockeyed look of dumbfoundery, then laughed. "Of course it did! Stole the crown from that chainsaw incident when we went camping."

"That was a fun trip! We sank a canoe!"

Sylvester smirked at the memory, remembering the unfortunate folks who'd been paddling it at the time.

He twisted his arm in rotational thought, showcasing that it still functioned, some semblance of pride poking through, "This landed me in the hospital for days. Took months to recover. Got fired. It was a fun experience."

Felicia reached out and took his hand, turning it back and forth inspecting it, a sushi chef studying the bluefin. The scars were mottled and twisted, wrapping up his arm like Damascus steel.

"It looks wonderful!! I'm so impressed Vest."

"Only you would have a compliment."

"Are these third or fourth degree?" she asked as she poked a particularly brutal spot and hoped it still hurt.

"Third."

"So you wussed out?"

"Passed out."

"I'm sorry I wasn't there to help hold you down."

Sylvester scowled, "Lots you missed while gone…and broken up."

Felicia dropped his hand as her eyes tilted toward the ceiling, considering the past, "Sorry about that. I probably coulda handled it cleaner. Oops."

Sylvester's mouth pursed with frustrated anger, "Oops?"

"Oopsie?"

Sylvester turned away, quenching an unexpected anger, "It was a weird way to end it."

"It was…" she paused, a strange bit of wishful hope creeping into her voice, "…but it might've been for the best? We both needed space."

Sylvester shrugged, "I don't know that I did."

Felicia shrugged in disagreement as a vapid elephant of awkward silence sat down at the table with them. Coffee was refilled. Pie was delivered. They spent minutes sipping and chewing before Felicia finally broke the moment, reaching out a forkroach and propping it on the table.

"My thumbs got strong," she said.

The forkroach's antennae curved upwards majestically, its legs evenly balanced. It looked almost machine made by elves, if that were possible.

Sylvester's eyes went wide and his mood softened. "Wow," he said, picking it up tentatively, "this is great." There was true appreciation in his voice as he rolled it over in his hands, examining its underside discreetly to avoid making it blush. "This is better than I can do with pliers."

"Thanks. Add it to the herd," she nodded to him. It wasn't much of a peace offering, but it was something. It connected them and their past back together.

Sylvester wasn't sure how to respond. Forgiveness or fear? Wanting or rejection? He wasn't even sure of his own mind. He was still stuck distantly dreaming of Natalie and her percussive existence, thoughts built on a mix of abject guilt and clinical loneliness, both of which seemed to be conspiring to propel him toward any distraction they could find.

He watched as his hand twitched imperceptibly toward the middle of the table, clearly having intentions of its own. Felicia eyed it and feared it, her hands drifting to safety.

"I don't know, Vest…" she began.

"Me neither." He paused. "We used to be a good match."

"We did. But now? Now I don't know."

Sylvester nodded in agreement. Now was throwing him for a loop as well.

"For years I just wanted to play my games and have my fun. Every thought was about scratching that itch of everlasting injury."

"Me too," Felicia smiled back.

He inhaled deeply, committing to himself that he believed what he was saying.

"Now…I'm not so sure anymore?"

"What changed?" she asked, waving for more coffee with her middle finger.

"Perspective? I see a few paths and I'm not sure which one to take. Does that make any sense?"

Felicia laughed and snorted, nodding her head, "Let me guess – one is the 'easy path to the past' where you and I get back together, while another's more of a 'run like the wind in the opposite direction'?"

"Just about."

"That's not so bad, is it?" she asked. "To see different futures? To see options?"

"No, not at all. But it's also a tease. Which road leads to the happy ending? Seems like dumb luck that you pick the right one at the right time."

Felicia nodded, familiar thoughts having bounced around her head recently as well. "I don't remember seeing two paths before prison."

"Me neither." He paused, jumbling his thoughts. "I see a few now, but I suspect most dead-end just out of sight."

"Which am I? The good path or the dead end?"

He grinned at her, "Probably both."

She smirked and took it as a compliment. "Funny, I was thinking the same about you."

Their eyes caught, looking deep, and a moment of palpable, anxious silence rose between them, and she knew what was coming next. She could see it on his face as his willpower failed.

"Felicia…did you want to…"

But she didn't let him finish. She saw Sylvester as the biggest cog in her addiction, the one drug she craved a relapse into, evidence of both her personal success and her personal failure, teetering on the wall of potential collapse and potential salvation. For now, she was enjoying the role of rebellious villain-in-training and she didn't want to regain her morals and ethics.

"Sorry Vest, I'm not interested in being anyone's path or dead end. I have six months of fun to catch up on without a ball-and-chain-conscience yapping on my shoulder."

A braincloud of sadness drifted over Sylvester as he collected his second rejection of the week, his esteem continuing to be pummeled by gut punches.

She eyed him, curiously. "Come on, why so needy? You haven't been all chaste and virtuous while I was gone have you? I know I wasn't."

"Does it matter?"

"To my curiosity it does."

"Too bad for your curiosity," he said with a tiny twist of a smirk.

Felicia read the confirmation between his lines, a subtle morsel she couldn't ignore. "Oooh, now I'm curious what my mischievous little pincushion has been up to. Tell me about her. It was a 'her' I assume? Or was it a 'them'?"

"Seriously? You haven't seen me in months, you make it clear you have no interest in getting back together, yet are somehow dying to catch up on my dating habits?"

"What can I say, I live a tabloid life."

Sylvester shook his head, focusing on the forkroach.

"You're such a no-funsy! C'mon, gimme a hint. Was she tall? Short? Good at math? Bad at baking? I deserve a nibble!"

"No, you don't."

Felicia pressed, "Did you replace me?"

"With another sociopathic felon?"

"I prefer 'institutionally-trained pain engineer'…but yeah."

"I don't want to talk about it."

A delicious grin crinkled her dimple. "Oh, you still have a thing for this girl don't you… Come on, just that crumb. Did she like to…ya know…" she began, before making a shiv-like stabbing motion with a coffee stirrer.

Sylvester smiled, finally conceding, "No. She wasn't like you. She was a bit of a klutz."

"A klutz?"

"A klutz."

"A literal klutz? As in, drops all the dishes, walks into walls, knocks over the knickknacks?"

"Yes. Exactly like that, although I'd go with a 'literary klutz' more than a literal one…"

"What does that even mean?" Felicia asked as her face bent into a baffled look of befuddlement.

Sylvester shrugged, enjoying his inside joke.

"Far more creative than I was expecting! But oh, how the mighty have fallen…again and again and again…" she laughed as her sense of humor cheered on its own witty self, before a grin caught up to her mind and spread across her face. "Can I meet her?"

"No, of course not."

"Why not? She sounds…fun."

"Don't even think about it."

"You do realize what happens when you tell someone they can't have something, right?"

Sylvester glared, white-knuckling the forkroach, a dawning realization that this wasn't something to have let slip in Felicia's presence, before dropping his voice to a dangerous whisper, "Felicia, seriously. Off. Limits. I'm warning you…"

"Warning me? What're you gonna do, bleed on me? Run into traffic to distract me? You can't stop me. You should know that."

"Felicia…"

She gave him a look and a glare, seeing a hint of something she wasn't used to.

"Fine, fine, I'll leave your klutzy play-thing alone," she finally said with a mischievous wink.

"I'd appreciate that."

Felicia gave him another look, a final weighing, to certify to herself that she didn't want him, before standing up to leave.

"This's been fun, but I need to run. I've got a tech convention to book into an Amish community before they sell out of barn space," she said, before adding with a laugh, "and for some reason I can't do it over the phone…"

Sylvester shook his head, still impressed by her creative depths, "Thanks for coming out. It was nice to catch up."

"It was. I'll give you a ring if I get desperate or need a target to practice on."

"I'll do the same."

And with that she walked out, stiffing him with the bill.

CHAPTER 37
SYLVESTER BREAKS

With Natalie plucked from his life and Felicia refusing his uncertain advances, Sylvester's immediate instinct was to once again slip back into a depression of pain by buffeting, blistering, bruising, and battering his body with anything and everything within reach and available for mail-order.

He began with twice-pricked fingers and over-stubbed toes, and soon graduated to light bulb burns and dental floss cuts. He teased stray cats and used grapefruit spoons to eat pudding. He put broken bits of glass in his shoes and took up bottle dancing.

And like any good addiction he was able to hide himself away within it, punishing his body while avoiding his mind.

Over the next week he was admitted to the hospital four times for lacerations and bruised bones, a dislocated shoulder and a handful of loose teeth, each time getting no further than the emergency room before being sent home with stitches and antiseptic, medications and stern warnings.

He stopped dwelling on the thoughts behind his actions and let his id lead the way, his distant mind wondering if he was simply trying to close the distance back to Natalie; to be near enough to trigger some kismetic fated reunion, as if the hospital itself was their lodestone to the past and he could chase after her with the inevitable coincidence of injury.

But instead he was met only by disappointment, his life looping along in boring, lonely repetition. He thought often of Carl, once again wondering if he'd accidentally crossed back over to that path of distracted living and punch card politics.

Socket was little help, absorbed in his own world of hermitical electrocution, oblivious to the struggles of rejection Sylvester was dealing with. Socket didn't seem to suffer from loneliness, but whether that was a default setting or a calloused skin, one was never sure.

And so Sylvester pained and he pined and he dallianced himself with constant angry attention until he'd burned his wick of pain down to a stub, and when he'd finally reached past his limits, the normal torment no longer tickling, his eyes began to widen to what was outside his reach, the temptations beyond his skill level.

His subconscious had long ago found his new basket of bubbling oil, the zooplace perk HR never mentioned, an office surrounded by creatures that knew how to bite and mangle, to poison and puncture, who craved little beyond a vengeful desire to strike back at their captors.

And so, one night, Sylvester decided to take them up on it.

He had the place to himself after hours, the main-gate security guard slumbering away in the distance, but he still did his due diligence, lessons learned from Felicia long ago, ensuring no headlights pierced the parking lot, no office light signaled a late night, and when the cameras were all off and the doors were all locked, he meandered off toward his destiny.

"Is this really what I want?" he asked the brisk night air as he spent a dawdling tease listening to the chill, quiet darkness that creaked its silence across the zoo, occasional snortles and gurps echoing through the night.

He thought of the oil briefly, his last painful flourish of failure, but somehow it didn't weigh on him like it should have.

He was wedged firmly into the addict's moment of corrupted reflection and he knew it. That moment when you recognize you're about to fail yourself but still rush headfirst towards it, your energy focused not on saving yourself, but on turning off that pesky part of your brain that's desperately trying to stop you.

"Just one moment of rule-breaking recklessness to scratch the greater good," he tried to convince himself, before taking a final breath of the fresh night air and caving to inevitable temptation and barreling himself inside.

He ignored the mild and the meek, his attention focused on the biters and the blowhards, the pint-sized and powerful, the branch walkers and the disease bringers, whose exhibit signs hung with hot pepper fangs marking their powers and potency.

He skipped past the twig ants and the paper wasps, the hornets and the honey bees, the harvester ants and the tarantula hawks, buffet aspirations ignored in favor of a singular, succulent dessert, the temptation that had to be tasted, the mighty king of the hymenopteran insects, the bullet ants.

Bullet ants were not your normal sidewalk mound-makers, barely noticeable beyond their easily crushed villages and towns. No, the bullet ants were devil-fanged and demon-ridden, the midnight marauders, the sheep stealing beasts, and they called to him from their glass enclosure, tree-dwelling Sirens like his oil enchantress.

He watched them wander and weave, learning their penchants and personalities. These were his golden fleeces, the white whales of a lifetime, creatures destined to cross his path in this life or the next. They were the apex of what the planet had to offer, and they sat behind a lock he held the key to.

"What do you guys say? Want to help a fellow out?" he asked as he knocked, friendly and polite, imagining their feeble voices cheering him on, drowning out his own legitimate ones that pled for him to change course.

Sylvester had no idea what to expect, no concept of their power or willingness to assist, so he started with the first six in line, tiny wristbands seeming to indicate they'd been waiting since morning for their tickets.

He scooped them into a bag, their wrinkled hairy carapaces pitter-pattering around the plastic like the first attendees in a concert hall, their footsteps thunking off the walls as they scraped madly at their confinement, a palpable sense that they wouldn't need much encouragement.

"Are you excited for this? Do you get excited? I'm not really sure what spectrum of emotions ants go through, but I hope you enjoy yourselves."

Sylvester smiled at his new friends and playmates, elevated above their station of workplace wards, they were instant confidants and partners in crime and they'd be in his wedding party.

"I hope you're in a nibbly mood…" he said as he triple-clenched his arm, loosening muscles and circulating blood, before taking a final shot of courage and slipping his arm into the bag, strapping himself in, the escape route duct-taped around his elbow.

The ants seemed taken aback and confused, seeking some final confirmation that this succulent morsel being offered was, indeed, theirs for the stinging. Sylvester simply nodded and closed his eyes, his senses attuned to his arm, curious and hopeful.

The ants looked to one another and shrugged, curiosity bundling them toward the target. Some stepped and some leapt, settling on the scar-marked terrain, craters of injury and tripwires of arm hair scattered about, and when the last ant finally arrived, its pincers primed, its footing established, they nodded to each other and began their feast.

It didn't start with a modest nibble or a brief and curious taste, but a gluttonous sting, downright angry and insolent, decisive and painful, a small sextet symphony of strikes.

It took a moment for Sylvester to register what had happened; a moment for the neurons in his pain receptors to send the message along his spine to his brain, and his brain back out to his eyes and mouth and thoughts. A message of blistering, molten, instant, fever-inducing pain that staggered Sylvester to his knees in an instant.

"Ouch..." he said under his breath, as he looked down on swiftly swelling stings blistering into sight.

He wasn't sure he'd ever uttered the word before.

His eyes blurred and refocused and he saw the ants holding onto his arm like sailors on the ocean, their stingers dug deep trying to avoid shaking loose. If they owned cowboy hats, Sylvester was certain they would've been waving them.

Pulsing surges of awfulness throbbed in pounding pain through dozens of tiny wounds unexpectedly machine-gunning into existence across his arm as his eyes teared and his hands clenched, making the memory of the bubbling, boiling oil feel like a feather on his skin.

And then Sylvester felt something break, something dangle, bouncing loose from its mooring, unable to plug itself back in.

It was the car part you hear falling away before you know what it did.

What it meant.

What you lost.

Like a child with a treat, Sylvester had indulged himself past the point of failure.

He had broken his addiction.

*****

Sylvester crashed on the couch, his arm swollen and sore, dribbles of some strange liquid bibbling out of the bite marks. He'd lost count of the many tiny holes adrift in the chaos of swelling lumps that were spreading further and wider as time moved on. It hurt to move. Even to wiggle.

The ants had looked exhausted when he'd returned them to their habitat, their rumps sore and overworked, their bodies in welcome need of a nap, but still they smiled and waved their thanks, their compunctions punched, their own personal addictions satisfied.

Sylvester's were not.

His tears had only stopped a few minutes before, his ducts emptied, a combination of pills and ice finally numbing and slowing the spread of anguish as his mind wandered and wondered what'd happened.

The pain was unbearable and energetic, surging through him with an angry torment that tickled nothing. It didn't hold the happy satisfaction it once did. It was agony with no ecstasy.

But it wasn't just pain he felt. He also felt an absence.

It was awakening to a missing limb, phantom feelings permeating and teasing you with a sense of incomplexity you can't quite place. Even as a toddler gamboling around the playground, leaping from swings and face-planting under jungle gyms, Sylvester remembered that strange feeling of enjoyment buried beneath the scrapes and scratches.

He could not remember ever feeling the absence of something so integral to him.

It was a memorable moment, the life-altering point you think back on, forever frustrated by the poor decision-making of your past.

He still hoped it would pass, a hiccup of his super powers brought on by a cold, an infiltration of some poison into his system that disguised a knack that would inevitably return, but he wasn't confident, lost in the unchartered waters of unhappy pain that he didn't know how to deal with.

As with most problems in his life, he tried to attack it with personal violence.

He noticed a conclave of forkroaches meeting en masse, an overthrow of his dictatorial ways seemingly being plotted, and he took the ringleader, a majestic forkroach Socket had made for his birthday, and squeezed it hard, the tines pushing deep into his skin as he hoped to inject his addiction back into himself.

It did nothing but hurt. Normal, arrogant, angry hurt. There was nothing to tease him, nothing to tempt him.

"Maybe it's the 'what' that matters?" he thought to himself as he got to his feet, his arm dripping ice, and began to wander, looking for inflictions to tease himself with.

He circled Socket's playhouse, touching everything he could, hoping for shocks and stutters that would defibrillate his obsession back into being, but the few he got were meaningless sizzles, brief burns and surprises with no lasting effect.

He found Poke, happily napping away in the living room on a bare stretch of floor devoid of oddball collectibles and electrified knickknacks. The porcupine greeted him happily as Sylvester bear-hugged him with love, the quills diving deep, and he held and he hoped, as if love itself would rekindle what he needed, but still there was nothing. An absence of even the knowledge that it ever existed; that his addiction was anything more than a dream unproducible in life.

He moved on to other tests, other inklings, bouncing from splinters to Legos to fingers in doorjambs, all with only a hollow silence returned.

And then Sylvester cried, not from the pain slowly denumbing through his arm, but for the loss of his most passionate friend, the most personal part of his life, the grift that had kept him going.

His pain.

CHAPTER 38
STRONGER THAN A SNOWFLAKE

Natalie lay curled and castled in a cornered nook of her bookstore, fuzzled in fleeced pants and a comfy shirt, picking at plaster casts while she stared out the window. Snowflakes flitted and flubbed on the wind, teasing the sill and melting after a moment's rest. She watched as each one came down, its life full of cold potential and freezing energy, only to be snuffed out by the cruel warmth of the strange manmade creations awaiting it on Earth.

"Am I stronger than a snowflake?" she asked to nobody in particular. She talked out loud to herself a lot these days. Nobody seemed to mind.

She looked down on her broken body and cast-ridden limbs where her fidgety fingers had long since moused small nibbles in exposed edges, the surest sign that boredom was within reach. She'd already picked clean through two arm casts that had to be replaced, but luckily the behemoth wrapping her hip and thigh was so large and thick that no amount of wandering fingers could scrape away enough to matter.

She was healing slowly, but steadily, as she always did, life's cruel way of preparing her for the next failure it had in mind.

She'd been free from the wheelchair for days, the casts scheduled to be removed the next week, and in the interim she'd begun to take advantage of her more mobile self, slow-lapping around the store and clawing back her life of shelving books and dusting spiders.

"Physical therapy for stay-ins," she liked to say.

She didn't go out, and if anything stayed further from the door, sometimes leaving it unlocked rather than approach it, fearful the outside world would reach in and pull her out.

There was an aspect of her future that both enticed and repelled her, a Stockholm prisoner who'd tasted freedom only to be paroled back in. These days she saw the path paved with gold and the path paved with risk and interwoven between them the path of least resistance.

On her lap sat *The Hobbit*, her favorite book, about an adventureless fellow who decides to give one a try. She always appreciated and admired old Mr. Baggins for taking such an unexpected leap into life, and now here she was, herself burrowed away, having taken that leap briefly and having nothing to show for it but scars and medical bills.

She frowned, jealous envy creeping out, "Lucky hobbit…you had it easy with only trolls and dragons…no staircases in Middle Earth, huh?"

She looked back out the window, trying to spot optimism in the alleyway. She saw it hiding behind a dumpster, nervously waving back.

Natalie smiled to herself, happy at least that it still existed.

Maybe the treasure, as Bilbo had found, was not in the gold that they brought back, but in the memories of the adventure? And she did have memories. Deep, wonderful, heart-pounding memories she treasured immensely. Her adventures didn't involve dwarfs and goblins, but pumpkin hills and carnival slides, hospital chats and deep-fried pancakes.

"Were the adventures worth the cost?" she asked aloud as her anxiety looked ahead to a closeted life.

She thought of Sylvester, her fellow adventurer, and his humor and passion for all things pointy that the world could offer.

She'd had boyfriends over the years, school chums and bibliophiles who'd found the store, but they never lasted past the first few injuries. They each had their own reason. Too much guilt. Too much fear. Too much responsibility. There was one who simply wanted to collect her.

But none had been quite like Sylvester, curious and challenging and wanting to sidekick along for the fun of it. She found it intoxicating that someone would not only accept her for her own bit of oddness, but was jealous. Nobody had ever been jealous before.

And where had that intoxication gotten her? Beaten to a pulp and chair-bound for months. Were those moments of adventurous bliss worth the pain? Probably not. But maybe. And she had gotten a t-shirt out of it.

She looked down and watched as her toes wiggled happily. They seemed to be working properly once again, no worse for wear. Like any injury it took time for the wound to heal and the confidence to return.

It was then that Grandma Norris wandered by, seemingly distracted and in conversation with an apparition only she could see, a purchase perched on the moment, her salesmanship on display.

"Two bits! Brand new. That's a great price! Even includes that new Krakatoa!" she was arguing.

"Gran?" asked Natalie, spooking her grandmother into losing eye-contact with her imaginary buyer.

"Oh, hello dear," she said as her head swiveled briefly, wondering where her patron had gone. "I almost sold that set of map-making books, but the gentleman seems to have vanished...such a nice hat, too..."

Natalie smiled sadly at her grandmother, age continuing to take its toll on her in strange ways. "It's OK. I like having those in the store."

Her grandmother smiled sweetly at her, a belletristic love between bookswains. "Always the dreamerous adventurer. Always loved your maps."

Natalie's head dipped, "I'm no adventurer..."

"Of course you are! Always were. Injury-prone, sure, but adventurous to the core."

"Are you confusing me with Grandpa again?"

"I don't confuse anyone!" said Grandma Norris with a suspicious glare that accused Natalie of convalescent thinking.

"I don't remember ever feeling adventurous..."

"Bah! Too many falls on the noggin knocked it outta you. But I remember! Book forts and treasure maps! Always planning, you were. Escapades and adventures! Such a mess to clean up... Do you know how many hardbacks you scribbled cartography in? We lost count!"

Natalie regarded her curiously, uncertain whose memory this was and if it could be accurate. She certainly didn't remember drawing maps and making book forts, but that didn't mean it wasn't a casualty of youthful repression.

Grandma Norris suddenly perked up, spying down the aisle a bobbing and familiar spectral hat, and she headed off towards it, their conversation forgotten, her shuffling feet wappling into the distance.

Natalie looked after her, a forlorn smile on her face at the uncertainty of memory. The subconscious was an interesting beast sometimes, wasn't it?

And as if on cue, her mind drifted back to her adventures with Sylvester and a forgotten memory clicked into place. A memory of a winded voice of reason begging her not to descend; to not risk it. A voice of reason that was overruled.

Now here, removed from the events, it all seemed as clear as day.

She'd been safe at the top of the stairs. It wasn't Sylvester's reckless ways, but her own adventurous spirit that was responsible for her fall.

Her tongue slipped between her teeth, tasting the emptiness where her broken tooth had once lived, a subtle reminder of her own undoing, and she pondered more of her life and her memories and what truths they still hid from her.

She looked out the window and watched as the snowflakes continued their fluffy, plodding fall to the sill, a few of them starting to stick, their fallen comrades paving the way for their arrival. She wondered what their goals were and if they were content to simply pile upon one another or if they dreamed of something more.

She watched their dance and then opened the window, letting the flakes filter in and frolic on her skin, a far more exciting adventure for them than looking in from the outside.

CHAPTER 39
SOCKET TRIES TO FIX SYLVESTER

Socket clamped down on the car battery and let loose a stream of electric anger that coursed and twizzled, arcing along Sylvester's body in its mad dash to reach the ground.

"Anything?" he asked.

Sylvester lifted his hand and stared as small wisps of smoke twisted and drifted away. It seemed like it belonged to a recently escaped cadaver, scarred and stitched together, faint red lines and wrinkled white flesh signaling its unfinished medical history. He played coy with his hand for a moment, lulling it into a false sense of security, before suddenly jabbing it with a fork.

"Oww! Damnit. No, nothing."

Socket crossed off 'car battery'. "Ok, another infliction to cross off the list. Moving on..."

The two of them sat in the kitchen, still surrounded by the day's activities; a spent defibrillator tossed in a corner, pliers and burned forks lining the table, the tattoo kit and a variety of rented tools piled in the sink. They'd spent hours attempting to spark Sylvester's habit back into being and thus far had simply collected blown fuses and scorch marks.

It'd been almost a month since the bullet ant game, and while the pain had faded, his habit had not yet returned. Whatever Sylvester had done, whatever breaker he'd tripped, he'd still not found a way to turn back on.

For weeks he sat sadly and silently, poking and prodding himself, hoping for a sudden surge of surprise, a spark of happiness, a pinch of awakening. Instead, he felt only numbness, surrounded by phantom feelings that could never be found.

Socket's skillset was limited, but focused, and they'd pushed it to the limit over the course of the afternoon. He looked down at his list and its bumbling rows of electrified ideas, almost all of which had been tried and crossed off. They'd even mixed in some of the basics like sharp rocks and rug burns and paper cuts, none of which had worked their magic. Sylvester had even run the Halloween course twice, touching everything in reach like an escaped OCD patient after an earthquake, a final electrified attempt to reignite whatever pilot light existed within him.

"What about an electrical outlet?" Socket asked as he hefted a 2x4. "Stab it with a fork and I'll smack your hand away after a few seconds, cool?"

"Not sure I want to go quite so 'last resort' just yet..."

"Well I'm out of ideas," said Socket as he tossed the jumper cables and the 2x4 on the table and threw up his hands in frustration.

"Where's your creative spark?" asked Sylvester.

"Listen pal, my creativity is limited to tattoos and cross-wiring doorbells, not rekindling weird addictions in bug-hugging idiots. And speaking of idiots, I still need to rewire the Halloween course today while it's nice out, so I can't waste my entire afternoon on you."

Sylvester bristled at Socket before grabbing the cables and clamping down on the battery, giving himself another hard shock.

"Come on man, don't drain it!"

"Damnit! Why won't anything work?!" said Sylvester, as he kicked off the clamp.

"Why not embrace the break?" asked Socket as he started coiling the cables and casually shifting the battery out of reach. "There could be some good to come out of this, right?"

"No."

"Optimistic thinking here!"

"C'mon man! I don't live for the job perks or the pretty flower smells or some stack of kids you drive to ballet class. I live for one thing and one thing only and it's not working, which in turn means I'm not working."

"Maybe that's life's way of suggesting you change it up? Do you remember that time we had a blackout and I thought about giving it all up? It's like that."

They both stared at each other for a moment before breaking into caustic fits of laughter.

"Oh, that was a good one," said Sylvester, wiping tears from his eyes. "I needed a good laugh."

"What about the ants?" asked Socket, the idea flitting in. "Why not head back and offer 'em up a second course? Maybe it's a frog prince kinda deal? Kiss the ant queen, get your powers back?"

"I was tempted, believe me."

"But…?"

Sylvester paused, realizing with frightening clarity what he was about to say, mumbling his voice into a whisper, "I'm scared it'll hurt."

Socket's head cricked to the side, confusion breaking into his conscious as he absorbed what Sylvester had almost certainly just said for the first time in his life.

"Excuse me? Did I really just hear you say that?"

"Yeah, no shit, right?" said Sylvester, shaking his head. "But you can't imagine those ants, you really can't. Did I tell you I cried? I can't remember the last time I cried."

"Jeez, you're such a wussy without your binky…"

"It's like I'm stuck in someone else's life and I can't operate the controls."

Socket glanced around at the dangling wires littered about like a robotic autopsy, confirming to himself that at least he was still assigned to the correct life. He hoped that whatever was wrong with Sylvester wasn't contagious.

"Listen pal, I'll do anything I can. You know that. But there's a point where I'm just electrocuting you for giggles. Now, as your friend, I'm fine with that. I like electrocuting you. But it's not gonna fix whatever's wrong unless you're holding a radioactive spider or some magic beans."

"I'd kill for some magic beans right about now," said Sylvester as he looked down on his scar covered arm and his crackling tattoos, years of abuse having left him with a chronic soreness that now rudely teased him.

"I'm sorry man, but there's only one direction you can take from here, and you know what it is. You need an expert, and for that you're gonna have to pay the piper her penance."

"Yeah, I know…" said Sylvester, a sullen feeling of personal corruption seeping in.

"Maybe she'll be in a helpful mood?"

"I doubt it. She'll probably charge by the lashing."

"Think she'll go overboard?"

"Without a doubt. You don't shove your head down a lion's throat expecting a Swedish massage."

CHAPTER 40
FELICIA GOES TO THE MALL

Felicia flicked her finger, launching another steel ball bearing down into the mall, the vast American wasteland of layered shops encased in glass and advertising.

She watched as it dropped two stories before it bounced and cascaded, caroming off carts and indoor awnings, finally angling off a pretzel vendor and beaning an old woman in the head, knocking her to the ground and sprawling her coffee around her.

"Oohh, extra point for the latte!" Felicia said to herself as she made a mark in her notebook, happily satisfied with the luck of her aim, pleasant childhood memories drifting up of tokens falling off arcade game ledges.

She took aim and flicked again, launching her final salvo and watching as it bounced itself harmlessly down the thoroughfare before catching a bad edge and hobbling itself into a roll, skittering away into a corner.

"Such a sad note to end on..." Felicia said with a scowl, her missile wasted, before emerging unnoticed from her perch behind a seasonal sunglass shop.

She had gamboled along for hours now playing smaller games and killing time, a balletic dance of destruction, bubblingly building and pacing her day towards a crescendo of fun. Patience and delayed gratification were prerequisites for her doctoral program.

Freedom was fun these days, a lion let loose in the pasture of a land without wolves. She'd already knocked two people down escalators, kicked out the canes on three retirees, spent a half hour screaming at a salesman who'd done nothing but wish her a nice day, and wasted an hour slipping tacks into shoe soles, an anxiety-indulging nudging of her previous downfall that only made the game taste sweeter.

"Where to go, what to do, and who to do it to..." she mumbled to herself as her eyes danced over shop signs. She only had a few minutes left for a final appetizer before the dinner bell rang and the main course was served.

Her wandering feet suggested the kitchen and cutlery store, lobster crackers and clam knives always fun to pramble about with, but they were overruled when the smell of coffee twisted by, a distracting temptation of boiling potential teasing into her conscious. There were some songs she just couldn't help but sing along to.

Felicia sidled in, a well-advertised (but poorly caffeinated) hipster destination for those who wanted status and attention more than the addictive fix of a tasty brew. The walls were papered with fake brick and coffee-house kitsch, while elegant and teetering small-tall tables lounged about like weekend flamingos.

She ordered herself a blazingly hot coffee and brutalized it with sugar, a beaten down beverage that no longer wanted life, before surveying the room, calculations flitting by as she took in her playground.

"Now who, who, who, looks like they want to wear their coffee?"

There were a variety of options to choose from, ranging from the schoolmarm grading papers to the recovering junkie nursing a hangover, but instinct hooked her hard when she spotted a tall and slender cup, topless and piping with wisps of steam twisting through the air in escape. It sat precariously perched and teased for a tumble, an unleveled coaster mismanaged to integrity issues.

The coffee's owner was an arrogant man with an arrogant face, a basement haircut and a tilting nose, the snobbish look of someone who deserved far less than a pleasant cup of coffee on a chill winter's day.

A Cheshire grin spread across Felicia's face as her targeting system flickered to life, centering on points of impact and temperature patterns. For a twinkling moment her conscience joined the party, only to sit down and wave from the stands, a tub of popcorn in hand.

Her body moved on its own, smooth and silent, a breeze whipping up to the table, before culminating in a stumble that made the man hop from his seat, a chauvinistic savior at the ready. There was a look of actor's shock on her face as she fell, but hers was a stumble of calculation that let her direct a teetering coffee at a wobbly target, her fingertips tipping the coffee to guide it, instinct aiming and angling it, splattering it across him, his fashion instantly stained from business casual to crunchy bohemian.

"Owww!" the man shrieked as he tried to dance the heat out of his pants.

"I'm so sorry!" Felicia exclaimed in apology, reaching in with a handful of napkins as she leaned her own coffee on the same corrupt coaster, a brief smirk of evil twisting on her lips.

"It's fine, it's fine," stammered the man, trying to maintain his visage of 1800s handlebar masculinity.

Felicia dabbed at his shirt, seemingly trying to help, her napkins flashing as the man let her hands wander, reading a flirtatious interest into her actions. She smiled up at him, sweet and delicate, before suddenly reaching, seeming to spot something, her napkin-hand swinging wildly as it knocked her coffee off the same coaster at the same target, a second sticky splash that seemed certain to burn anything the first one had missed.

The man wailed and screeched, waving and slapping her away, cringing and cowering from her deadly assistance, his eyes wide in terror as his tears leapt to their death.

Felicia was already stepping back, bowing as she gushed pleasantries of apology, the pick-pocketing gypsy grasping her bag handles as she slipped away into the crowd, lost in the distraction as a smile spread across her face.

She'd barely left the coffee shop when, as if on cue, she heard the clock chime and knew it was time for her finale, the swan song reward for her day of undelayed gratification.

Felicia giggled, excitement bubbling as her mind danced, her grin growing wide as she stretched her bellicose muscles, anticipation throbbing in her veins as adrenaline replaced blood. She pulled on blinders as she zigzagged across the mall, passing easy marks and teetering targets, a skip to her step as she focused on future fun.

The food court was half empty by the time she arrived, the draw of unhealthy extravagance at its afternoon lull. She didn't bother walking in, instead leaning against a railing on the far side of the escalator canyon, her final game available from a distance.

"Quite the crowd, quite the crowd," she commended herself as she took in the late lunch cattle and their piles of tray food, her self-discipline rewarding her patience.

She squinted towards her audience of dinner tables, silhouetted wires dripping beneath them, diner lessons learned and long since improved upon, a dozen petulant pizza lunches and a game of musical chairs giving her the cover she needed. Sylvester had told her not to do it blindly. Prison taught her how to target.

She took a casual glance around, a safety check for sanity as unobservant eyes napped away their attention, while the taste of infliction teased her lips, preparing to let the monster within her twist and prance.

Her fingers danced a drumbeat on the railing as her hand slipped into her pocket and around a small remote. "It's a good thing you're not here Vest, because I doubt you'd approve…" she said with a smirk as she pressed the button and looked out on the crowded court.

A dozen tables sparked in unison, launching a synchronized set of shrieks from their tenants, a strange cacophonic display of preplanned brilliance and violence.

Felicia beamed, a spoiled child being pelted with Christmas gifts, excitement vibes branching through her nervous system as she saw food fall and soda spill and children cry, permanent scarring and a fear of food courts now burned into their juvenile psyches.

"I'm getting downright devious," she thought proudly as echoing screams bounced in the background, a wild wail of anger at the injustice of the world piercing their thoughts.

But then Felicia paused, her finger slipping off the button, her mouth crinkling in concern as her subconscious mind poked out its head and flagged her down.

She had finally ascended to a level of evil that she'd never known, and even now, she looked on with a dappling of concern and second guessing, her immediate happiness followed by the aftertaste of regret and embarrassment.

Was she really this evil? Someone who injured children and the elderly? It was one thing to poke and prod, but quite another to cripple and maim.

And at that moment she realized that she'd lost herself, finally cut adrift from morals and ethics and a sense of how dark her actions had become. Her mind clouded with confusion as an absent conscience returned, a long vacation retreat that'd gone unnoticed.

"Is this who you want to be?" it asked her.

She didn't have a response.

But life did.

It was then that her phone rang, a vibration of destiny that pulled her back from her rare moment of introspection.

It was Sylvester.

CHAPTER 41
FELICIA TRIES TO FIX SYLVESTER

Felicia was leaning impatiently against the hardware store window, her fingers distractedly flicking the air, hoping to swat flies that foolishly wandered within reach while her mind plotted the potential malice within sight.

There wasn't much to see, which in its own way made the game all the more challenging and fun. There were uneven curbs and potholed crosswalks and fast-moving cars, all of which seemed to indicate that gentle nudges and elbow shoves were the convenient currency of the realm.

But Felicia preferred the creative, the unexpected, and focused her eyes on the often ignored. The dangling holiday decorations and festive electric lights, the photogenic snowmen and mistletoe draped doorways. She chuckled at the faded reindeer littering the common and sensed an angry potential nestled inside them. The herd had stories, she could tell, but she didn't speak plastic to hear them.

Lots of opportunities, lots of choices. This was going to be a fun place to live.

She spotted Sylvester, slow-walking the sidewalk, a slump-shouldered plodding that dragged his confidence along behind him, the hobbled has-been who needed help. He didn't seem her type these days.

"Hey, 'Licia..." he said with a half-hearted wave as he approached.

"Hi Vest," she giggled, smuggling her thoughts away, "So the punctured pincushion comes back pleading for a professional..."

He smiled crooked, hopeful and nervous, "I appreciate the alliterative appointment."

Felicia regarded him, cross-eyed and doubting, but uncertain, "This better not be some pathetic attempt to get back together..."

"Scout's honor. I just want to use you for your bloodthirsty elbow grease."

Felicia smirked, inflated, "Go on..."

"I broke myself..." he began, squinting into the sky as if it held answers. "Got too greedy with a game I didn't understand and now the tickle's gone. I can't seem to get it back. Tried everything. Even had Socket go to town with everything but the full grid. Nothing doing. I'm out of ideas. Figured maybe you had some I hadn't thought of?"

Felicia pondered him, powerless and dejected, a failed knight reduced to a squire. She couldn't help but look on him with pity, the lion with the sharp teeth beginning to understand the drawback of dentures.

"How'd you do it?" she asked.

"Ant bites," said Sylvester.

"Oh, how low the mighty have fallen…"

"Don't knock it 'til you try it. Easily the most painful thing I've ever experienced."

"Really? More than the oil?" she asked, suddenly intrigued.

"More than the oil."

She gave him a respectful nod, filing away a mental note for future research. "I can't say you aren't inventive."

Sylvester looked sheepishly at his feet as his voice wobbled, anxieties of hope and fear mixing together, "So you up for trying? No strings involved."

"How about rope? Can I use rope?" she asked.

"Sure."

"OK, I'll take a stab. I can appreciate a good challenge."

"Let's leave out the knives."

"Wimp," Felicia smirked as she opened the door beside the hardware store, gesturing him up the stairway.

Sylvester couldn't help but steal a glance at the bookstore across the way, before finally stepping inside.

Felicia followed a step behind, her own quizzical glance having followed his.

A 1960s soundtrack emanated from a 1990s movie as she opened the door to her apartment, gesturing Sylvester inside. He made it a few feet before grinding to a halt; Felicia's post-prison apartment was a frighteningly different world without Sylvester's personality to offset it.

The kitchen table was littered with batteries of all shapes and sizes, solar cells and chargers working overtime, while a pile of dog biscuits and a lathe sat beside a few open boxes of similarly colored cookies. A pegboard against the wall dangled an inspiringly large set of tools Sylvester had never seen and doubted the hardware store below was even capable of special ordering. There was a weed-whacker poking out of the cabinet where normal people kept dishware, just above the fruit bowl full of paint-stripping drill bits, which in turn sat above a drawer that was rattling about as its contents struggled to escape.

Sylvester's eyes went wide as a flutter of nervous butterflies tried to escape, but Felicia had already closed the door, trapping them inside.

"You seem to have taken up some new hobbies..." he began.

"Nah, same hobbies. More effort."

An envelope sealing machine was whirring off to the side, a set of round sanding wheels attached, sharpening the envelope edges as they spun through and fell into a box. Sylvester's eyes pointed towards it as his head nodded.

"I do coupon mailers now," she replied. "I actually make a profit off those!"

His eyes continued to wander, pausing on old photos of them nestled on the shelves and the unexpected smattering of forkroaches scattered about the apartment, the missing Entwives to his collection of Ents.

Felicia watched as he took it all in, a mischievous grin of malicious pride on her face.

"Nice place, eh?"

"Yeah…" Sylvester stammered, "…you've done a lot with it."

"Thanks!" she replied, joining him in admiration of her interior design choices before turning to business. "OK, catch me up. What've you tried? Pins? Prods? Punching bag practice? Shocks and stubbed toes? Kickboxing with vice grips? Hot coffee leg waxing? What did what?"

"I tried it all."

"Rope burn?"

"Made of sisal and tied to a car bumper."

"Salt in a wound?"

"Both iodized and kosher."

"Sharkskin massage?"

"Couldn't afford the real deal, but I *did* visit the aquarium and vigorously pet one."

"Ankle-twisting dance moves?"

"Pulled three muscles, but I did master the windmill."

Felicia leaned into her chin, an analytical air of studying his puzzle, her body twisted into that ponderous posture TV show detectives use when preparing to solve a case, before clapping her hands together, "Then let's get creative!"

She slid open a deep drawer and began to rummage, pulling out a strange variety of odd implements, some of which Sylvester recognized from his hospital wish list. A few items looked like kitchen utensils that'd been bred for combat with a lawnmower. Others seemed likely remnants of 1800s farming equipment that had been repurposed for the Inquisition.

"I don't even know…" began Sylvester, a strange type of fear coursing through him as he realized how different this version of Felicia had become.

"…what they are? Me neither! Great finds, right??"

Sylvester gave a nervous thumbs-up.

Felicia held up one that looked like an egg whisk, but with pointy ends and serrated edges, "I made this one myself!"

"You don't say…"

Felicia smiled, deviously proud.

"OK, hop on the bed. Face down. No shirt," she began, before handing him a small rubber dog bone, "…and you may want to bite down on this."

Sylvester flopped onto the bed, anxious and uncertain, a sense of clattering fear circulating through him as Felicia began dropping her ammunition on the mattress beside him.

A minute later she straddled his waist and dug her nails into his back, greeting her favorite cratered scars with a loving whisper, "Oh hello my pretties, how I've missed you so…"

Felicia's fingers trailed off over his scar arm, testing the crackled oilskin, before wandering into the scandalous site of the ant bites, small marks still strangely visible as if the ants had signed their handiwork.

"These must've been big ants..."

"Size of your thumb," he said.

Felicia nodded, raising one of hers to eye level in measuring respect.

"You ready?' she asked.

Sylvester took a final, resonating breath, knowing that this was his final, desperate gamble.

"Do your worst."

Felicia grinned and threw him a batter's salute before laying into him like a demon on a sugar high.

She squeezed and she kneaded, soft hands abrading the skin off anything they touched. She moved from fingers and nails to crimpers and clamps. She tried wood glue and whips, pry bars and pliers, the mound of cast-aside equipment growing on the floor as they went. She went through her entire repertoire, bludgeoning and beating, scratching and skewering.

Sylvester took it all, whimpering beneath her, desperation letting him ignore the unpleasant pain, memory his only hint there was hope, shock and surprise his forced anesthetic. He gave Felicia her time to work, hope carving out his patience, a barrel-chested faith that a corner would be turned, a knob twisted, and that he'd sense some hum or tickle as his world flickered back to life.

But there was nothing, not even an inkling or a snore of restive existence. Nothing but an increasingly alarming amount of pain and anguish and blood loss.

He lasted an hour before he caved, his body numb to her attempts, his small crumbs of hope pecked away and forgotten.

"I gotta stop..." he muttered between shallow sips of breath.

"Whatdya mean stop? I only just started! It's barely been an hour!" Felicia growled as she tossed the latest toy into the pile and dismounted, slapping his back as she went. "What's wrong with you, Vest?"

"I told you, I broke something," said Sylvester as his sore body curled itself into a husk, his back bruised and bleeding, his legs whipped and smacked, his armpits poked and prodded, his moans too exhausted to emerge. Even his eyelids hurt. He had taken it all, unconditional confidence in Felicia's abilities regardless of her methods. But nothing had worked.

"You made it sound like you had a splinter, not a rod through the head…" Felicia mumbled as she dug into a cabinet full of lawn tools and began ticking off new ideas, a second wind emerging as she gathered more gear.

"Whatever's wrong with me…it's not getting better," he said as he forced himself up, shaking the pain and numbness from his limbs as he reached for his shirt, a sudden urge to escape competing with a desire for immobility.

"C'mon Vest, one more round and we can break for dinner. I have so many more things I want to try! We didn't even get to the sandpaper and steel wool. You always loved steel wool! And what about the belt sander? You don't want it to feel left out, do you?"

Sylvester struggled to his feet, angling himself toward the door, "I can't take anymore, Felicia. Thanks for trying. I think I just need to find a good morgue to lie down in…"

Felicia stepped between him and the door, her arm out in a policeman's posture, "Nonono, you don't get away that easily. That's not how this works. You can't wind me up like that and then leave. You leave when I say so; when I've tried everything. This is a full-service establishment!"

"Felicia…come on. It's not gonna work. I'm too far gone."

"But that's no reason to take away my fun!" Felicia shrieked, brazen and belligerent and determined to collect her payment, the schizophrenic leg breaker to her own lousy loan shark.

Sylvester's mouth twisted into a sad look of disappointment, "I'm just a toy to you, aren't I?"

"Of course! And a deliciously fun toy at that. Or at least, you were."

The clattering reality of the moment was not lost on him. She was right of course, on both counts. He'd always been a toy to her, and these days, a broken one at that.

"Come on, Vest, what we had? That wasn't love. That was mutual codependency. You turned my knobs, I turned yours. That's all most couples have."

"Is that why you broke it off? You needed new knobs to turn?"

"No," she said with a hint of sadness. "I needed knobs within reach, and you weren't."

Sylvester's mouth crinkled in restrained heartbreak, holding back his emotions. Maybe a prison sentence wasn't the only thing that split them apart.

"I'm sorry, Felicia…" he finally said, stepping around her and out the door.

Felicia stared, dumbfounded and confused at the rejection and uncertain how to proceed. It took a moment for reality to settle before her voice returned. "Get back here you little pincushion! You owe me!" screamed Felicia as she hurled a forkroach across the room, embedding it in the door behind him. "You better not come back begging for round two!"

Her banshee shriek made Sylvester cringe as he hobbled himself down the stairs, desperate to escape, an honest fear that she was moments from bursting through the door in axe-wielding chase, and with each step of freedom his fear shifted to uneasy regret, knowing full well that he'd just set a trap someone else was going to set off.

Felicia continued to scowl at the door, her voice dropping to a mumbling rage of adolescent fury as she regretted not owning axes. "I waste hours getting worked up and then you leave like that? No. No! You can't give me an itch and not let me scratch it!"

She heard the downstairs door clatter and ran to the window, her teeth grit in constipated anger as she prepared to hurl screaming tirades of profanity at him.

But before her lungs could erupt Sylvester did the strangest thing.

He stopped.

Right there on the sidewalk.

He stopped and he stared.

Not back at her apartment, but across the common. He was staring at the bookstore.

Felicia glanced over, curious if it had burst into flame, but it looked the same as always, dark and arrogantly educated. Sylvester was already shuffling away when she looked back, his eyes bouncing between his feet and the bookstore.

There were only so many longing looks he could throw before a fishy smell wafted up to her window, and it was then, in that moment, that everything clicked into place, and Felicia finally knew what a 'literary klutz' was, and where to find one.

CHAPTER 42
THE BOOKSTORE BATTLE

Felicia stared across the common at the bookstore nestled beside the ice cream shop, a sense of vindictive jealousy flowing through her, an unsatisfied itch still begging to be scratched.

The store looked old and awkward, a relic from centuries long past, a wooden edifice in a sea of siding. Few people seemed to notice the store or enter it, and the ones who did exited moments later, glazed looks indicating it wasn't the kind of best-seller-bookstore they'd hoped it would be.

She watched as a little old lady wobbled out of the store in deep conversation with herself, a senile geriatric dalliance chuckling through Felicia's mind that this was who Sylvester had replaced her with. The little old lady spun in circles three times before finally calibrating her direction and careening off into the street, tires screeching in avoidance while she happily waddled through traffic.

Felicia grinned at the bookstore's potential as she plucked and packed her favorite toys, setting out a few minutes later, a Swiss Army Knife of prepared infliction.

She slow-stalked across the common disguised in tourist actions, shopping bags dangling from fingertips while upward eyes took in the skyline, before sidling up to the store, fingers tickling the moldings as her eyes squinted in at the drowsy darkness. The place looked like it'd been closed for decades.

A wry smirk of anticipatory excitement spread across her face as an afternoon of wasted aggression and accidental detective work had rewardingly convinced her that somewhere in this store sat her prize, a romantic nemesis and injury-riddled klutz custom designed for her to trifle and toy with.

She vacuumed in deep breaths of chilly air as she tried to steady her wild smirk, and with a final heft of breath she gave the door a shove and barreled her ego inside, following it into the enemy's nest.

The door jingled its jangle as it opened, a dustless gust twisting inside before turning around and heading back out; this was clearly not a place for illiterate breezes that were afraid of the dark.

The silence of the store won the first battle as the overly flammable contents absorbed the ambience from outside. Stacks of books littered the tables and stands near the doorway, intimidating and old, reminiscent of Smithsonian libraries and flea market dowagers. Felicia's hand slid over a nearby book, a soft layer of bunnies rushing off with a touch, plugging her nose with must and dust. This place was not a franchise, she was certain.

Her eyes scanned the gargoyled ceilings and bookends, flicking past the squinting blinds that never fully opened. The floor squeaked as slants of sunlight filled with pufts of dust as she slowly walked the aisles, listening to the air cycle and the wood creak. The sound of old, thick pages flipped softly on the air, pulling her toward the center, and she followed, happily curious what she would find.

She emerged in view of a small counter, an old-fashioned register propped on top, stacks of leather-bound books crisscrossing in a wall of returned knowledge. Behind the counter sat Natalie, a side-bun of twizzled hair peeking out, a lone unused sling her final hurdle to recovery.

Felicia's eyes thinned, measuring and weighing her. The girl looked more than a little canaried, small and slight, thin and brittle, with the look of something meant to be crushed in a magician's trick. She wore a thin and wispy dress that hugged her legs (which were themselves layered with leg warmers), as well as a pair of gloves and the type of headgear you'd expect to see on someone prone to seizures or triathlons. And strangely out of place, a fluffless mismatch from the rest, the girl wore a simple t-shirt with a pangolin in a bib, happily eating pancakes.

Felicia pulled on a face of ignorant interest as she approached the counter, perfectly playing the part of the passing shopper.

"Hello..." said Felicia with a sudden inclination to offer up a poisoned apple.

"Oh, hello!" said Natalie as she looked up from her novel and slipped in a bookmark. She was smiling and pleasant, bookish and angle chinned, with glasses rounding her eyes and giving off a sense of spelunking. "What can I help you with?" she asked with a tilt of her head, one ear clearly not as good as the other.

"Oh, you wear glasses, too!" erupted Felicia, the excitement getting to her.

"Excuse me?"

"I like your glasses."

"Oh, thanks! They're thick because they're bulletproof."

"You are a darling little creature..." smiled Felicia.

"Can I help you with something?" Natalie offered again, cocking her head in confusion, unsure why this strange woman was saying strange things.

Felicia's eyes darted around, processing acceptable requests in a den of gilded pages.

"I'm looking for a gift," she lied, a slight smirk dancing on her dimples. "I was hoping to find something...quaint."

"Sure, did you have anything in mind? We mostly deal with old books here. First editions, hardbacks and the like. Did you want to get a favorite of something?"

"I'm not sure, but I'll know it when I see it!" Felicia replied, knowing and embracing the irritation of indecisive shoppers.

Natalie hobbled to the ground and reached for a cane, propping herself up as she shuffled toward a far wall. "We have some great gift books..." she began cheerfully, her steps echoing as she wobbled down an alley of books.

"This almost seems too easy," thought Felicia, "A fish in a shot glass, more than a barrel." But who was she to argue?

She followed a step behind, smiling and nodding while she ignored whatever Natalie was saying about dustcovers and bindings, some doddering talk of bookish boredom. She was busy plotting and planting as they walked, nestling future attacks while worker eyes weren't watching.

She began by slipping a pouch of foul-smelling fish into the heating vent, followed by a light drizzling of olive oil on the floorboards, before finishing with a small box of wasps nestled snuggly into a gap between books, their doorway slid open with her thumb, before quickstepping into Natalie's wake as she rounded the corner.

She hadn't missed much, Natalie now rambling on about *Moby Dick*, "...we sold out of that edition last week, but we've still got seven other versions, the earliest going back to the 1930 Lakeside Press Edition, but that's a bit costly. If you're just looking for a reading copy we've got a 1981 Oxford University in decent shape..."

Felicia nodded in blissful ignorance and counterfeit competence.

"This is the gift section," said the girl as she pondered a shelf, one hand on her chin while the other balanced her weight on the cane. "If *Moby Dick* doesn't grab you, maybe a first edition of *The Silmarillion* or *Uncle Tom's Cabin?*"

Felicia feigned interest, her fingertips dancing over spine titles while her mind was busy planning. She wasn't bothering to pace herself, her thoughts set on quantity of injury more than quality.

"No, nothing here is grabbing me," she finally said, turning with a casually swift kick, an appetizer-attempt to knock the load-bearing cane from Natalie's hand.

But what happened next surprised them both.

Felicia's foot did indeed make quick contact, but the effect was quite different, the cane pivoting on Natalie's wrist and wheeling about overhead, coming down hard on Felicia's head as stars burst into view.

Both of them stared, speechless, in doe-eyed confusion.

"How odd..." thought Felicia, unaware that she'd said it out loud. She'd never before had something so simple backfire so badly.

"I'm...sorry?" replied Natalie, unsure what had just happened but feeling somehow responsible.

"What? Oh!" said Felicia as she shook her wits back into place, "No, no, completely my fault. My foot got away from me...entirely my mistake."

"OK, if you're sure..." said Natalie, still a bit confused, before turning back to the wall and trying to remember her place. "Umm...books, right? Books... We have a few new ones that I haven't put out yet...how about a *Brothers Grimm* in German from the 1800s?

Or a signed 1926 *Winnie the Pooh*?"

Felicia shook her head, "No, still not quite right. I want something a bit quirkier. Something unexpected."

Natalie scrunched her face in thought as her eyes searched.

"How about a book about shuffleboard?"

"Shuffleboard?"

"The game of retired baby booming kings? We have a lot of books on shuffleboard. Figured it qualifies as both quirky and unexpected!"

"A bit too…fossilized…I think. Anything more useful?"

"I didn't think you'd bite! Useful, sure. This way," Natalie laughed as she waddled off the way they came, her cane clacking in exuberance as she went, a bookswain in her bailiwick.

Felicia glared at the girl's back, her anger ascending. This girl had not only dodged her attack but had the bubbling gall to giggle as well!

But then a grin of realization started to spread across her face as Natalie turned down the aisle with the oil, a sashay emerging in Felicia's step as she followed, her eyes twinkling as she dawdled out of cane range, watching as Natalie fobbled and wobbled, closer and closer, her eyes focused more on her feet than the glistening, rounded drops dabbling the woodwork.

But again, strangely and unexpectedly, the oil didn't work as intended.

Natalie stepped in the oil sure enough, but instead of slipping and falling, her balance skittered backward like a cartoonish banana-peel skit, legs kicking the air as she careened towards Felicia's fading grin.

Felicia took the brunt of the charging momentum, swapping her collapse for Natalie's, her jaw slamming into a bookshelf as a chipped tooth cackled along the floorboards in ecstatic escape. Taken aback and slightly concussed, Felicia crooked her head at the bookshelf, a stubborn suspicion that it was out to get her.

Natalie stood in shock, a look of dazed confusion plastered across her face. She was at a complete loss, unable to recall a single instance of avoided injury in her entire life, let alone two in the span of as many minutes. That should have been a cataclysmic fall. She should be nursing at least a sprained ankle and, more than likely, something far worse. She was tempted to fall over on principle alone.

Felicia sat sprawled on the ground, her tongue testing her tooth while she waited for the birdies to fly off, a curious sense of unexpected failure tiptoeing through her. She wasn't used to making mistakes.

"I'm sorry," said Natalie, still unsure what to make of the situation. "I don't have very good balance."

"S'okay," said Felicia through a whistling tooth as she pushed herself to her feet, a dizzying world greeting her at the higher altitude. She watched distantly as Natalie tented open a Wet Floor sign over the remains of the oil spill, a variety of them clearly scattered across the store for just such an occasion, before toweling off her feet with the sign's companion.

"Was a vent dripping or something…?" Natalie asked aloud as she looked up at the dry, empty ceiling, still unsure what had caused the slip, before offering the towel to Felicia.

"Don't worry about it, these things happen," said Felicia with a frothy slur as she joined her in looking up at the ceiling, hoping to distract her away from the evidence.

Natalie smiled, nervous, before finally wambling off again toward the far wall, her free hand bracing against the cabinetry.

Felicia followed, curious and concussed, a doubt of unexpected uncertainty dancing through her mind. Her most bullish tricks had backfired spectacularly, her confidence had been crushed, and like a gambler trying to break even, she saw no choice but to double down on the next hand.

"Here's our general reference area," said Natalie as she sat on the closest bench, an absolute certainty that she was overdue for danger. "Tools, tactics, turnips, and travel. Maybe something grabs you?"

Felicia glanced at the shelf of mismatched spines, *Merck Manuals* and horse-race handicapping mixed in amongst the *Tulip Investment Guides* and the *History of Straw Hats*, before finally scaling her eyes north. "What about those ones? On the top shelf? They look eye-catching."

Natalie followed the pointing finger up, spotting the green and gold gilt books on the top shelf, an immediate shiver of nervousness shuffling through her. She never liked getting books from the high shelves; it seemed to be pressing her luck to an extraordinary degree.

"That's an old encyclopedia set," said Natalie, hoping to dissuade her. "It's not accurate anymore. It was written in the 1800s and still lists Hawaii as having a king."

"That's just what I'm after! Can I see it?"

Natalie crinkled her mouth, uncertain if she should simply refuse the sale rather than risk it. It was a rather large and expensive set that had sat untouched for as long as she could remember, so it would be nice to finally move it, yet something about the customer's tone threw her off.

Natalie squinted, holding her in a reserved glance for another moment, weighing her motivations and her credit line, before finally hobbling down the aisle and grabbing the ladder, wheeling it along the wall and locking the feet to steadiness before taking her first step up.

"You're absolutely sure?" she confirmed.

"Absolutely!" Felicia replied, barely containing her excitement, her anxious foot tapping precipitously close to the ladder brake. This would put her ahead for the day, she was sure of it.

Natalie's anxiety was screaming, a bubbling fear in her fingertips that sensed a disaster in the making. She risked a glance down at her pancake pangolin, hoping it would infuse her spirit with bravery, and with a deep breath of confidence she began to climb the ladder.

Felicia barely gave her a handful of rungs before her self-control snapped, her foot leaping out to release the brake, the ladder wobbling as a sense of foreboding filled the room.

Natalie glanced down at the wobble as her hand touched the book, watching as Felicia's body twisted on her pivoting ankle in a fake fall with a sham scream, a façade of acting as she lost her footing, a kicking shove of accidental collision that sent the ladder shimmying down the bookwall.

But again, inexplicably backwards, something had gone wrong.

The weightless ladder had moved too quickly, and Felicia found herself sprawled on the ground where she'd expected her prey to now lie, confused stars twisting around her as she once again wondered what had happened.

She spotted Natalie still above her, one foot perched on the bookshelf, the other dangling in midair, her unused sling caught in the mouth of a wooden gargoyle as her hands scrabbled to free herself.

"What the...?" began Felicia in verbal confusion before a second set of stars appeared, a heavy green and gold gilt encyclopedia toppling down on top of her, a stabbing corner to the eye that turned an instant black and blue.

Natalie, still unaware of Felicia's malicious intent, took the brunt of the explanation as she tried to free herself. "I'm so sorry!! I lost my balance when I reached for the book! I must not've locked the ladder down!"

"No problem…" said Felicia with a cobwebbed headshake as she struggled to get to her feet.

She barely made it to one knee before the next five volumes of the encyclopedia set cascaded down, imparting a stuttering bassline of knowledge.

"Ouch!" cried Felicia as her spinning stars gained constellations of their own.

Natalie looked down on the unfolding disaster, confused beyond belief and fearful of lawsuits, "Oh jeez, oh jeez, I don't know what's going on! These things always happen to me, so I'm at a bit of a loss!"

Felicia said nothing, her focus solely on scampering around a corner to safety, her eyes scouring the bookshelves, fearful the rest of the alphabet was preparing to pepper her with obscure facts. She barely noticed that Natalie had somehow freed herself, managing the few steps back down to the ground, unexpectedly graceful and injury free.

"I have no idea how that happened…how could it have?...this is so weird…" Natalie rambled to herself, confused and uncertain, knowing she'd never escaped so many perils and pitfalls that so clearly should've ended badly. It was as if a bizarro version of herself, impervious to injury, had somehow taken control of her body. She scratched her head as she reached for her cane, intent on steadying herself before gravity swung a retaliatory punch.

Felicia faltered and stumbled as she tried to stand, colliding with globes and bookends and spilling their contents. "I think I'm...gonna pass...on the set," she finally managed with some difficulty. "What about...something else...ummm..." Felicia paused, dizzy wheels spinning as she desperately tried to extend the game, "...children's books?"

Natalie scowled. She could understand some animosity toward the encyclopedias that'd just attacked her, but you'd think she would've at least flipped through one to know if it was worth the injury and the effort. But no, the books still sat untouched and ignored where they fell as the customer rushed her attention off to another book and another destination.

Natalie began to step away, her eyes thinning, a sneaking suspicion finally dawning that these were not honest intentions. "Do you even like to read?"

"What?" said Felicia, taken aback. "Of course. I read all the time. I read something just last week."

"You don't come across like a person who reads. In fact, you come across like a person who's never entered a bookstore in her life."

"You don't say..." said Felicia, a crooked, grinching smile curving along her cheek as she tossed away what was left of her tourist disguise.

And it was then, as Natalie looked on, a weird and violent anger so clear on Felicia's face, that it finally clicked into place who this must be.

"Are you...Felicia?"

"And you must be the mystery fling," Felicia smiled back, happy to finally confirm that she'd targeted correctly.

"Are you trying to...hurt me?" Natalie asked.

"No, of course not."

"You just pulled a D battery out of your pocket. I can see it."

"Oh this? This is nothing. I use it for balance."

Natalie nervously nibbled her bottom lip, scared and confused and uncertain what to do. She knew little of Sylvester's ex beyond her stint in prison, which seemed enough to warrant concern.

Felicia was equally at a loss behind her bluster of bravado, her expected advantage having turned itself against her.

It was as if some cosmic balance had decided to play tricks on them, the close proximity of elemental forces wreaking havoc on their individual gravities. Neither of them could explain what was going on as odd thoughts rambled around their addled minds.

And then the door jingled its jangle and interrupted their trance as Grandma Norris' senile muttering began to trickle through the stacks, ranting and raving about the dangers of margarine.

"We should do this again. I'm sure I'd have better luck next time," said Felicia, realizing her window had closed.

"I'd rather not," said Natalie with a look of disbelief, her growing dread molting into rumbling anger. "Why don't you try somewhere else? I'm sure the prison library must have some coloring books you'd enjoy…"

Felicia glared, a hint of smoke escaping from her nostrils.

"How about one for the road then?" she asked with a wink as she hurled the battery full strength, all attempts at subtlety lost.

But as with everything else, it unexpectedly backfired, Natalie's own klutziness preempting Felicia's failed attack, toppling her sideways into a comfortably cushioned couch while Felicia's battery caromed off the wall, reflecting back and beaning her in the head, tumbling her into the travel section where a greedy gargoyle took a vengeful bite, splitting open her lip.

Anger erupted as Felicia's composure finally broke, "What the hell!! This was supposed to be fun and easy!"

And then, as if offering nature's commentary, a small swarm of wasps suddenly appeared, happily ignoring Natalie while they stung Felicia unmercifully.

"Why does today suck so much?!?" Felicia shrieked as she ran, arms swatting at the swarm of tiny demons as they chased her from the store.

The door slammed shut as Natalie slid to the ground to safety, her heart still pounding, unsure what had just happened. "That was certainly unexpected."

Across the store, as if to underscore that the world had returned to its normal rotation, three bookcases collapsed and a strange smell of fish began to emanate from the heating ducts, culminating in the final volume of the encyclopedia set toppling off the shelf and hitting Natalie in the foot.

"Finally!" she said, happy to have broken the pattern, before her mind drifted back to her visitor.

For all of Natalie's fallings and failings in life, it'd always been accidental. This was the first time someone had actively tried to injure her, and of all people, Sylvester's ex-con ex.

Her mind dabbled in curiosity, wondering if jealousy had prompted the visit and how Felicia had even found her. Sylvester could certainly solve the riddle, but first she had to decide if he was a wound worth reopening.

But then her eye caught the oddest oddity of the day - in the midst of fallen encyclopedias, random and askew, sat a volume that had landed on its spine, forcing itself open, and there, scrawled in crayon, was a treasure map.

Apparently, Grandma Norris wasn't as senile as she appeared.

Natalie had indeed once been an adventurer.

CHAPTER 43
THE MEETING OF ADDICTIONS

Socket flipped the breaker, sending power flooding back through the obstacle course he'd spent the afternoon rewiring. He gave it a few seconds, then smiled. Nothing had burst into flames this time and the rest of the neighborhood still had power, so that was a good sign. Far better than the last time he tried to take the course off batteries.

He closed the breaker box and climbed out of the basement, dropping the bulkhead behind him as he stepped over the pile of garden batteries he'd spent the afternoon plucking from various traps scattered about the yard. He'd need to decide where to use them next; maybe he'd finally get around to wiring the driveway.

But first he had to test things.

He glanced over at Poke, snorily sunning himself in a snowdrift in the crisp winter air. He'd be safe enough as long as he didn't wake up and wander.

Socket grabbed his voltmeter and started wandering the edges of the yard, slowly spiraling his way in as he tested every surface, every obstacle, and every object. There were almost two hundred electrified items he could remember, ranging from lawn gnomes to spare tires to tree branches, and he wanted to make sure none of them were wired wrong. The last thing he needed was another accidental five-figure electric bill from an overzealously wired birdhouse.

He'd been testing for half an hour when the gate creaked open, Sylvester's willpower dragging his hobbled and beaten body inside. He made it halfway across the lawn before crumpling into tears, slumping against the large metal beetle that glowed on Halloween and electrocuted the trick-or-treaters who foolishly chose the direct path.

The noisy gate awakened Poke, who now stared alongside Socket toward Sylvester, their matching heads hung with curious uncertainty.

"No luck with the old missus?" Socket finally asked.

Sylvester's mouth barely moved, gurgling sounds, "She couldn't do it. Did her worst, not even a whiff."

"I'm sorry, man."

Sylvester said nothing, his body exhausted and internally bleeding, his mind focused on self-pity and the inevitable crawl to his deathbed.

"Anything me or the walking sea urchin can do to help?" Socket asked. "I could strap him to the bumper and run you down with the van. Ya know, if you wanted."

For a minute Sylvester said nothing, watching his tears fall as his mind scrabbled for options and hope in a directionless life.

"I don't know what I'm supposed to do."

Socket searched his jukebox of emotions for 'sympathy', but when he couldn't find the record, simply played whatever seemed closest (which turned out to be a Billy Ocean song).

"Bummer to hear it, man. Maybe that's life's funny way of telling you that when the going gets tough, the tough become a test dummy?" he said with a smirk and a grin, trying to raise his friend's spirits. "I could use the help. Might help take your mind off things. Maybe after that we hook you up to the full grid and try to Frankenstein's monster you up proper?"

Sylvester shrugged, unsure if even Victorian science could help him now, his apathy and self-pity knowing no bounds. "Sure, why not."

The pair spent the next hour testing the yard, Socket checking voltages while Sylvester played guinea pig to the baitshop of clutter strewn about. They found a dozen oddities that'd been disconnected completely, a few more still hooked up to batteries Socket had overlooked, and even a small handful that'd been miswired so badly that they shocked Sylvester off his feet.

The sun was starting to dip as they finished spreading the last of the fresh walkway mix, preparing to test it, when the gate suddenly slammed open and Felicia barreled in, a look of maleficent intent on her face as she descended upon them.

"OK Vest, round two. Let's go!" she barked, her finger waggling.

"'Licia? What're you...how did...?" began Sylvester, confused where the black eye and wasp stings had come from.

"You owe me and I'm gonna collect!"

"Hello Leash," said Socket with a wave as he took a protective step back, instinct jingling the fear bell in his brain.

"No!" screamed Felicia, pointing towards him. "Inside!"

Socket scampered back, wide-eyed and fearful, suddenly certain that things were about to escalate to personal danger.

Sylvester caught him by the arm, "Can you take Poke, too? I don't want him getting winged by shrapnel."

Socket paused, fearful if she'd allow it, before grabbing the sleepy porcupine and hurrying into the house, cringing as loose quills jabbed him in the midsection. The pair slid into the living room and started shoving the boxes and books and holiday supplies away from the window, clearing a path toward the action, before Socket finally dropped Poke on the window bench and snuggled in to join him.

"This's gonna be good!"

Poke looked up and nodded, clearly agreeing, before settling in to watch the festivities, hoping for fireworks.

Sylvester watched them go before turning back to Felicia, her shoulders still heaving in carbonated anger. It'd only been a few hours since her failed attempts to fix him, but it was clear her mood hadn't softened.

"I'm gonna fix you, right here, right now," she began as she took a step toward him, a clear indication she intended to break him properly.

"Felicia, I told you, I can't…"

And then Felicia swung, a surprise right hook that knocked Sylvester to the ground.

"Don't think that did anything…" he said as he stretched his jaw and held his hands up defensively. "…and I don't think I can be fixed just by beating the crap out of me."

"I'm fine with trying it."

"I'm not!"

"What happened to you? When did you become such a wimp?!" she screamed at him.

"And when did you become such an asshole?" he shouted back, sadly wondering what had happened to the fun girl he used to play fire-poker games with. This one seemed like she'd spent a hot day melting on the dashboard of a car.

Felicia scowled, chewing her lip, trying to rein in the anger. She only lasted a few seconds before erupting, "Because of that bookstore bitch! I couldn't touch her!"

Sylvester's eyes flashed red, "Wait, what? Natalie? I told you to stay away from her!"

"You can't tease me like that! You can't dangle that carrot!"

Sylvester leapt to his feet, anger surging through him, "What'd you do, Felicia?!"

Felicia glowered, pulsating, enjoying having at last gotten a rise out of him, happy that some of her skillset still worked.

"What??" he demanded.

She grinned, trying to enjoy it, before caving to criminal pride, "Nothing! I couldn't touch her. It was ridiculous! It was like some game to her, sidestepping everything I tried!!"

Sylvester took a step back, confused.

"Wait, are we talking about the same person? Glasses? Padded clothing? Covered in band-aids?"

"Yes! In that stupid geriatric bookstore!"

Sylvester couldn't help but smirk, a chuckle of ironic calamity bubbling out, "You couldn't touch her? Really?"

"No! And it wasn't funny!" screamed Felicia as she shoved Sylvester with both arms. "I thought she was supposed to be a klutz!" She shoved again. "I thought she was going to be easy fun after your broken ass!" She shoved again. "But no! She kept getting out of the way before I could touch her!"

Sylvester laughed as Felicia attempted another shove, bouncing him off the beetle, "Oh man! That's great!"

"No, it's not!! How did she do it?!"

"How would I know? How do any of our weird idiosyncrasies work?" he paused, still smiling, proud of Natalie and wishing he'd witnessed it. "Sure sounds like she gave you a taste of yourself, though."

"Screw you," said Felicia. Given how well her day had started, it had taken a decidedly negative turn since leaving the mall.

It was then that a taxi slid to a stop outside Socket's house, puttering its engine as small gassy spurts of smoke burped out of the tailpipe. It puttered for a second minute, and then a third, before the door finally opened and a cautious and nervous leg stretched out, tapping the ground as if testing the surface of a strange planet.

The leg was shod in a heavy, sturdy boot, above which thick downy ski pants puffed and wrinkled, a dozen more layers clearly buried beneath. The strangeness continued as the rest of the body emerged, an over-poofed jacket layered on top of a variety of lesser coats, while the hands wore gloves, which in turn wore mittens, and the head hoisted a tall set of winter hats topped with a bobble, giving off the appearance of someone wearing their entire winter wardrobe at once.

Natalie had barely placed her second foot on the ground and straightened her legs before the taxi sped off, the door bouncing shut as it went, the driver sick of waiting for her grandmotherly movements to extricate her from the car.

She looked around briefly, checking for dangers, ignoring the quixotic tilted stares the neighbors threw at her, before finally moving to the sidewalk.

The gate itself was next, rickety and unshorn, intimidating her with its passivity, as if the handle itself had a streak of meanness within it waiting to flail out. She watched it nervously for a moment, but it stayed steady and near silent, the creak of an old bent nail the lone sound as it begged for help.

Taking a final breath of courage, she closed her eyes and pushed forward into the yard, the twittering hinges drawing the attention of Sylvester and Felicia as their conversation dwindled in surprise.

"Natalie?" asked Sylvester, wholly perplexed at the continuing oddness of the day.

Socket and Poke's tipping attention thudded against the window in rampant curiosity, the carnival show having thrown a surprise twist to the audience.

Natalie waved and they all watched, the long gravel drive throwing off her balance, causing her to wander and waver and tumble across the grass, a drunken duck of a walk that took three times as long, but eventually landed her at their feet, a handful of injuries buried beneath the layers.

Felicia stared in awe of the performance, certain it was staged, a desire to cripple and maim bursting to life within her.

Unexpected and confused, Sylvester's thoughts leapt between fiddling happiness and uncertain intent, unabashed curiosity and pickled fear, but he kept his wits and extended his hand, pulling Natalie to her feet.

"Hey, Sylvester…" she said with a happy smile, before turning her thinning eyes to Felicia, "…and you."

"Hello trollop," said Felicia as she flipped her the bird.

Sylvester's eyes bounced between them, fearing fireworks.

"What're you doing here?" he asked as his hands pocketed placebo forkroaches, determined to gather strength from his hobbled habit, his mind cluelessly confused by his grail girl abruptly appearing after weeks of failed crusades.

"Thought I'd swing by for a visit."

"I didn't think you swung anywhere? Don't tell me there's a Morlock tunnel to my place?"

She smiled, happy he wasn't sad to see her. "The big secret is that we Morlocks know how to call a cab."

He laughed. She fell. Felicia looked on curiously, a fuse briefly blown, amazed that someone like this existed outside of small undiscovered island tribes.

"Well, after her visit," Natalie continued with a nod to Felicia as she returned to her feet, "I had a few questions."

"I didn't send her, if that's what you're wondering," Sylvester began as he turned to glare at Felicia. "In fact, I explicitly told her you were off limits."

"Oh right, like that ever works…" said Felicia with an epileptic eye role.

"How'd you even find her?"

Felicia smiled, proud of her makeshift detective agency and wishing she had business cards to hand out. "You need to control your fawning, dreamy looks, is how. You kept staring at that stupid old bookstore!"

Sylvester grumbled, angry at his oversight, before turning back to Natalie, "Are you OK? Did she hurt you?"

Natalie surprised him with a smile and a laugh as she thin-eyed Felicia, "She certainly tried!"

"And why is that funny?" iced Felicia.

"Because you kept missing!"

"I don't miss."

Natalie shrugged, "Coulda fooled me."

Sylvester's eyes brightened as his butterflies flapped free. He adored this girl. Not only had this seemingly delicate creature sidestepped Felicia's Olympic-level skillset of violence, but she also didn't take any lip from her.

Felicia glared under her breath at Natalie, "I couldn't even get a paper cut on her…"

Natalie rolled her eyes in a dismissiveness that instantly collapsed her to the ground, as if mocking Felicia's failure and how easy it should've been.

Sylvester helped her back up before turning to Felicia, "It still doesn't explain why you thought this was even remotely OK to try? What if you'd succeeded?"

"It would've been a blast!" said Felicia as her hands conducted her exuberance. "After that crap you pulled earlier to wind me up? I needed a release! What better way to scratch that itch than with a toy that falls down on its own? It was too tempting to pass up!"

"Felicia, seriously. People are not toys!"

Felicia laughed, heartily and arrogantly, "Of course they are."

Natalie scowled, unsure what to make of the subtle puzzle piece that had just been dropped through the cracks: what exactly had preceded Felicia's bookshop visit? She searched for only a moment before a boomerang of jealous realization suddenly struck her. "Are you two back together?"

Felicia smiled and winked, lying and trying for a quick jab of jealousy.

"No, still broken up," said Sylvester, before putting a bullet in it. "For good."

Natalie couldn't help but smirk.

"She was just trying to...help me," he added.

"Scar-boy here broke his little habit and came back begging," said Felicia as she gave him a shove.

And for the first time, Natalie noticed the sadness etched in Sylvester's face, the dangling hands that no longer danced in his pockets and picked at his surroundings, a lobotomized shell of what he once was.

"You...broke?" she asked, her own familiarity with the term landing on him with a thud of obviosity.

Of all the people he knew (which wasn't that many), she was the one who could best understand being broken. The enormity of the awareness staggered him, both for how foolish he'd been to overlook it, as well as how serendipitous her timing was, and before he knew it he was spilling his story of self-destruction, beginning with the triumph of the bullet ants and the failure of his fun, before rambling off to his quest to rekindle it.

Felicia rolled her eyes, bored of his biography, and began to circle, her shark-like need to feed propelling her blindly along as she searched for an injury to inflict. Here sat two subtle morsels, floating in her tank smelling of bubblegum chum and begging to be chewed.

Socket was enthralled as an animated Sylvester told his tale, seemingly unaware of just how much he was starting to look like a seal dinner to the circling predator. This was far more fun to watch than Halloween and there weren't even costumes involved.

Poke lumbered over and yawned, his naptime imminent, his swashbuckling tail knocking off knickknacks as he searched for a path down from his perch. Socket smiled and lowered the porcupine to the floor, tossing him a treat, before returning his attention to the action outside, hoping he hadn't missed the climax.

Felicia's head weaved as she circled, sniffing the seawinds for blood, curious if Natalie's avoidance was a conscious choice or some instinct running in the background. Natalie was still oblivious to the dorsal fin and the theme music, her eyes focused on Sylvester's rambling tale as Felicia's finger inched forward, scientifically slow and curious, preparing to test her.

But the finger never made it, Natalie unexpectedly falling sideways and bouncing off the beetle, popping back up in a different spot a moment later, continuing her conversation without batting an eyelash, the lab rat who'd accidentally sidestepped the syringe.

Felicia tried again, this time moving faster and more randomly, hoping to catch gravity unaware, two fingers attacking from different directions. But again, now almost expected, Natalie fell first, her proximity to Felicia's outstretched hands seeming to work like a forcefield of protective enchantment, a crooked carnival game you weren't meant to win but kept plunking down quarters to try.

When Natalie bounced up a third time and a fourth, still clueless about what was being asked of her, Felicia couldn't help but sputter, "Did you see that?!?"

"See what?" asked Sylvester, mistily having forgotten Felicia was even there as his lovelorn eyes looked elsewhere.

"Her! Watch!" she said as she reached toward Natalie, her finger extended, trying to touch her, and as Sylvester watched, the poor girl toppled and fell, again and again as Natalie's frantic attempts to stand were immediately thwarted by Felicia's restless attempts to make contact.

Sylvester was frozen, enthralled and perplexed, uncertain what he was witnessing but unable to turn away. It reminded him of the bees on that common walk long ago, where the rules of the road only applied to certain travelers. It took a flailing kick from Natalie to finally regain his wits and insert himself between them, holding Felicia back while he helped Natalie to her feet.

"C'mon 'Licia, that wasn't cool..." he finally got out, his mind still reeling and curious.

"Why can't I touch her?! It doesn't make any sense!" Felicia fumed, her eyes orange and enraged, perpetual torment teasing her. She'd always led life as the aggressor and had never before been dealt the hand of the easily dispatched distraction.

"I should get going," said Natalie as she sensed a growing urgency to escape while she could, Felicia's predatory wanderings indicating another attack was imminent.

Sylvester's face fell with the pulp of crushed emotions, the temporary tease of his missing friend being ripped away too quickly.

Natalie sensed it too, and after a step, she paused, turning back, "But maybe visit the shop again sometime? I'm sorry I scared you away. I'm a little sturdier now."

"I'll do that," he smiled, an ebullience of fluttering happiness busting forth as his grin spread. Had he thought about it, he'd have realized he wasn't even thinking about the preponderance of injuries he was dealing with or his dormant need to injure himself.

Natalie smiled too, big and broad, boastful and happy. She was happy to be an adventurer, at least for today.

The third member of the trio did not share their bliss, and somewhere in that smile Felicia found the final nudge of encouragement she needed to tumble down the rabbit hole of retribution, a crooked smile spreading across her face as the peripheral world vanished and she let loose her full potential, her body slithering and slaking as it launched an elbow-shoving, body-thrusting hip-check at Natalie meant to hobble and topple an easy target wobbling on bad luck's spindle-threaded tip. An attack meant not only to injure, but to cripple and to maim, the built-up failure of her day bursting forth in cataclysmic retribution.

And it was then that one of those strange moments of life popped its head up, as if the universe itself had decided to crack its karmic disc and relieve the pressure of a world tweaked out of alignment, as time slowed and a lot of things happened at once.

The first was Sylvester, expecting the worst and instinctively diving between them, a fundamental urge to shield Natalie from Felicia, a selfless bulwark of protective affection. But Natalie's body had already made plans of its own, collapsing in on itself before Felicia's attack had even arrived, causing Felicia's nudge to become her own domino of tumbled gravity as she fell into the maelstrom and joined them.

To the outside world it simply looked like a fall between fools, but to the game at large it was a far more forceful fluttering, slow motion to even the gods above. The balletic arc of a lost mitten, the whip twist of hair as it snapped at the empty air, a drawling dance as they corkscrewed together.

And then, as their twisting collapse made landfall, the final thing happened, the oddest of them all.

Poke the Porcupine, mid-yawn and mid-step, fell asleep, a narcoleptic seizure of suddenness that dropped him onto the small plastic box that Socket had shoved to the side and ignored. The box with the purple button that was only used on Halloween.

Immediately and without warning electricity funneled through the graveled metal path of nuts and washers, caps and lugs, all mixed together and vibrating to life as electrons coursed through them.

A brilliant blue arc danced briefly, pirouetting around, desperate to find the ground as it leapt from Sylvester to Felicia to Natalie and back again, their bodies shaking but unmoving, lashed in place by mother nature's magic, a masochist, a sadist, and a klutz, and for a brief moment their addictions danced between them, mixing and matching, a thousand-million dance steps contained in a millisecond.

And then the circuit breaker broke, the spark was sundered, the thrum of electricity grew silent, and they all collapsed their separate ways, remnants of crackling currents tumbling over them, thin wisps of singed smoke the only movement still twisting in the air.

CHAPTER 44
AFTER THE BBQ

It took Socket a moment to realize what happened.

He dove for the controller, his thumb stabbing the button as he tried to rip the batteries from the back, his neck twisting toward the yard as the fuse finally blew and the house went dark.

Socket vaulted a confused and newly awakened porcupine and tore the door open, a sizzled shock coursing through him as he cursed his own randomized battery games, before jumping the stairs, a defibrillator in hand.

Poke sprinted out the door behind him, tumbling over himself in a mad rush to reach Sylvester, his quills sensing trouble as his guilty conscience regretted his never-ending need for sudden sleep.

The trio of bodies lay prone on the ground, dribbles of spittle escaping their mouths as their eyes fluttered with the look of chaotic, scrabbling dreams, occasional sparks and crackles murmuring beneath them.

Socket fell to his knees, his hands reaching out to shake them as he shouted their names and warmed up the defibrillator. His mind was continuing to race, a frightening fear for his friends mixed with a desperate desire to delve into the outage, brownouts and blackouts his bowl games. He felt like the kid who could see the puppy wrapped in paper wagging its tail under the tree but had to wait for the family photo before he could open it.

Sylvester was the first to awaken, his turtle-shelled skin used to sudden electrocutions and thudding injury, doddering into awareness with an unexpected taste for pancakes and pie as his eyes and his ears took in the quiet dimness of dusk, slowly remembering where he was.

The power was out everywhere. Their house and the next and the streetlights and the store lights. Whatever they'd blown was more than just a fuse and it was a wonder he wasn't dead.

He glanced down at Felicia and Natalie, curious about their sturdiness and hopeful he'd somehow taken the brunt of it. Natalie was already stirring, her beaten down body also used to the unexpected punishment, her elbows supporting her as a confused and awakening head nodded into clarity. Felicia was the last to join them, needing another minute to awaken, her body the least prepared and the most confused.

They all sat in a daze, recognition slowly rekindling as they tried to ponder the pieces, still unsure what had happened.

Poke was frantically licking Sylvester's face as he ignored the random arcs of electricity that continued to erupt, an overwhelming fear of lost love and a grateful animalistic sense that danger had barely been averted.

"It's OK Poke...I'm still here..." he said as he scratched the porcupine behind the ears.

"I'm thirsty..." sputtered Felicia as she lip-smacked loudly and absently, her sharp edge palpably dulled.

"I'm on it!" said Socket, jogging back inside and returning a moment later with three glasses of something blue and full of electrolytes, which they all sipped slowly and silently as their heads unscrambled.

"OK, I gotta say, that was awesome! What a zap!" erupted Socket, his concern having given way to excitement and professional curiosity. "Anyone know what happened? It looked like some kinda trust-fall exercise gone bad."

"I fell down, but that's nothing new…" said Natalie as the worms of dizziness continued to wander across her vision. "Maybe my aura of calamity pulled the rest of you in? It'd be a first, but I don't put it past myself."

Sylvester eyed Felicia, knowing the true culprit but uncertain if he should out her. Even if it was her fault for starting it, what followed was certainly not.

For once, Felicia's conscience surprised him.

"No, this was my fault," Felicia admitted. "I was trying to knock you over but lost my balance. Sorry about that. It was a mean thing to do."

Sylvester and Socket's jaws dropped at once, the unexpected flavor of an apology throwing them off, while Natalie's eyes thinned to a glare, a resentful desire to lash out at this foe who'd repeatedly tried to hurt her.

"I think something's wrong with The Leash..." said Socket as he reached for the defibrillator.

"Honestly, I think there's been a lot wrong with me lately, but for right now I'm just incredibly thirsty," Felicia added as she downed the rest of her drink and reached for Sylvester's. "Does anyone else have a headache?"

"Yes," chimed in Sylvester and Natalie together, a strange feeling of ansible kinship circulating between them.

"And how did you get involved?" Natalie asked as she turned to Sylvester, stifling an unexpectedly violent urge to shove him.

"I faintly recall diving in headfirst..."

Natalie arched an eyebrow as she shook her head, "Of course you did."

Sylvester shrugged.

"And the electric chair treatment?" asked Natalie, still not fully comprehending whose house she was visiting.

"Oh, that's on me and the urchin," said Socket with a thumb toward a now-napping porcupine. "Poke face-planted on my Halloween button."

"That would explain the teeth-chattering electrocution alright..." added Sylvester.

Natalie perked up, a random thought suddenly popping into her head that she was certain wasn't hers, "You electrocute trick-or-treaters, don't you?"

"Maybe..." said Socket as he eyed her, wondering if she should be defibrillated instead.

Sylvester cocked her a glance, certain he'd never mentioned it.

"I'm sure I deserved it," interjected Felicia, a crinkle of regret on her face. "I think I'm a bad person sometimes. I don't mean to be. Well, no, of course I do, but I mean...deep down. Deep down I don't think I mean to be mean."

And then Felicia waffled and squiggled, her face contorting with surprise emotions, before suddenly bursting into cataclysmic tears, a torrent of unexpected guilt from a lifetime of pent up peccability. It was as if a hole had been drilled in her conscience to allow the bile to pour out and a waterfall had decided to take advantage of it.

Socket's jaw dropped as he whispered to Sylvester, "I didn't think she was capable of crying..."

Sylvester nodded, equally in shock, not at Felicia but at himself, a sudden and unexpected surge of sympathy, followed immediately by an impulsive and vindictive urge to laugh.

Natalie on the other hand actually did, cackling and pointing and hurling a torrent of giggles at her rival, before abruptly clamming up, a shocked and embarrassed look on her face that made it clear she didn't know where it was coming from either.

They all seemed a bit out of character.

Sylvester's eyes danced between them as waffling urges to cry and laugh pickled around inside him. Something was clearly off, and he began to wonder just how much power had flowed through them, and if it had melted some of their inner circuitry.

They all sat in silence for a few minutes, Felicia's weeps and Natalie's cackles slowly dissolving while they organized their waffling thoughts.

Natalie was the first to crack, her dominating need for safety overwhelming her rambling and unforeseen thoughts of vengeance.

"I think I'm gonna try to get going again," said Natalie as she climbed to her feet, "...before a piano somehow falls on me."

The others each nodded, a newly common fear of falling objects shared between them, before following her to their feet, the dizziness dissipating as they stumbled uneasily upright.

And then the oddest thing happened.

Sylvester's world wobbled a little strangely, a little crookedly, and he suddenly lost his balance, toppling down, a bungling sputter onto his backside. His eyes immediately caught Natalie's as she cocked her head, pug-like and curious, his fall feeling strangely familiar.

But there was something else, too.

An elusive and familiar feeling that began to tease around the edges, dappling him with goosebumps as his eyes crinkled in confused excitement. And before he knew it, he felt it, as the tickle of his habit flickered back to life, a pocket full of forkroaches stabbing joyously through his pants as a thrilling sense of pain tore through him, unleashing a scream of pure joy and happiness as he ground himself into the earth, determined to embrace it.

Everyone else stared, confused and lost by his grinning, giggling happiness.

But only for a moment.

Because Natalie's legs had started to wiggle and wobble like a jealous yawn trying to play mimic, kinking and bobbling her towards a matching collapse, but as the gravity gods tried to take their toll she felt an instinct, a sudden angry urge to pass off the pain, and in that moment, she learned how to shove, her arm shooting out violently and knocking Felicia to the ground as her own balance centered itself back to stability.

Natalie was still standing.

And again, everyone else stared, confused and lost by her grinning, giggling happiness.

But only for a moment.

Because Felicia, having hit the ground hard, her elbow plowing into the walkway of metal below, smirked and smiled, her afternoon of failures forgotten, a smile spreading across her face as an unknown happiness floated through her, tingling her senses in a way she never expected, an enjoyment of the hurt more than the hurting.

And for the third time in as many seconds, everyone else stared, confused and lost by her grinning, giggling happiness.

Socket and Poke were completely confused, foreign spectators watching a game they didn't understand and struggling to understand the score.

But Sylvester, Felicia, and Natalie did, and they all stared at one another, a strange awareness that some sliver of their selves had somehow splintered and shifted, as if their minds and their memories and their very being had been shuffled together like a deck of cards and dealt back out. Felicia found herself staring appreciatively into a mirror of masochism, while Natalie was paired with a shard of sadism, and Sylvester was now served with a side of clumsiness.

It was a dawning moment of insight for all of them as they looked upon each other with a new perspective.

And then Felicia broke the moment by doing the strangest and most unexpected thing of all, reaching for one of Sylvester's fallen forkroaches, a casual "Can I borrow one of these?" tossed into the air, and without waiting for a response, she stabbed it hard into her thigh, a sudden inexplicable urge to injure herself, giggling and laughing as a true appreciation for the creatures finally dawned on her.

CHAPTER 45
THE HAPPY ENDING

Sylvester awoke with a start and immediately fell out of bed.

A moment later Natalie joined him, her own circadian alarm clock popping to life and encouraging her to follow, the same confused and bemused look on her face as they both looked around, twin dodos curious for food and disappointed in the room service.

Sylvester scratched his head, noticing the mattress that lay flush with the floor, slowly remembering where he was. "Is that how you wake up every morning?"

"Pretty much!" said Natalie as she crinkled her face and pushed her arms into the sky in a full body stretch. "Except I've never had anyone to cushion my landing before!"

"My life as a pincushion continues..."

Natalie stood up and wobbled into the bathroom and dove at her toothbrush, scrubbing away the sleep, while Sylvester kicked out his feet, bumping into the wall that he swore was further away moments before. Clearly the small details of his new living arrangement were still being hammered out.

The morning cobwebs were still fresh and it took him a minute to gather his feet before stepping out of the bedroom and into the bookstore, popping out near the unusually large section devoted to Canadian Fishing Hotspots that disguised the door. Natalie's grandparents had done their best to ensure her suitors had a challenge in finding her.

Sylvester looked up at the morning light filtering in through the skylights and evaporating the overnight dust parties. It was a different atmosphere here. A different world. Different from Socket's. Different from Felicia's. This was Natalie's. It was funny that Sylvester always seemed to live in someone else's life and never his own. He shook his head as he smiled at the thought.

But the head shake was somehow too much, too violent, and his gravity twisted a little strangely, a little crookedly, and he toppled over, unexpected and unintentional, crashing elbow-first into a growling and grumpy gargoyle, its pointed teeth gnashing out a token pound of flesh, hobbling the new resident before his morning coffee.

Sylvester's eyes caught Natalie's as she glanced over from the bathroom sink, cocking her head, the toothbrush paused, before meandering out and helping him to his feet, toothpaste still foaming from her mouth.

"So? Was that an accident?" she asked, excitement bubbling out through the bubbles.

"I don't know *what* that was..."

"You fell over."

"I know I fell over," he said with a smirk. "But I didn't even see it coming!"

"That happens sometimes. Was it dizziness or gravity?"

"A bit of both, I think? I just...fell."

"How exciting!" exclaimed Natalie as she clapped her hands together, the violent act seeming to unsteady her for a moment. "And hey! We have a matching set now!" she added as she skirted down her pajama pants, revealing a similar gargoyled tattoo scarred on her hip, mates for life from the same bitter foe.

"Great," said Sylvester as he hopped back and forth from foot to foot, testing his balance as it wobbled him in teasing jest. "I didn't realize you got dizzy," he added, smiling, the pupil to the master.

"I don't even notice it anymore. When I was a kid I got the dizzies something fierce. Missed the whole second grade. Couldn't get past the bus stop."

"I'm so envious of your childhood."

"Now I don't even...yup, I'm dizzy right now and didn't even notice," she began as she felt the wobbling, bobbling, morning dizzies and started to topple her way to the ground.

Yet instead of accepting it, the barrel over the waterfall, she parlayed her new instinct into service, Felicia's spark dancing within her, and shoved whoever was nearest, saving herself with a selfish bit of aggression.

Sylvester collapsed in a heap of happiness as he collided with the bookcase, his head tilting at an odd angle as the butterflies of happy habits fluttered through him and a storm of hardcovers rained down.

He smiled up as she glanced down, comfortable happiness shared between them, before she turned and tripped over the yawning porcupine and tumbled out of sight.

Between them it took an hour more to get ready, wrapped and strapped and ready for an injurious adventure.

They stepped out of the bookstore together, the fresh snow and ice collected on the ground as the frost fairies dusted their domain, a crisp chill burrowing through their clothes. They both wore helmets now, his more reminiscent of the bike-riding variety, their poufy coats seeming like Sumo suits made for carnival roughhousing, not sunshine speckled meanderings down the sidewalk.

Sylvester took a deep breath and smiled at the crisp air, his limbs shaking with uncertainty, his addictive mind both wanting to fall and refusing to fake it.

He glanced over at Natalie and saw her smiling apologetically, her arm extended to help an elderly gentleman extract himself from the snowdrift she'd just knocked him into.

Life was somehow different with Natalie. Simpler. Happier.

"Ready?" she asked as she appeared again next to him, her eyes dancing with adventurous potential.

Sylvester nodded.

Then she lost her balance and shoved him into a fire hydrant.

Acknowledgements

Many, many, many thanks to Stephen Wolfson, Erica Scialdone, and Patrick McCarthy for reading the first *and* second drafts of this story and giving me honest and helpful feedback that was invaluable. Thank you.

Thanks to my parents, family, and friends for reading, providing feedback, and supporting the book as I inched along with it.

Thanks to Charlie Robinson and Cutlip.com for the wonderfully fun and eye-catching cover design.

Thanks to Tofu for taking dictation and typing up my notes.

Also by Pug Grumble

Farlaine the Goblin ~ Book 1: The Tinklands

Farlaine the Goblin ~ Book 2: The Saltlands

Farlaine the Goblin ~ Book 3: The Racelands

Farlaine the Goblin ~ Book 4: The Twistlands

Farlaine the Goblin ~ Book 5: The Vaultlands

Farlaine the Goblin ~ Book 6: The Winglands

Farlaine the Goblin ~ Book 7: The Final Land

www.PugGrumble.com

Printed in Great Britain
by Amazon

39918811R00158